Music and Society

From blues to rock

This book is dedicated to the memory of Mike Leadbitter: friend, scholar, writer, researcher, drinker and reluctant guru.

David Hatch and **Stephen Millward**

From blues to rock
An analytical history of pop music

Manchester University Press

Published by Manchester University Press,
Oxford Road, Manchester M13 9PL, UK
27 South Main Street, Wolfeboro, NH 03894–2069, USA

British Library Cataloguing in Publication Data
Hatch, David
    From blues to rock: an analytical history
    of pop music. – (Music and society)
    1. Music, Popular (Songs, etc.) – History
    and criticism
    I. Title   II. Millward, Stephen   III. Series
    780'.42'09   ML3470
    ISBN 0 7190 1489 1 *hardback*

Library of Congress cataloging in publication data
Hatch, David.
    From blues to rock.

    Discography: p. 203.
    Bibliography: p. 207.
    Includes index.
    1. Music, Popular (Songs, etc.) – History and criticism.
I. Millward, Stephen.   II. Title.
ML3470.H38 1987   780'.42'09   87–11008
ISBN 0–7190–1489–1

Photoset in Linotron Plantin with Gill Sans
by Northern Phototypesetting Co., Bolton

Printed in Great Britain
by Billing & Sons Ltd., Worcester

Contents

Preface

From Blues to Rock was written as a result of the authors' involvement in undergraduate and extra-mural courses at the University of Manchester as well as similar courses within adult education. The experience of selecting suitable reading matter for these courses, in addition to feedback from enthusiasts, revealed a need for a serious study of pop music as a historical phenomenon, since much of the available literature has concentrated either on extra-musical and biographical details or commercial statistics (such as the discographies and compendia of hit records). Obviously, therefore, a number of people should be acknowledged for having made a contribution. These are: Paul Berman, Jane Davies, Andy Firth, Tony Johnson, Chris Lee, Simon Napier, Jaki Siers, Mary Singer, and Judith Wills. Special thanks are due to Tony Batey, Dave Driver, Craig Harris, Pete Martin, and Pete Peterson. We should also like to thank John Banks of Manchester University Press for his support and encouragement.

Foreword

We live, we are often told, in a museum culture, clinging on to artefacts of the past because we cannot invent appropriate ones ourselves. Yet even if this is true, it is also true that more people than ever before are interested in and enjoy some form of music: people who attend concerts of some or other kind and people who play music themselves, as well as the countless millions who buy records and tapes (themselves the products of a major industry) or simply experience the pervasive effects of music on radio and television and in films. Though heterogeneous, this public is enormous, including both those who are professionally involved in the production of masterworks and those who just 'know what they like' when they chance to hear it. For despite another of the claims often made about contemporary societies – that their rationalistic and utilitarian values have all but erased the spiritual, the emotional, in a word the distinctively human qualities of life – it is evident that the clamour for music not only survives, but indeed is intensified, in such societies.

In short, music matters. For some it is the paramount expression of human creativity, for others the symbolic affirmation of the Western cultural tradition. Others again hear in their music an explicit denial of the values of such a tradition: for them music may mean the sound of protest, rebellion or even revolution. What is common to each of these, and other, orientations is an undeniable, if usually unstated, belief in both the power and the importance of music in society. In this context, the usefulness of the books in this series – to students, teachers, and the general public – should spring from the fact that they aim to enhance enjoyment by way of understanding. Specialist knowledge will not be assumed, the volumes being written in a lively style, primarily for non-specialist, albeit thoughtful, enthusiastic, and diligent readers.

We take it as axiomatic that, since music is made by human beings, it cannot but be a manifestation of human experience – of the problems and despair, the triumphs and joys which are an integral part of living together in particular social contexts. Some of the books have a musical, others a sociological, bias, but in all the musical and sociological aspects are inseparable. We are concerned simultaneously with the external manifestations of music as revealed, historically and anthropologically, in ritual and in religious, civic, military, and festive activities, in work and in play; and also with the social, psychological and philosophical undercurrents inherent in music's being made by human creatures. Although matters have been complicated, over the last century, by the fact that industrial capitalism in the West has to a degree fragmented the cultural homogeneity of earlier societies, this interdependence of music and society has not been radically changed. It is true that in our 'pluralistic' society we may detect at least three overlapping musical discourses: a folk or ethnic tradition, a classical or art tradition, and a commercial or commodity tradition. Even so, Music & Society starts from a recognition of the fact that these 'discourses', however distinct, cannot be independent, since they are coexistent manifestations of the world we live in.

The point is emphasised by the present volume, in which Hatch and Millward trace the evolution of pop music forms from their emergence in the 'folk' musics of nineteenth-century America to their manifestations as the rock, soul, and punk styles of more recent times. The influence and significance of such forms in contemporary culture can hardly be exaggerated, yet in spite of a general awareness that such phenomena ought to receive serious scholarly attention, they have seldom been investigated in any depth. Here, Hatch and Millward base their arguments on the musical evidence itself, as displayed by recordings: for this, they point out, is above all an 'aural' tradition, a fact which distinguishes it clearly from the 'popular music' of Hollywood or Tin Pan Alley. Inevitably, their analysis is challenging. The authors are sceptical, for example, of the widely-held view that the blues was in some way the forerunner of jazz: rather, the two should be seen as very different plants growing alongside each other in the same soil. Similarly, on purely musical grounds, it is impossible to distinguish 'black' from 'white' styles. Such conclusions hardly square with recent orthodoxy; suffice it to say that the authors do not duck the consequent issues.

Most unequivocally of all the arts, music is a social activity. It has evoked and does evoke strong collective sentiments; it has generated and will support complex social institutions. Even the solitary composer, who may think that his personal motivation is to transcend the society he finds himself in, owes his 'loneness' to the world that made him. Beethoven himself – who in his middle years believed that his music should and could change the world, and in late years knew that his transcendent music had changed the self, ours as well as his own – could not but be dependent on his music's being *heard*; and this inevitably involved other people – as performers and listeners, but also as patrons, sponsors, agents, managers, instrument makers and the whole host of unseen but vital others without whom musical performances would be no more than unfulfilled dreams. Unlike the solitary experience of novel readers or contemplators of paintings, communities of musicians and listeners, whether in tribal gatherings, peasant communities, 'classical' concerts, jazz clubs or discos, depend on contact with one another, and on a shared cultural perspective.

Music does not create or realise itself, but is always the result of people doing things together in particular places and times. To understand music is to understand the men and women who make it, and vice versa. The approach promulgated in Music & Society is, we believe, basic. It needs no further explanation or apology, except in so far as its self-evident truths have sometimes, and rather oddly, been forgotten.

Wilfrid Mellers
Pete Martin

Acknowledgements

Acknowledgement is made for permission to quote material from the following songs:

'Matchbox', 'Dixie Fried', and 'What'd I Say' all used by permission of Carlin Music Corporation, 14 New Burlington Street, London W1X 2LR.

'Long Distance Call' used by permission of Tristan Music Ltd.

'Mama T'ain't Long Fo' Day' used by permission of Southern Music Publishing Company Ltd.

'Are You Sure Hank Done It This Way' used by permission of the Welk Music Group.

'I Never Loved A Man' used by permission of CBS Songs.

'God Save The Queen' © 1977 Glitterbest Ltd and Warner Bros Music Ltd.

'Alison' © 1977 Plangent Visions Music Ltd.

Introduction

It is our intention to offer in this book a new approach to pop music history. That is, we shall concentrate upon the factors, both musical and extra-musical, that have produced succeeding developments in pop music during the present century.

We use the term 'pop music' as locating a body of music which is distinguishable from popular, jazz and folk musics, though obviously having connections with all of these throughout its development.

By 'popular music' we mean the music associated especially with Tin Pan Alley and the sheet music publishing industry, and also with Broadway and the 'musical show', plus the cinematic connections of these traditions through the Hollywood musical.

For our purposes the distinctive characteristic of popular music is its method of publication – that of sheet music. Thus it shares with 'art music', or at least the art music of recent times, the procedure of being initially *written* and subsequently performed.

Pop music, on the other hand, is, in common with jazz, primarily an aural and improvised music. That is, both musics are transmitted (i.e. published) and learnt through 'live' performances, radio and television broadcasts and, especially, gramophone records.

In other respects pop and jazz represent parallel, yet only indirectly related, developments, despite their sharing a common folk music ancestry. Apart from the obvious difference of pop being a music which typically combines the human voice with other instruments (especially the guitar) there are other more fundamental distinctions between the two musics. The materials which make up their repertoires are, for example, quite different. By far the most common external source for jazz materials is that of popular music. Thus a great many jazz standards are former popular music hits – or transformations of such material, as in, for instance, the many variations on 'I Got Rhythm' employed by bebop musicians.

In contrast, pop music initially drew its repertoire from the folk traditions of the US, and thus indirectly from previous African and European traditions. By the end of the twenties those musical sub-types which comprised early pop, namely country blues, boogie-woogie, gospel and hillbilly, had evolved repertoires which had as much in common with each other as with any other musical traditions (including those forming their folk musical 'roots').

Given the tradition among jazz historians of describing blues as a 'precursor' of jazz, it is especially interesting to note that no country blues numbers have become jazz standards. Those numbers common to both jazz and pop, such as 'Careless Love', evidence the common folk heritage of the two musical traditions.

Pop music can therefore be legitimately seen as a continuation of both formal and substantive elements of the folk tradition. The continuity of the oral/aural tradition is exemplified by the common practice among pop audiences of treating the initial gramophone recording as the original 'publication' of a song, even comparing subsequent *live* performances to the recorded version. Thus references to 'interpretations' and 'copies' (or 'covers') of songs typically denote versions, recorded or live, following the original recorded version of a pop song.

Though there have been periods in pop history, notably during the fifties, when 'cover versions' have largely been vehicles with which artists and record companies have competed for the major share of a song's potential sales in recorded form, the practice of 'reviving' songs from an earlier period has constantly been a method of evolving new types of pop. As a result of this practice songs can reappear in a number of manifestations, as succeeding musical generations of musicians give them new rhythms, or alter slightly their melodies. This development of the potential of songs gives rise to what we shall call 'song families'.

Song families are constructed out of the lyrical, melodic and rhythmic structures of a song by means of adapting those structures to the requirements of new musical developments. A number of song families have seen constant revival and extension over a period of up to sixty years. Songs emanating from the country blues tradition have subsequently contributed to the evolution of rock & roll and post-sixties rock musics. Thus Elvis Presley's first record reinterpreted a blues song, 'That's Alright', and a hillbilly number, 'Blue Moon of Kentucky', which not only helped to form the new musical traditions of rock & roll and rockabilly, but also, to an extent, contributed to the development of blues and hillbilly (i.e. country & western) forms.

The procedures of song revival and song family extension have a number of uses in the context of pop evolution. They provide, for instance, concrete exemplification of a new movement for fans and musicians alike, showing, in the case of Presley's 'Blue Moon of Kentucky', how rock & roll and rockabilly differed from earlier hillbilly (and in particular 'bluegrass') styles. A similar function was performed by the Rolling Stones' recording of 'Not Fade Away' (1964), in that it differed from the Buddy Holly original (of 1957) through its accentuation of the 'hambone beat' popularised in the fifties by Bo Diddley. Such examples of song family extension have the facility to demonstrate the 'before and after effect', thus giving definition to the musical development in the most concrete way. And this documentation is particularly effective when, as in the case of 'Not Fade Away', both (or all) of the versions are readily accessible to the public.

Song extension was similarly employed by Muddy Waters at the close of the 1940s to transform the Chicago blues. This was achieved by reviving the repertoire he had learnt during his youth in the Delta region of the State of Mississippi, using a small band and gradually increasing the amplification. Muddy's recordings of Robert Johnson's 'Walking Blues' (his first version, of 1949, was retitled 'Feel Like Going Home') and 'Rollin' And Tumblin' ' were sufficiently accurate renditions to be dubbed 'downhome' blues. It is ironic that Muddy thus inaugurated the modern pop tendency to innovate through the use of song families from a previous era.

Some fifteen years later the Rolling Stones, and subsequently Cream an Canned Heat, followed his example in substance as well as spirit by themselves drawing on the same source. Thus the Stones recorded Muddy's 'I Just Want To Make Love To You' (1964) and 'I Can't Be Satisfied' (1965), Cream made versions of a number of Delta blues, and Canned Heat took their name as well as their inspiration from the Delta bluesman Tommy Johnson (see Chapters 1 and 4).

The equally time-honoured practice of *copying* earlier recordings has played a similar role in pop music development. As with song extensions, song copying allows the novice to become a competent member of a musical tradition. This applies to both musicians and audiences. One obvious example is the birth of rock in Britain through copies of American rhythm & blues hits such as the Stones' version of Arthur Alexander's 'You Better Move On' (1964) and The Moody Blues' recording of Bessie Banks's 'Go Now' (1965). As the first generation of British pop musicians, bands such as the Animals, Beatles and Stones lacked a native pop song and instrumental tradition: it was therefore natural to copy particular examples of American pop music as a first step in the creation of a native tradition. In the case of the British 'R & B' copies the choice of material also had an ideological aspect, serving to display the musical credentials of artists and audience (thus staking a claim for inclusion in the 'black music' tradition).

Those developments in pop often seen as revolutionary, in other words as creating new musical types or sub-types, such as rock & roll in the 1950s and British rock in the 1960s, are commonly initiated through the use of song family extension and song copying. A further and more mature stage is reached when original songs conforming to the same model are produced. Thus British rock groups, such as the Beatles, the Stones and the Who, soon began to write their own material. This subsequent material, though composed by Britons, was recognisably within the American pop tradition. British pop music had thus become established.

There are thus at least three possible stages available to new generations of pop musicians in the development of their musical competence. A recognisable first stage is that of song/performance reproduction (or copying) of examples taken from selected musical types. A second stage requires the competence to improvise on given patterns (usually manifested as song-family extensions). A third involves the writing of new songs composed of elements derived from the material in 'stage one', which thus can be described as *musical family extensions*. This appears to be a generally applicable model in pop song development, as stages one to three are constantly repeated.

This pattern is clearly documented in the work of Muddy Waters, the Rolling Stones, Cream (as detailed above) as well as many others who will be discussed in the rest of this book.

This model of pop development may be illustrated by the following diagram:

Artists	Recordings		
	Stage One	*Stage Two*	*Stage Three*
Frank Hutchison	—	'Cannonball Blues' (1927)	—
Jimmie Rodgers	—	—	'Blue Yodel No. 1' (1927)
Larry Henseley	'Matchbox Blues' (1934)	—	—
Robert Johnson	—	—	'Ramblin' On My Mind' (1936)
Muddy Waters	—	'I Feel Like Goin' Home' (1948)	'Young Fashioned Ways' (1955)
Pat Boone	'Tutti Frutti' (1956)	—	—
Rolling Stones	'You Better Move On' (1964)	'The Last Time' (1965)	'Satisfaction' (1965)
Cream/Eric Clapton	'Ramblin' On My Mind' (1966)	'Sitting On Top Of The World' (1968)	'Layla' (1970)
Elvis Costello	—	—	'Mystery Dance' (1977)

The musical types which comprise pop are manifestations of musical family development in that tradition. By this we mean that the pop music tradition has evolved by means of a compound series of developments from the core musical family *blues-boogie-gospel*. This basic musical family contains virtually all the elements out of which the musical types in the pop tradition have been constructed. In the main the melodic structures of blues and boogie plus the rhythms of gospel have been perennial elements in the various evolutionary stages of pop. For example, the hillbilly (or 'country') sub-tradition inaugurated by the recordings of Jimmie Rodgers, especially those of the 'Blue Yodels', combined the melodic structures of blues and boogie with at least intimations of the off-beat accentuation of gospel.

Thus continuity and change in pop music, apparent in types such as rock & roll, soul and (post-sixties) rock, have *compounded* the number of basic musical structures available to each succeeding musical generation. The use of boogie structures in rock & roll is therefore related to, but nevertheless distinct from, the use of those same structures by Jimmie Rodgers and his disciples.

This accounts for how the more recent developments in pop such as punk and New Wave are related *indirectly* to the American tradition: that is via the British rock of the 1960s. Thus the Dr Feelgood version of 'Rolling And Tumbling' (1975) owes its particular conception of that song family more to the recording by Cream (of 1966) than to any version by a Chicago blues band.

On the other hand, artists such as Elvis Costello and Bruce Springsteen have begun their development at stage three of our model (see the diagram above). The originality of composition and exposition consistently found in the work of Costello and Springsteen results in performances such as 'Mystery Dance' (1977) and 'Ramrod' (1980), combining the quality of originality with those associated with the classic rock & roll tradition.

Thus the achievements of these artists, because of, rather than in spite of, their originality, owe a great deal to those of earlier generations.

From the mid-1970s onwards the growth of the 'reissue' album industry has meant that virtually the entire history of pop music has become universally available. Prior to this development in the record business most parts of this corpus were available only to specialist collectors. Now any contemporary fan has the opportunity not only to compare recent copies with the original versions but also to appreciate the connections between, for example, Bruce Springsteen's 'Ramrod' and the work of Dion and Gary 'US' Bonds. There is no reason to suppose however, that this universal availability of what amounts to the entire pop tradition will eliminate completely either song copying or song-family extension. Thus there have been very recent examples of copies (or 'late covers'): for instance, Shakin' Stevens' 1985 version of Joe Turner's 'Lipstick, Powder and Paint' (1956) and the Rolling Stones' 1986 remake of Bob and Earl's 'Harlem Shuffle' (1963). But the very existence of the reissue industry allows artists of Costello's and Springsteen's calibre to quote from the pop tradition in very subtle ways. It also allows the equally subtle, but otherwise different approach of the band Big Daddy, who, in their reworking of the Springsteen song 'Dancing In The Dark' (1985), use *musical* quotations from Pat Boone's records 'Moody River' (1961) and 'Love Letters In The Sand' (1957), presumably with the intention of parodying Boone.

The reissue arm of the record industry is, on the whole, the result of erstwhile consumers becoming producers. Thus many reissue labels, such as Ace, Charly, Flyright and Yazoo, are run by people who were formerly specialist collectors and enthusiasts.

The commercial success of the reissue movement highlights the fundamental differences between pop and popular music. For though the two musics have shared 'productive forces' for the last sixty years, in that they have been manufactured by the same record, publishing, radio and television companies, the two traditions involve radically different conceptions of musical development. In particular, pop music, because of its peculiarities of 'composition', has never been comfortably absorbed into practices of the song publishing industry. Equally the pop tradition conflicts with the popular music obsession with 'new material' as manifested by the emphasis placed upon the contents of the 'latest charts'. However, if only because of their constant proximity, pop and popular music have often influenced each other, and on occasion one has seemed to be about to completely subjugate the other. For instance, in the mid to late fifties pop in the form of rock & roll was seen as an enormous threat to the popular music business (and in fact spelt the end of the prominence of the sheet music industry); ironically, a few years later the positions were reversed as the popular music industry found ways of manufacturing an alternative version of rock & roll, but one produced by means of the traditional popular music methods of songs being first *written* and then marketed for recording purposes. This phenomenon is widely referred to as the Philadelphia answer to rock & roll (see Chapter 4, p. 94).

That pop music self-consciously combines continuity with change, which constitutes the central argument of this book, is illustrated perfectly by the fact that yet another wave of 'minor' labels (that is, the reissue companies) has in the 1980s come to challenge the domination of the established record companies, just as earlier waves did through the introduction of rock & roll during the fifties, rock during the mid-sixties and punk during the late seventies. The fact that the largest generation of successful small labels is run by ex-consumers confirms that record buyers as well as musicians orientate to the pop tradition as a distinct phenomenon.

Popular music historians typically delineate the pop music tradition by implication. That is by excluding it from their considerations, or by dating its inauguration from the period when pop, in its rock & roll manifestation, first began to seriously threaten the hegemony of the popular music establishment. Thus Hamm (1979), for instance, mentions blues and hillbilly musics in passing, as part of his discussion of the precursors of rock & roll. He thus, quite rightly, both recognises the existence of a pop tradition and treats it as being of marginal importance to his central concern, the history of *popular* music. Hamm therefore limits his coverage of pop to the impact of that tradition upon the popular music industry. In particular, his concern is with the effects that the success of rock & roll (followed by soul and rock) had upon the established record companies and the sheet music publishing industry.

The commercial success of rock & roll promoted the gramophone record to the position of being the most successful medium for the dissemination of music in the United States: overtaking, after more than thirty years of competition, the medium of sheet music. This change in the balance of marketing power resulted from location of rock & roll within the oral/aural tradition. Thus the music was learnt by its established musicians and novices, and appreciated by its fans, by means of gramophone records alone, sheet music exposition being a redundant medium in the dissemination of rock & roll. Therefore, for the first time in the history of the American popular music industry, sheet music sales associated with hit records became commercially insignificant. As Hamm remarks: 'At the root of this switch of power from music publishers to recording companies was perhaps the most fundamental change in the entire history of popular song in America – from a music existing in a written tradition to one in oral tradition' (1979, p.402).

Yet the recording companies were also, at that time, mostly run by men whose perspectives were closer to those of popular than to pop traditions. And through these popular musical connections rock & roll and later manifestations of pop were subject to pressures to conform at least to the marketing values with which the popular music industry had been familiar. As a result of these influences pop music did, of course, take on at least some of the traits previously associated with the products of Tin Pan Alley. Among these was the orientation to short-term sales – universally described as 'chart success' – an approach to music production which encourages artists, as well as record company personnel, to concentrate upon songs with the potential of mass appeal for a few weeks, without straying too far from what are often called 'proven formulas', thus conforming to the *general* formula of 'success rather than innovation'.

The relationship between pop and folk musics is at once relatively simple yet often opaque. The two traditions obviously have many formal and substantive characteristics. And at least in the very early days of pop the distinctions between the two musics was extremely blurred. Thus the first generation of pop musicians, for instance Blind Lemon Jefferson, Jimmie Rodgers and Charley Patton, *learnt* their techniques and repertoires by means of the old folk ways of personal contact with those who taught them. Yet by the early twenties these and other musicians were teaching the next generation through their recorded performances (the example of Blind Lemon Jefferson is discussed in some detail in Chapter 2, pp. 53–6).

The media of the recording and radio industries therefore effected a qualitative change in the music they disseminated within a very short time. And an effect having important consequences for 'folk /pop' distinctions was that involving the breakdown of regional and ethnic differences in the musics so mediated. For it is normally axiomatic in definitions of folk musics that they are clearly the product of a specific population of a specific geographical (and perhaps temporal) location.

Though we are prepared to argue for a folk–pop continuum as being the most appropriate descriptor of our subject matter, the additional step, taken by Belz (1972), of proposing that pop music is the *real* folk music of the contemporary world is unnecessary for our argument. Such a step would surely bring charges of the misappropriation of the term 'folk' by those who continue to use it to describe musics other than those of rock & roll, soul and rock, and, perhaps more importantly, musics using mainly acoustic equipment (i.e. not amplified guitars, etc.).

The concept of 'folk music' does, however, mean many different things to different sets of people. Thus a formula apparently intended to strike a balance between definitional rigour and public acceptability, promulgated by the International Folk Music Council in 1954, is perhaps worthy of being quoted in full here. It stated:

Folk music is the product of a musical tradition that has been evolved through the process of oral transmission. The factors that shape the tradition are: (i) continuity which links the present with the past; (ii) variation which springs from the creative impulse of the individual or the group; and (iii) selection by the community, which determines the form or forms in which the music survives.

The term can be applied to music that has been evolved from rudimentary beginnings by a community uninfluenced by popular and art music and it can likewise be applied to music which has originated with an individual composer and has subsequently been absorbed into the unwritten living tradition of a community.

The term does not cover composed popular music that has been taken over ready-made by a community and remains unchanged, for it is the re-fashioning and re-creation of the music by the community that gives it is folk character.

(Quoted in Woods (1980) pp. 10–11.)

. . . the connection between listener and song is an immediate one; no aesthetic distance separates the two, no gap that would provoke art-consciousness. With rock, as with any folk idiom, a consciousness of art is unnecessary for grasping the full impart of a particular work.

(Belz p. 7)

To define a music in terms of spontaneity of performance and response is to lead one's analysis up an unnecessary blind alley. Belz's logic requires that the existence of an audience which responds to the music of Bach, Vivaldi or Mozart in a 'spontaneous' manner, destroys the 'fine art' status of those musics. Likewise either the music or the audience are expelled from the 'folk' category if an audience (of one or more persons) responds to a rock record in a 'self-conscious' (i.e. analytic) manner. The very notion of any large audience having a uniform response to any type of music (or, for that matter, any form of entertainment or art form) seems improbable. And it is certain that such a proposal is beyond the bounds of *rigorous* examination given the currently available techniques of the social and psychological sciences. Furthermore, Belz's equation of 'folk-art' with an 'immediate' and 'spontaneous' response on the part of the audience to an equally 'spontaneous' method of production is not only unforgivably but also *unnecessarily* patronising. His argument shows a marked improvement when he discusses the relationship between the 'folk revival' of the sixties and the folk music tradition. He points out that performers like the Kingston Trio and Joan Baez, and at least some of their admirers

. . . seemed to equate folk music with songs telling a story or conveying a moralistic point and accompanied by the acoustic or solo guitar. To its enthusiastic audience, this type of music was pure, eschewing the so-called falsifications of recording-room manipulations. . . . The artists and audiences of this new trend failed to realize, however, that folk styles change. The acoustic guitar may have been all that was available to the folk artist of the 1930s (sic), but his counterpart in the 1950s and the 1960s could work with electronics, with echo chambers, and with complicated recording techniques. (pp. 8–10.)

Belz may well have pointed out that the introduction of *any* type of multi-stringed instrument to the performance of Anglo-American folk songs, as occurred during the latter part of the nineteenth and the first decade or so of the twentieth centuries, alters the music much more drastically than the mere introduction of *electronic* hardware. For the old European folk songs of the early American settlers were *modal*, therefore sung either solo or in unison. The introduction of instruments such as the guitar, the fiddle and the banjo to accompany the vocals involved an adaptation of the music to *diatonic* scales through the instrumental *harmonic* accompaniments.

The familiar antipathy to electronic hardware and 'commercialism' in folk music circles is itself the best argument in favour of a 'pop as modern folk music' thesis. For the prevalence of the attitude regarding folk music as something to be preserved, rather than stimulated, turns folk clubs, societies and concerts into musical museums.

The widespread belief among folk music devotees that they are preserving an idiom of the past has a lengthy history itself. As Woods points out, even the Victorian collectors of folk songs, such as Cecil Sharp, assumed the music to be of a dead or rapidly dying tradition, when in fact the tradition had merely migrated to the towns and cities with the younger musicians, where it was combined with the popular and music-hall songs of the period.

A similar pattern emerged in early twentieth-century North America, particularly with respect to ragtime, blues and white country musics. From the 'discovery' of the great Blind Lemon Jefferson country blues was regarded as something from the past. The Paramount Record Company thus promoted Jefferson's early recordings as the last examples of a dying tradition, of interest as novelties; and clearly assuming that the urban blues of the vaudeville-influenced female vocalists were the 'modern' variety of blues.

The 'folklorist' approach to blues has, in fact, proved to be very persistent indeed. Its longevity probably owes much to the work of John and Alan Lomax for the Library of Congress folk music archives. Their field recordings, particularly those of Delta bluesmen like Son House and Willie Brown, definitely have a more 'folksy' sound than the *earlier* commerical recordings of those blues musicians (see Chapter 6). Without the efforts of the often abused commercial recording companies, the country blues of the twenties and thirties would not only, via the Library of Congress recordings, be somewhat distorted in terms of our present picture of them, but also they would probably have developed in a different way. Eventually the 'folklorist' approach to blues culminated in the rather bizarre recordings of Sam 'Lightnin' ' Hopkins and John Lee Hooker in the early sixties, with those artists accompanying themselves on acoustic guitars (instruments they had possibly forgotten about). More than twenty years earlier Huddie Ledbetter, the protégé of the Lomaxes, would occasionally use his Library of Congress recording sessions to do 'cover versions' of current commercial blues hits (compare, for instance, his August, 1940 version of 'Bottle Up And Go' with Tommy McClennan's November 1939 version of the song for the RCA Bluebird label). Whether or not the Lomaxes were aware of Ledbetter's sources in these instances, his 'cover versions' add an interesting twist to the Library of Congress folk music archives.

In schemas designed to distinguish 'folk' from 'pop' musics blues is a persistently difficult case. Usually the problem is solved by consigning blues recorded before various dates (from around 1935 onwards) to the 'folk' category, or alternatively, reserving the 'folk-blues' category for the variety accompanied by acoustic instruments and having some rural connections. Yet such categorisation criteria ignore the dissemination of blues songs and styles (and likewise hillbilly musics) via records and radio programmes in the 1920s.

From the point of view of this book, pop music commenced with the advent of commercial recordings and radio broadcasts of the various regionally-located musics of the southern US states during the 1920s. Principally these were ragtime, blues, 'hillbilly'-'country' and gospel musics. We shall argue that these recordings and broadcasts had a crucial effect upon the development of the 'folk' music of the southern states. In particular, what are now known as 'blues' and 'country music' had their separate identities established largely through these processes. Country music, for instance, can hardly be said to have had anything like a singular 'form' before the early thirties. Its emergence as a coherent music owes much to radio shows like 'The Grand Old Opry', but probably more to the career of Jimmie Rodgers. He, undoubtedly, was the first pop star; he also acted as a unifying factor for the musics of the Old and New South through associations with Mississippi (his birthplace), the Carolines and the Virginias, and finally Texas, his 'adopted' state during the last years of his life (see Chapter 2, pp. 52–3).

The emergence of the blues as a recognisable type of music was more or less simultaneous with the currency of that term in the popular music world, following the publication and widespread acceptance of W. C. Handy's compositions, just after the First World War, and the use of the label 'blues' in the title of numerous vaudeville songs. The exact relationship between the popular song compositions of people like Handy, the early vaudeville (sometimes called 'classic') blues and the development of the country blues remains largely a matter for speculation at present, but certainly the importance of Handy as a populariser of the music has been underestimated by blues writers to a similar extent that it was previously overestimated by jazz writers. And the influence of at least some of the vaudeville singers, particularly Bessie Smith, on the country blues musicians has probably also been underestimated of late.

As Gunther Schuller (1968) has argued so eloquently with respect to jazz, the essential evidence upon which discussion of aurally transmitted and improvised musics must be based is that of the gramophone record, or some functional equivalent. In pop music publication is of this form, and written versions of the music (e.g. sheet music publication) are to be regarded as accurate or inaccurate *transcriptions* of the primary recording.

Unlike most researchers of human culture, musicologists in the pop music field, as well as that of jazz, thus have at their disposal a fundamental source of evidence which is quantitative, incontrovertible and available for continual analysis and review. Many pop music writers fail to maximise the effectiveness of the gramophone record as a resource. And this often leads to sloppy analysis, especially in the categorisation of musical types. We accept that music existing prior to the availability of physical methods of recording such as the gramophone record cannot, by our own definition, be analysed with the same degree of rigour. Yet many writers in the modern era decrease the value of their conclusions through their neglect of recorded musical evidence; either through an attachment to the art and popular musical traditions of *written* publication and transmission or through an unwillingness to delve into technical analysis.

We understand an analytical history to be an investigation of the technological, social and other relevant factors in the development of a music, or body of related musics. Within such research the evidence showing musical changes and continuities has to be found in the most relevant materials. In the case of pop this involves an adequate familiarity with both the details and the broad themes of a large number of records, including evidence of typical and actual musical structures.

Two exemplary studies in the field of analytical history of music are those of Gunther Schuller (1968) and Jeff Todd Titon (1977). Schuller's study of the early stages of the development of jazz clearly rests upon both a broad and a detailed knowledge of the basic relevant evidence (i.e. early jazz records). Likewise, Titon's study of early blues is based not only upon a long familiarity with the material, but also upon comparative analysis of forty-eight blues records and transcriptions of the same. Titon, even more than Schuller, provides the reader with both his evidence and his criteria in as explicit a manner as is possible. Thus his categorisation procedures are as fully available as possible to the reader. This is a particularly useful feature in the field of pop history, for many of the arguments and controversies which surround the subject are concerned with problems of categorisation. Distinctions such as those between 'spirituals' and 'gospel', 'rhythm & blues' and 'rock & roll', the various types of 'blues', and many others are constantly debated in books and journals, and in discussions between music enthusiasts.

Many critics and commentators would argue that pop music does not merit an analytical approach. Even Charlie Gillett has been quoted as saying that pop music '. . . doesn't really hold up to that much analysis and attention' (Sunday Times, November 1983). Interviewed for Binia Tymieniecka's film *Da Doo Ron Ron* (1983), Albert Goldman asserted: 'Rock & roll is basically institutionalised adolescence. And the bottom line of rock & roll is that it's a baby food industry.' In fact it is the norm in music writing to use, either implicitly or explicitly, an aesthetic model of stratification having 'art music' (otherwise known as 'classical' or 'concert' music) at the pinnacle, then descending through jazz and popular musics to folk music and, finally, pop music. This model has many obvious, but also many more obscure, relationships with social-status stratification as found in the Western world. It is, for example, common to equate pop music with what is often called 'working-class culture', and folk music has traditionally been seen as the music of agrarian workers. Also, both forms have often been described as crude and unsophisticated, especially when compared with art or even popular music. It is common to find critics who favour popular music using the term 'sophisticated' to describe it, and also those types of pop music influenced by it. It would not, we feel, stretch our stratification metaphor too far to see the popular music community as very much like lower-middle-class persons with upper-class pretensions. The notion of popular music being more 'refined', more 'grown-up', than pop music, may have been argued less frequently and with less bitterness since popular music came to terms with the rock & roll phenomenon at the beginning of the 1960s, but, as Albert Goldman demonstrates, it remains a feature of the popular music world.

As might be expected within a stratification system it is normal to find deferential behaviour within the pop community towards art music. This often involves behaviour suggesting an orientation to art music as the source of standards of excellence. Typically, however, the nature of those standards and the method of their derivation remain opaque. Their explication consists of isolated statements of a comparative nature. Thus Tony Palmer, in his role of music critic for the *Observer*, was seen as bestowing some form of 'artistic' credence upon the music of the Beatles when, during the sixties, he compared their work favourably with that of Schubert. This kind of comparison soon became grist to the mill of the more pretentious pundits in pop music criticism. For a time it became fashionable to write extended pieces known as 'rock operas', the most famous example being that of *Tommy* (1969), by Pete Townshend. In 1970, moreover, the rock group Deep Purple produced a piece of music they entitled 'Concerto for Group and Orchestra'. And from around this period it became customary in some quarters to discuss 'rock music' as a possible 'art form'; that is, 'rock' rather than 'pop'; a distinction which became more common as the 1970s progressed.

This type of aesthetic stratification model does not, however, have any demonstrable justification. It consists of nothing more than either misconceived deference or status-seeking prejudice (and often a combination of the two). For though it may reasonably be argued that the music of, for instance, Mozart has a structural complexity not present in any example, or type, of pop music, such an argument does not furnish any kind of aesthetic licence; unless the arguer is also prepared to define quality of music *merely* in terms of structural complexity – a very peculiar definition indeed. In fact, such comparisons are not merely odious, they are analytically and philosophically naïve. They ignore, for instance, the long-standing controversy in the philosophies of aesthetics and ethics of the possible relationships between 'normative' and 'empirical' propositions. In other words, the possible connections between 'matters of fact' and 'matters of moral/aesthetic opinion' are *many*. Many eminent philosophers have denied, very persuasively, *any* basis in 'empirical facts' for any single aesthetic or ethical conclusion. From such a view relationships which are commonly accepted to exist between 'factual' and 'aesthetic' phenomena do so *only* to the extent that they *are* generally accepted. In other words, any such relationship is a matter of common opinion, and as such can only thrive in what may be called a vacuum of serious and sustained objections. Where that vacuum is breached and the relationship is persistently called into question it becomes no more than one more way of seeing things.

We recognise, of course, that aesthetic arguments are commonly formulated in ways that link a number of value judgements to a number of presumed facts in a complex manner. Thus, whether the disagreement concerns the relative values of, say, the Rolling Stones' versions of songs first recorded by Bo Diddley, Arthur Alexander and Chuck Berry, or the relative merits of 'guitar wizards' such as Blind Lemon Jefferson, Robert Johnson, Buddy Guy and Eric Clapton, *some* of the points at issue will be open to empirical research (were notes missed out or added by mistake, thus showing incompetence, or deliberately, showing competence plus a talent for innovation?); but equally, some of the points disagreed upon will be matters of taste. We have found during our research, for instance, that many listeners are uncomfortable with recordings made either before or after the period in which they became familiar with pop music. Thus some records have too much, or too little, bass, or treble, for some people to find their overall 'sound' acceptable. Thus Blind Lemon Jefferson may be rejected as a guitarist not worth listening to on the grounds that the 'primitive' qualities of the recording equipment of the twenties makes it *difficult* to listen to his performances. In the case of Jimi Hendrix, on the other hand, many persons accustomed to earlier recordings have found the accompanying bass and drums intrusive and the prevalence of electronic 'interference' difficult to overcome in attempts to appreciate Hendrix's performance.

The obvious rejoinder to both types of reaction is to point out that the obvious, but often ignored, fact that the human ear, like the human mind, can be educated. Pop music, from the twenties to the eighties, contains a wealth of magnificent performances. To miss the enjoyment of *any* of it is a great loss to anyone.

Given that pop music was a product of the rural working-class of the southern United States, it is perhaps no wonder that the picaresque theme, so important in the mythology of that group, is such a constant one within the music; for the theme is prevalent in all the American arts, especially where they are folk-derived or folk-oriented. It is noticeable, for instance, that where the American novel deals with working-class life in any persuasive manner – from Mark Twain's *Huck Finn*, to the works of John Steinbeck and Jim Thompson, to Kerouac's *On The Road* – it does so within a picaresque tradition. Likewise, the Hollywood movie has created and/or sustained the legends and myths of the cowboy, the pioneer and backwoodsman, the okie and the hobo, the private eye and the gangster, the hell's angel and the long-distance trucker, and many more images of what the *Oxford English Dictionary*, in its definition of 'picaresque', calls the 'adventures of rogues'. A valuable documentary account is that of Kenneth Allsop's (1967) investigation of the American hobo, which details the extent of the phenomenon from the time of great movements of western-bound settlers through to the huge displacement of working people during the various depressions, to the modern, motorised, wanderers.

The theme fairly saturates pop music, especially (white) country music and the country blues. The urge to 'travel on' is both celebrated and bemoaned in both these sub-traditions, providing succeeding generations of musicians with a corpus of picaresque themes, phrases and images, as well as complete songs. These songs and thematic elements were eventually intertwined with those of the sacred tradition, so important in the early days of American music. Many of the images and themes of the spiritual–gospel tradition were, quite naturally, Biblical in origin. But Biblical places and concepts were used to describe the American experience, dreams, and attitudes. Thus concepts like 'Jordan', 'Egypt', and the like, were used as thinly disguised *double entendres*, having political as well as religious connotations. 'Egypt' could, after all, easily symbolise the Slave States for the American Black, with either the North, or Abolition representing the 'new Promised Land'.

Pop music accelerated the secularisation of these images and themes, combining them with other picaresque images. It is interesting, for instance, to combine Alfred G. Karnes's 1928 song 'I Am Bound For The Promised Land', with its more or less straightforward religious imagery, with the Chuck Berry song 'Promised Land' (1964), where the 'Land' in question is identified as

California. Berry's number is possibly the American picaresque song *par excellence*, combining most of the 'travelling' images of the genre with a facility few song-writers or poets could match. The song tells the story of a 'poor boy' who leaves 'my home in Norfolk, Virginia', to travel, via Greyhound bus, train and plane, through Carolina, Georgia, Alabama, Mississippi, Louisiana and, finally California. Berry shows a masterful grasp of the metaphor describing his bus ride with a pun on the name of the bus company – 'I straddled that Greyhound and rode him into Raleigh . . .' – and describing the aeroplane by means of imagery from the spirituals – '. . . swing low chariot, come down easy, taxi to the terminal zone . . .'. Berry's song can surely be described as a masterpiece, combining the imagery of the American picaresque tradition with that of the American song through the years.

Thus many of the songs and themes to be found in pop are derived from musics which existed before the gramophone was invented; that is, from a period properly thought of as *prehistoric* from the pop historian's point of view. From the period between the initial settlement in North America and the 1920s came a large number of songs and themes which Tony Russell (1970) has called 'common-stock' material; that is, shared by black and white musicians. In the 1920s and 1930s, as blues and hillbilly musics achieved their now familiar identities, the 'common-stock material' was recorded by both black and white artists in a number of styles and modes. Many of the songs and themes from this common stock were of the picaresque variety, including the 'railroad hero' themes, such as 'Casey Jones', 'John Henry' and 'Railroad Bill', gambler and 'rounder' songs like 'Skin Game', 'Stack O' Lee' and 'Jack O' Diamonds', and the songs with the melancholic theme epitomised in the 'Poor Boy Long Ways From Home' song-family.

The pioneers of the blues and hillbilly traditions, such as Jimmie Rodgers, Charley Patton and Blind Lemon Jefferson, adapted the lyrical and musical elements of the common-stock material and added new images, themes and structures, thus creating new traditions from the old. Because of these factors the recordings of their work are a crucial legacy of that era of transition preserved, fortunately for us, by the pioneers of large-scale production and marketing of America's music on gramophone records.

The construction and reconstruction of the songs commonly followed a discernible pattern, giving the historian and the *aficionado* sufficient clues to the resultant thematic and structural development. The 'mechanisms' of that development involved, then as now, a constant experimentation with forms, structures and their elements.

The interactions between song families and musical families, and their elements, can clearly be seen as having pivotal roles in this development. Thus the blues-boogie-gospel family and hillbilly-country & western family had not only roots (or 'ancestors') in common but also progeny, their combination producing virtually all types of modern pop, including soul and rock.

Thus Russell's concept of 'common stock' needs to be enlarged so as to include, apart from songs, musical themes and elements, instrumental and vocal techniques, attachment to certain instruments, plus conceptions of particular traditions in terms of certain musical, instrumental and social elements.

The roles of wider socio-economic factors have also to be taken into account. For often pop musics are given shape and identity via the industry by which they are produced and the audiences they are thus able to reach. This was most obviously the case with rock & roll. But the more complex example of soul music can also be seen as having gained much of its identity through specific socio-economic factors (see also Chapters 3 and 5).

In order to concentrate upon the threads of continuity and change in the evolution of pop music, however, whilst giving due recognition to the effects of social, commerical and technological factors, we have focused our analyis upon musical elements. For though speculation concerning the effects upon music of the cruder types of sociological phenomena can be fun, the results of such speculation are, more often than not, sociologically as well as musicologically crude. Some of the more sophisticated sociological analysis developed over the last fifteen years actually contributes to musical analysis (rather than 'explaining' it), however. Thus we draw on ethnomethodological and linguistic techniques and findings in our approach to musical analysis.

Our principal methods of research have been those of the comparative musical analysis of pop as preserved on gramophone records, audio and video tapes as well as the available discographical information. We have also interviewed, and generally conversed with, musicians and fans (together numbering around 400). We have not followed Titon's (1977) example of using a finite sample of recordings on which to base our analysis. Rather, given the somewhat wider scope of our subject matter, when compared with his, we have taken as relevant all pop recordings, paying particular attention to those recordings having a crucial significance in respect of the *evolution of pop*. Consequently, those records mentioned often and/or analysed carefully in the following pages are adjudged by us to be either crucial to the development of the music or to typify the processes whereby pop has evolved. Thus, for instance, Larry Henseley's 'cover' of Jefferson's 'Matchbox' (1934 and 1927 respectively) evidences both the development of the gramophone record mediated aural tradition and the importance of the country blues to the early hillbilly musicians, as well as the importance of song families in pop development. Other songs featured prominently exemplify the melodic structure of boogie or the Delta blues, or were the vehicles for transformations of those and other musical types and sub-types.

Thus we have striven to explicate the mechanisms whereby the early musical families of blues-boogie-gospel and hillbilly have been exploited in respect of their formal and substantive elements in order constantly to create new types of families. That is, we have had as our goal the rigorous description of pop music as a *tradition* oriented to by its members (including musicians, fans and those who belong in both of these categories).

In view of the current confusion in the world of music literature with regard to the proper domains of musical analysis, musical theory and musicology – as discussed by Joseph Kerman (1985) – plus the demographic limitations usually imposed by ethnomusicology, we would wish to be aligned with the body of music writing which has come to be described, happily or not, as sociomusicology. Previous examples of this approach are to be found in the works of Gunther Schuller (1968), Watson and Hatch (1974) and Jeff Todd Titon (1977). This approach typically combines the comparative analysis of musical structures within their evolutionary context with the more compatible, and useful techniques from recent sociology, social psychology and linguistics. *From Blues To Rock* expands the scope of sociomusicology by applying it to pop history as a whole. As such it is intended to be read as an explication of a perspective and of methods of research, in fact as a 'puzzle' which *all* pop fans may help to solve, as well as a detailed history of pop. We hope that other contributions will follow.

The contents of the book are ordered in the following manner:

Chapter 1 presents an overview of pop development, linking more recent developments with early examples via an explication of song and musical families. It also introduces the crucial musical differences, and relationships, between country blues and boogie.

Chapter 2 concentrates upon the early period, detailing the evolution of country blues and hillbilly, giving particular attention to the positive relationships between black and white musical traditions.

Chapter 3 analyses the advent of rock & roll as a sociomusical phenomenon, relating it to previous musical types, including hillbilly and western swing as well as rhythm & blues.

Chapter 4 investigates the genesis of rock & soul, detailing the connections between sixties rock music and country, plus Chicago blues. Special attention is paid to the birth of British pop via the 'beat groups' of the sixties, and to details of white contributions to soul music.

Chapter 5 scrutinises the concept of 'black music', calling some 'established truths' into question, and underlines the socially constructed nature of racial categories. It also looks at the relationship of Motown to the gospel–soul continuum.

Chapter 6 investigates the ways in which categorisation has influenced pop development, with particular attention paid to how the effects of perspectives derived from jazz and folklore approaches have led to distortions in the way the music has been perceived by both fans and musicians. Particular attention is given to jazz writers' and folklorists' descriptions of blues.

Chapter 7 looks at rock in the seventies and eighties, tracing the decline of established rock and its 'rebirth' via punk and New Wave. It also looks at the question of pop music's future in the light of the increasing availability of sophisticated electronic hardware.

Appendix A provides an explication of our central theme via the means of musical analysis. It concentrates upon the musical structures of the blues-boogie-gospel family, and the development of those structures via later branches of the pop tradition.

Appendix B, the discography, provides detailed information of the current availability of those recordings most important to our argument.

Appendix C, the bibliography, lists all books and articles mentioned in the text. It should be noted that all such references are denoted in the text by author and date of publication.

Chapter 1

Continuity and change in pop: something old, new, borrowed and blue

When the leading groups of the British 'beat' movement recorded rock & roll, rhythm & blues and 'country' blues during the sixties they were both exploiting and contributing to a lengthy pop tradition. Some of the songs recorded by the Beatles, the Rolling Stones, the Animals, Them, and Cream, to name but a few, had been part of the American pop music scene for over thirty years, whilst others were products of the rhythm & blues, country & western, and rock & roll booms of the forties and fifties.

The song 'Matchbox', for instance, recorded by the Beatles in 1964, was first recorded by the legendary blues singer and guitarist Blind Lemon Jefferson in 1927. In 1934 Jefferson's recording was undoubtedly the inspiration for a recording of the song by a white, country singer/guitarist by the name of Larry Henseley. This version of the song bears every sign of being learnt, virtually note for note, from Jefferson's original recording. This was probably the first white copy (or 'cover version') of a black record; and whilst Henseley seems to have had some difficulties in coping with the more complex of Jefferson's guitar patterns, it is a very fair copy.

Later still, in 1956, the song, with a somewhat modified tune, was a minor hit for Carl Perkins. Furthermore, Perkins is widely reported to have played as a session musician on the Beatles' recording of the song, contributing the heavy 'boogie-bass' guitar pattern present throughout the record.

The history of the song is thus almost the history of pop music in miniature, taking in the 'folk-music' roots of blues and country (or 'hillbilly') musics, the combining of these two, and other traditions, in the rock & roll revolution and, eventually, the emergence of a significant British contribution to the development of pop music in

the sixties, several generations of Blacks, Whites, and, latterly,
Britons singing the elegantly ironic theme of:

> I'm sitting here wondering will a matchbox hold my clothes.
> I ain't got many matches but I've sure got a long way to go.

Similarly, a song recorded by Van Morrison's early band Them, as
'Baby, Please Don't Go' began its recording career under the title of
'Don't You Leave Me Here' when it was recorded by Papa Harvey
Hull and Long Cleve Reed in 1927. As 'Baby, Please Don't Go', the
song was later recorded by Big Joe Williams (in 1941) and by Muddy
Waters (1953) before Them helped to make the song almost a
compulsory part of any aspiring 'British rhythm & blues' band's
repertoire during the sixties.

The emphasis on the country and 'down-home' blues tradition,
which was evident in the early work of the Rolling Stones and the
Animals, became a central theme with what may be called the 'second-
wave' of British rock bands during the latter half of the sixties. Led by
bands such as Cream, Fleetwood Mac, Chicken Shack, and Led
Zeppelin, a British *blues* movement became prominent, in both
commercial and artistic senses of the term. In the USA a similar
movement was led by bands such as the Grateful Dead, Captain
Beefheart's Magic Band, and Canned Heat, and by vocalists like
Grace Slick and Janis Joplin.

These bands also exploited the rich tradition of songs and musical
styles comprising the blues. In particular they combined aspects of
the earlier 'country' blues and the later 'down-home' blues styles and
songs; contributing on the way to many classic 'song families' (or
'tune families').

Continuity and change through song families

A song family, variously called 'Minglewood Blues', 'Roll and
Tumble Blues' and 'Forty Four Blues' for recordings during the
twenties and given a number of other titles for recordings in the
thirties, forties and fifties, proved extremely popular with what we
may term the 'blues-rock' movement of the late sixties. Cream, for
instance, recorded the song as 'Rollin' and Tumblin' ' in 1966, whilst
Captain Beefheart produced a version called 'Sure 'Nuff, Yes I Do'
and the Grateful Dead recorded a version called 'New, New
Minglewood Blues', both in 1967. Later, 1972, Neil Young recorded

the theme as 'Are You Ready For the Country', and Dr Feelgood cut a
version of 'Rolling and Tumbling' in 1975.

The song family seems to have been first recorded by Gus Cannon's
Jug Stompers in 1928, under the title of 'Minglewood Blues'. In the
following year Charley Patton recorded it as 'It Won't Be Long' and
Hambone Willie Newbern recorded it as 'Roll and Tumble Blues'.
The latter version is the start of a series of treatments linking the
recording by Cream to the earliest versions via recordings of the theme
by Robert Johnson (1936 and 1937), Muddy Waters (1950) and
Elmore James (1960). The versions by Captain Beefheart and Grateful
Dead, on the other hand, relied heavily on the 'Minglewood Blues'
'branch' of the song-family, at least in lyrical terms.

The 'Minglewood Blues/Roll and Tumble Blues' song family is
important on at least two counts: first, it has been recorded over thirty
times, by different artists, over a forty-year period, secondly it is as
typical of the 'heavy-Delta' blues tradition, which originated in
Mississippi and moved to Chicago via Memphis, as any single song
family, both in terms of lyrical content and, more importantly,
melodic structure. It also typifies the direct musical links between the
Delta and Chicago blues and the 'hard rock' of the sixties and
seventies, in terms of both guitar and vocal styles.

Due to its melodic structure the song family did not easily convert
to a boogie in the major mode (see Appendix A). Yet it was part of the
repertoire of New Orleans pianists. 'Professor Longhair' (Henry
Roeland Byrd) recorded two versions of it: 'Mardi Gras in New
Orleans' (1949) and 'East St Louis Baby' (1952). Fats Domino then
produced a version, also called 'Mardi Gras in New Orleans' (1963).
Otherwise the song-family did not appear in anything like a rock &
roll guise. Its recording history has two main strands; that of Delta,
and related blues, plus the later 'blues-rock' of the sixties, and that of
the piano-based 'forty-fours'. In the fifties, recordings by Muddy
Waters (1950), Leroy Foster (1950) and others established the song-
family as part of the Delta blues derived 'downhome' style which was
then revitalising the Chicago blues scene.

Other song families of a similar vintage were used in the
development of rock & roll, and its derivatives of the sixties. As well as
the already mentioned 'Matchbox Blues', these included some
interesting versions of a song usually called 'Milkcow Blues'.
Originally recorded by Sleepy John Estes in 1929, the song was a big
'race catalogue' hit for 'Kokomo' Arnold in 1934. Arnold's

intermittently 'off-beat' version was covered by a number of western-swing bands during the thirties and forties. One of these, 'Brain Cloudy Blues' by Bob Wills and his Texas Playboys (1946), contained most of the lyrics used in Elvis Presley's 'Milkcow Blues-Boogie' of 1955. And in 1960 Eddie Cochran recorded a version with the lyrics of the Wills and Presley recordings, a melody close to Arnold's and Presley's, but with a rhythm and a guitar accompaniment in the Chicago down-home blues mould. The central guitar riff used throughout Cochran's 'Milkcow Blues' is that used by Bo Diddley on his 'I'm A Man' (1955) and on a large number of Muddy Waters records of that period. Rhythmically too, the Cochran recording is in the down-home blues tradition. (A few years later Ry Cooder recorded a most curious version; one which virtually duplicated the 1929 Estes version in terms of lyric, melody and instrumentation, and which derived its title 'Ax Sweet Mama' (1972) from a peculiarly phonetically-inspired rendering of the initial phrase of Estes' recording, 'Now I asked sweet mama . . .'.)

Many of the 'revivals' and adaptions of songs, in the development of song families, have been used to inaugurate and to consolidate new musical traditions, and branches of the same. Where a song family has developed via a number of what today would be called 'crossover' recordings, as in the case of 'Milkow Blues', later versions benefit from a range of explorations of the possibilities available in the song.

This method of musical development has been so prominent in the pop tradition largely because most of the musics comprising that tradition are constructed in such a way as to make such developmental procedures not only readily available but also logical. The form and structure of blues is a particularly good example of this characteristic. The blues form, particularly the twelve-bar form, is constructed lyrically out of two or four phrases, forming two sentences (or sentence-like utterances). Thus a typical blues of the twelve-bar, AAB, form can look like Leroy Carr's 'Prison Bound Blues' (1928):

	1st phrase	2nd phrase
A	Early one morning/the blues came falling down.	(repeated)
	3rd phrase	4th phrase
B	I was on my way to jail/I was prison bound.	

or it can appear as in Robert Johnson's 'Me And The Devil Blues' (1937):

A	Early this morning/when you knocked upon my door. (repeated)	
B	And I said hello Satan/I believe it's time to go.	

And though often stanzas A and B could be constructed from what apparently are the long phrases, each a stanza in length, in practice these normally break down into the double-phrase stanzas as required.

The lyrical construction reflects a musical structure which is also composed of phrases of between one and two bars (or, roughly the length of the corresponding lyrical phrase). (See Appendix A for musical transcriptions.)

Thus in lyrical terms the blues form has a flexibility not found in, for instance, the ballad form, in which a coherent story is told. The blues form does not require distinct beginnings, followed by chronologically structured verses, as does the ballad form. In fact many of the old 'joint stock' ballads like 'Casey Jones' and 'Betty and Dupree' were divested of their ballad structure when adapted by blues musicians. Thus where the ballad is part of a long tradition, also including the parable, the epic poem and the classical play, which illustrates 'life' by means of particular stories with general applications, the blues form is closer to the epigrammatic tradition. And where blues songs have episodic characteristics these are seldom part of a coherent narrative as is the case with ballads. This particular characteristic of the blues tradition appears in most varieties of pop music, including those of the (white) country tradition.

The basic lyrical and musical phrases of songs in the pop tradition are the elements out of which song families and musical families are created and maintained. They give the music a technical coherence, providing, as it were, landmarks lending some consistency to an otherwise changing terrain. The phrases and themes of a song can thus be tinkered with to produce either a further development of the song family or a new song in the same, or a related tradition. That is, if a new song is produced it can nevertheless be treated as 'another example of' soul, rock & roll, or whatever, in that it has the 'sound' expected of a song in a particular musical category. Often, of course, it conforms to the requirements of more than one available category. Thus many records of the fifties and sixties, for instance, can be described equally well as examples of rhythm & blues, rock & roll or soul; including a number of records by Sam Cooke, Jackie Wilson and Ray Charles.

Song families and musical families

In pop music the notion of properly separate musical *forms* is a very difficult one to sustain. The constant borrowing of musical structures, ideas and practices within the folk and pop musics of the southern United States, plus the influences of the popular and other traditions, have produced a range of musical types and styles with both common and disparate characteristics. And whether these musics are distinguished according to geographical, racial or cultural criteria, or by any combinations of these, the resulting categories involve strong similarities as well as differences. The early country blues, for instance, had geographical and racial variations of awesome complexity. For though it is usual to distinguish blues as a whole according to racial criteria (that is, as being predominantly the music of Blacks) and secondly according to geographical criteria, the resulting range of sub-types are subject to a large number of exceptions. Some of the white musicians of the south-eastern states, for instance, produced blues resembling the Memphis and Delta varieties. Also the mixture of boogie and blues structures resulting in a distinctive sub-style were to be found in virtually all the regions by the beginning of the pop era.

Musical traditions resemble linguistic traditions in the way that discrete musical types and, for instance, dialects are created and sustained. The relationship between the two phenomena is not merely metaphorical, for they result from at least some common condition. In particular they both result from conditions of social isolation, which in turn are usually the result of geographical isolation. In the case of the musics of the US, the relative isolation of various musical communities has been, at best, intermittent during the last 150 years or so. There were unifying factors at work prior to those of gramophone records and radio. The migration westward to Mississippi, Arkansas, Texas and beyond, in the nineteenth century, the spread of the new religious music through the 'camp meetings' of the revival movement called the 'second great awakening' which occurred during the early part of the same century and the constant movement of peoples to new parts and growing cities, aided eventually by the building of the great railroad network of the later nineteenth century, all spread musical fashions and practices.

By the time of the commercial recording era these, and other historical factors had produced a host of folk types and sub-types

across the southern states, and this range was reflected in the records
produced during the twenties. This can be illustrated by reference to a
few of the first 'field recordings' trips by the Victor Recording
Company. At sessions in Bristol, Tennessee, in July and August of
1927, during their second trip south, the Victor crew recorded Jimmie
Rodgers, later to be the first country music star, the famous Carter
Family, the white gospel singer and guitarist Alfred G. Karnes, plus a
variety of duos and bands featuring guitars, fiddles, banjos and at least
one harmonica. Some of these combinations were racially integrated.
On two trips to Memphis in the following year, the Victor people
recorded the Memphis Jug Band and Gus Cannon's Jug Stompers,
plus various bluesmen from Memphis and the Delta and also a
number of preachers and sacred singers. In terms of the range of
musics, these trips were by no means untypical of field recording trips
in general during that period.

The regional tendencies in the early pop musics seem to reflect the
socio-economic conditions in which they grew. The blues of the Delta
is usually seen as the 'blackest' of blues, and it emerged in an area with
one of the highest densities of Blacks in its population. An area where
not only the racial laws and customs were as harsh as anywhere in the
South, but also where segregation often involved the separation of
some black and white communities in terms of large physical
distances. By contrast, the south-eastern states, often referred to as
the Piedmont area, produced black and white musics which
demonstrated a great deal of interracial borrowing. Both the blues and
the hillbilly musics of the area exhibit a marked ragtime influence. In
fact, if a single song title can ever sum up a family of musics William
Moore's 1928 recording of 'Raggin' the Blues' does just that for the
south-eastern area. The influence of various ragtime elements upon
the blues and country musics of the Piedmont region was probably an
important factor in what may be called an amount of racial
indeterminism in the music of the area. The constant interplay
between ragtime, blues and boogie and the relatively large number of
white musicians playing in black styles, narrowed the dividing line
between black and white musical practices in the area.

One interesting example of this racial indeterminism in Piedmont
music is provided by the recordings of a singer-guitarist called Bayless
Rose. Rose cut four sides on his one and only recording session in
Bristol, Tennessee, in June 1930. Of the four sides two were
instrumentals, and one of these was an instrumental version, called

'Jamestown Exhibition', of one of the vocal sides, 'Black Dog Blues'. This song was recorded a year earlier by a white singer/guitarist from the area by the name of Dick Justice. Justice, who was from West Virginia, made a number of blues records, some showing the influence of black guitarists such as Blind Lemon Jefferson and Blind Blake. Justice used the same lyrics and melody as Rose, but modified the guitar part somewhat. Rose's other vocal side, which he called 'Original Blues', was recorded by a duo named Tarter and Gay in 1928. They called the song 'Brownie Blues'. Apart from a common attention to the subject of 'browns' (i.e. brown-skinned women) the two songs do not share a set of lyrics in any strict sense, though they are close enough to speak of them as two versions of the same song (or as being parts of a song family). This is bolstered by the fact that Rose uses the same melody as Tarter and Gay.

Stephen Tarter and Harry Gay, the members of the duo, are both presumed to be black by those writers who have expressed doubts about Rose's colour. These doubts, or in some cases downright disbelief, are usually stated as deriving from Rose's voice tones and diction. In fact the musicologist Jeff Todd Titon argues that Rose 'was white' purely on phonetic grounds. He states his argument as being 'Rose tended to keep his tongue towards the front and roof of his mouth when he pronounced vowels, and he had a nasal quality to his voice which most black . . . blues singers lacked' (p. 76.). Yet the problem of his diction is not completely distinguishable from Rose's difficulties with the actual vocal techniques required for singing blues and ragtime songs. For he is rather hesitant in his vocal delivery on both 'Black Dog Blues', which despite its title is as much a ragtime song as a blues, and on 'Original Blues'. He certainly seems more ill at ease with regard to the verbal parts than do either Dick Justice or Stephen Tarter.

The doubts over Rose's colour are difficult to resolve either way, however. Comparisons of his voice tones and diction with those of Stephen Tarter, Dick Justice and a number of other vocalists, black and white, from the area provide less than conclusive evidence.

The more important musicological problem arising from the doubts about Rose's 'proper' racial category, however, consists of the very fact that experts find it difficult to determine Rose's racial identity from aural evidence alone (little is known about him apart from discographical details). Rose's records were published in the 'race' catalogue by his record company, Gennett, in 1930. But this does not amount to crucial evidence with regard to the racial question. For quite a large number of records by white musicians were issued as 'race' records (i.e. records by and for Blacks) in those days. Also, a number of records by Blacks were issued on the 'old time' (i.e. hillbilly) series. Tony Russell lists a number of cases:

The Mississippi Sheiks, that is the Chatmans, appeared more than once in the old time listings, while the white Allen Brothers turned up in the Columbia race series. (For this they sued the company for $250,000, but they lost the case and the record remained where it was.) Then the Carver Brothers, a black group including the young Josh White, were marketed largely through Paramount's hillbilly listing.   (p. 25.)

As with the US court which found for Columbia and against the Allen Brothers we are unwilling to contribute to the fetishism of 'racial identity'. It is enough that we have to recognise the phenomenon as a rather stubborn 'social fact'.

The case of Bayless Rose is useful, however, as demonstrating, for those who are as yet unconvinced, the extremely problematic nature of discrete racial identity in the US (and in Britain also). It is also useful as exemplifying the regional and cultural dimensions of the various musics comprising the folk–pop continuum. For the argument over Rose's colour is itself evidence for some degree of *musical* integration of Blacks and Whites in the Piedmont area (as evidenced by commercial recordings).

They all played boogie

A musical factor which contributed to *regional* integration was boogie (or boogie-woogie as it was called by many). It was an evident factor in the work of musicians in virtually all musical areas during the twenties and thirties, though the musical pieces which resulted were usually described as 'blues' on records. This was not an important source of musicological evidence, for the famous early boogie-woogie piano piece 'Honky Tonk Train Blues' (1927), by Meade Lux Lewis, suffered the same categorical fate.

The boogie is commonly thought of, at least in the early period, as a piano music. Furthermore writers generally refer to its rhythm ('eight to the bar') as being its pivotal characteristic. Many jazz writers have argued that it is *the* way of playing the blues on the piano, forgetting that there were other blues piano traditions, including one, the 'forty-fours' which differed markedly from other piano blues styles in terms of melodic progression (see Appendix A, pp. 182–3, for a more technical discussion of boogie structures).

Boogie also has a characteristic melodic, and therefore harmonic structure, however. And where it is adapted for vocals or guitar pieces it is this aspect of boogie which is utilised. In both vocal and guitar boogie pieces it is the bass line (in pianistic terms the left-hand part) which is used as a melody line. Whether the boogie was first played on the guitar or the piano will probably remain in the realm of speculation, but certainly the music was played on the guitar at an early stage in its development. It was also the mode for songs thought of as prototype blues by many writers. Sam Price, himself a fine boogie and jazz pianist, remembered Blind Lemon Jefferson '. . . using the term "booger rooger" and playing in that boogie-woogie rhythm as far back as, oh, 1917–18, when I heard him in Waco (East Texas) . . .' (quoted in Palmer (1981), pp. 106–7).

Jefferson actually recorded a piece called 'Booger Rooger Blues' for Paramount in 1926. Around the same time, possibly at the same session, he cut a track called 'Rabbit Foot Blues'. This record includes a number of boogie instrumental breaks, and it also has an instrumental introduction consisting of an extended boogie 'walking-bass' pattern (see Appendix A, pp. 186–7). Yet rhythmically, the piece often has a ragtime feel about it, at least in terms of the guitar part, which contains riffs and figures contrasting rhythmically and melodically with the vocal part. 'Rabbit Foot Blues' has often been referred to as Jefferson's masterpiece, in terms of early guitar boogie.

A somewhat different adaption of boogie patterns was recorded in New Orleans in 1927. This was a piece called 'James Alley Blues', cut by, presumably, a local musician called Richard 'Rabbit' Brown. This record is also an example of what was becoming a common compositional strategy, that is the blending of boogie with blues structures. 'James Alley Blues' has some verses constructed more or less straightforwardly out of a truncated boogie walking-bass figure and others following a typical blues melodic contour of a 'tumbling' descending run from the eighth (or the octave of the keynote) (see Appendix A, p. 187). The melody of the song is reminiscent of a number of pieces cut around thirty years later by Fats Domino. It is particularly close, in terms of melody, to Domino's 'Country Boy' (1960). And this similarity is enhanced by Snooks Eaglin's acoustic guitar backed version of 'Country Boy' (c. 1960).

In 1930 a certain Willie Walker cut four sides for the Gennett label, in Richmond, Indiana; his only recording session. Walker was famous in the area around his home of Greenville, South Carolina, as a ragtime guitarist. According to Bastin (1971, pp. 71–2) he was in fact thought of as the best ragtime player in the area by all his peers, including Josh White and Blind Gary Davis. Yet the first side Walker recorded was a version of the common-stock song 'Betty and Dupree', called 'Dupree Blues' by Walker. Like a number of the common-stock songs, 'Dupree' is fashioned from the boogie melodic patterns. Also, like many of the common-stock songs, it was 'revived' during the rock & roll era. Chuck Willis's 'Betty and Dupree' (1957) was a minor hit. It was also extremely close, in melodic terms, to the Walker version. This is probably no coincidence, for Willis was also from the Piedmont area. The Walker-Willis treatment of the song was probably part of a local tradition, for Brownie McGhee cut a similar version two years before Willis. Willis also revived the common-stock pieces 'C. C. (i.e. Easy) Rider' and 'Frankie and Johnny' (1957).

A year before Walker's 'Dupree Blues' recording, Charley Patton had his first recording session. Patton, who many regard as the 'father' of the Delta blues tradition, included for that session a piece called 'Tom Rushen Blues' (re-recorded in 1934 as 'High Sheriff Blues'). The tune is again one following boogie patterns. It also has some semblance of ballad structure in its lyrics. This has led John Fahey (1970) to refer to it as a 'blues-ballad', though the boogie melodic structure also links 'Tom Rushen Blues' to the old common-stock ballads.

Further members of the 'Tom Rushen Blues' song family were recorded by Leroy Carr, who cut a version called 'Midnight Hour Blues' in 1932, and by Robert Johnson, who recorded a version called 'From Four Until Late' in 1937. Carr's version of the song was an essentially northern and urban example of the vocal boogie piece, with his relaxed, mellow vocal accompanied by his own piano and 'Scrapper' Blackwell's jazz-inspired guitar work. The Carr/Blackwell duo began an urban blues tradition which came closer to the country variety than had most of the previous types of urban blues. They obviously had an amount of influence amongst country blues musicians as well as with those in the northern cities, for this is shown in a good deal of Robert Johnson's recorded output, including 'From Four Until Late', where he does a guitar version of the Carr piano part.

Johnson's approach to boogie was an important and widely

underrated legacy to the Chicago downhome blues of the fifties and sixties. Echoes of his style can be clearly heard in the work of Jimmy Reed, Sonny Boy Williamson (Rice Miller) and, of course, Elmore James. Many of James's recordings of Johnson's 'Dust My Broom' are accentuated expressions of the 'rocking' boogie style of Johnson.

Hillbilly boogie

The above examples show the extent of the spread of the boogie approach to what was still usually called 'blues' in the twenties and thirties. Musicians from Texas, the Piedmont area, and even the Mississippi Delta region and the northern cities were playing, as part of their repertoire, a boogie-structured music. And it was the boogie structure which continued to be the unifying factor in the otherwise regionally based 'rhythm & blues' of the forties and fifties.

The boogie approach to blues also pervaded white southern music. Initially, the melodic progressions of the boogie may well have found their way into hillbilly repertoires via the many common-stock songs having that structure. Possibly, of course, the origins of hillbilly boogie go back to the songs brought back from the camp meetings of the Second Great Awakening (c. 1800–30) (see Chapters 3 and 5).

Whatever the pre-pop origins of hillbilly boogie, there is no doubting the central role it played in the development of country music from the twenties to the present. The fundamental contribution of Jimmie Rodgers, for instance, was that of incorporating into 'white blues' the rhythmic and harmonic elements of hillbilly musics. That peculiar syncopation involving an 'off-beat' lilt was one element in the blend of country and boogie-blues associated with Rodgers; another was his mixture of common-stock, hillbilly and blues lyrics. He did not, as some of his contemporaries did, use phrases and expressions which were peculiarly black, with references to 'browns' and similar black idioms. He incorporated those idioms and images which were common to the southern working class, both black and white, in the twenties and thirties.

The musical structure of his blues, including the 'blue yodels', ranged from the straight major-scale, truncated walking-bass progressions, similar in structure to 'Rabbit' Brown's 'James Alley Blues', to those involving the popular boogie-blues progression of movements from the major sixth to the minor ('flatted') seventh and from the major second to the minor ('flatted') third (plus inversions of

n descending runs). His 'Blue Yodel No. 1 (T For Texas)' is an
le of the former, whilst his 'Train Whistle Blues' (*c.* 1928)
exemplifies the latter (see Appendix A for transcriptions and
analysis). The boogie-blues figures of 'Train Whistle Blues' have been
a common method of blending the major scale of boogie with the
minor and pentatonic scales of Texas and Delta blues. One early
example is that of Mississippi John Hurt's 'Got The Blues, Can't Be
Satisfied' (1928). Later, Elmore James used it as the basis for the
melody of his 'Shake Your Moneymaker' (1961). In more recent times
Bruce Springsteen used it for the initial notes of 'The River' (1980)
and for the first few notes of 'Downbound Train' (1984). And in the
fifties Bill Doggett used it as the basic melody for his instrumental
'Honky Tonk' (1956).

The boogie-blues of Jimmie Rodgers were to become the mainstay
of country music. The subdued, but definite, off-beat lilt of the 'blue
yodels' became gradually more accentuated through the western
swing, honky tonk and hillbilly boogie derivations of the thirties and
forties; eventually evolving into the rockabilly of the fifties.

Rodgers may thus be thought of as the first 'white boy who stole the
blues'; that is, stole rather than borrowed the blues, and thus
synthesised what became the dominant strain of country music.

The musics which together constituted early pop can be seen as an
extended family, or as a small 'clan'. And though country music and
blues, for instance, could be and were distinguished, they were
related both in terms of common musical elements and in terms of
common ancestors.

The blues-boogie-gospel family

Blues and boogie are obviously the musical equivalent of siblings.
Both are probably descended from a combination of the 'camp
meeting songs' of the Second Great Awakening (*c.* 1800), the 'sorrow
songs' of the latter slavery period and the 'common-stock' folk songs
and ballads of the late nineteenth and early twentieth centuries. Of the
two boogie is the easiest to describe in musicological terms, due to its
relatively small range of melodic and (therefore) harmonic
progressions, plus its equally limited set of rhythms. 'Blues', on the
other hand is a term at least partly the result of marketing practices
immediately prior to and during the early days of pop. It has been
used to describe musics ranging from the compositions of W. C.

Handy, through the Tin Pan Alley compositions stimulated by the success of Handy's songs, to vaudeville and minstrel songs of all kinds. Also, of course the term is used for jazz pieces having twelve-bar verses and a boogie-blues chord progression. Even within the country blues, which most writers consider to be the most 'authentic' of those musics carrying the 'blues' tag, there is a huge array of largely regional variations. Just within the state of Mississippi, for instance, a relatively large number of related yet distinct traditions existed in the twenties and thirties. So that even without the influence of popular music, the 'blues' has to be thought of as an amalgamation of a large number of musical traditions, some specific to a small town or country, others associated with one of the larger cities such as Memphis or Atlanta.

Thus boogie and blues, and also blues and ragtime, are related as are the poles of a continuum; with most of the ground between the poles consisting of various blends of the two polar traditions. The 'blues' pole would consist of those performances using the 'blues pentatonic' (see Appendix A, p. 190), many, if not most, of which would be from the Delta blues tradition. The far pole would be boogie, with the blues performed in the major scale adjacent, and so on. Diagrammatically the continuum would look rather like that below.

boogie-woogie ————————————————— Delta blues
major mode   major + minor modes   pentatonic mode

A more detailed picture of the structural relationships between boogie and blues is obtainable via the comparison of the key components of each. For, of course, the mode (meaning the actual notes of the scale used) is just one of the important elements in musical construction. The other key elements are the 'form', or verse construction; 'tonal distribution', meaning the tones most and least often, plus initial tone selection; 'melodic contours', which illustrate the melodic progression of the piece; and finally, 'rhythmic structure'. The following diagram compares the key elements of blues and boogie.

Form

boogie ◄ ──────────────────────── ► blues

Modes

boogie ◄ ─ ─ ─ ─ ─ ─ ─ ─ ─ ─ ─ ─ ─ ─ ─ ─ ► blues

Tonal distribution

boogie ◄ ──────────────────────── ► blues

Melodic contours

boogie ◄ ─ ─ ─ ─ ─ ─ ─ ─ ─ ─ ─ ─ ─ ─ ─ ─ ► blues

Harmonic progression

boogie ◄ ─ ─ ─ ─ ─ ─ ─ ─ ─ ─ ─ ─ ─ ─ ─ ─ ► blues

Rhythmic elements

boogie ◄ ─ ─ ─ ─ ─ ─ ─ ─ ─ ─ ─ ─ ─ ─ ─ ─ ► blues

(Where ◄ ─ ► = a weak link and ◄──► = a strong link.)

On occasion a blues can differ from a boogie, or boogie-blues, simply in terms of rhythm plus the flattening of the third and seventh of the scale. In such cases the two melodic contours would be almost identical. In the case of song families such as 'Minglewood/Roll and Tumble', for instance, there are boogie as well as various kinds of blues versions.

If gospel were substituted for boogie in the comparative diagram the picture would not alter very much. For during the pop era the gospel song has often been musically inseparable from the blues–boogie continuum. The most characteristic element of gospel during this period, apart from lyrical considerations, has been its strong off-beat syncopation. The 'beat' so closely associated with rock & roll seems to have been a feature of gospel music prior to its appearance in secular forms such as boogie, rhythm & blues and, especially, rock & roll.

The modern form of gospel is, of course, characterised by certain vocal styles and techniques, especially the extended use of melismata and the use of a wide tonal range in composition and performance. These vocal characteristics contrast starkly with those of blues. The latter are typified by their closeness to speech tones, at least in contrast both to gospel and European vocal techniques. That is, blues, or at least the early country blues, employ a rather *narrow* tonal range. This characteristic is particularly obvious when the vocalisation of early blues is compared with that of hillbilly musicians, who tended to use a much wider vocal range than that required for blues singing.

The vocal techniques of gospel were extremely influential from the late forties onwards. The techniques were popularised in the pop world by Roy Brown and Charles Brown during the late forties. And the 'crying' inflections of the sound were accentuated by a number of disciples of these pioneers in the early fifties. Little Richard's first recordings, in October 1951, sound very much like an amalgamation of the styles of the two Browns. Bobby 'Blue' Bland also adapted the gospel sound, and had a rhythm & blues hit with Charles Brown's 'Drifting Blues', which he called 'Drifting From Town to Town', in 1952. Bland's version of the song accentuates the emotional possibilities in the lyrics, which were relatively understated in Brown's performance. Despite the fact that he cut a number of up-tempo, rocking, numbers in the early fifties, Bland, unlike Little Richard, did not achieve fame as a rock & roll vocalist. Perhaps this was due to the wider range, particularly of texture, in Richard's voice, a voice which, probably because of his emphasis on the dramatic during his rock & roll career, has not been fully appreciated.

Ray Charles was another early disciple of the gospel-influenced vocal style. His first records, in the late forties, were very much in the Charles Brown vein. Later, with Atlantic, his recordings emphasised the gospel influence in their vocal style whilst sticking to the blues melodic contours. Occasionally Charles recorded an up-tempo number, such as 'I've Got A Woman' (1954), which was covered by Elvis Presley (1956), and 'Leave My Woman Alone' (1956), recorded by the Everly Brothers in 1957, and therefore, virtually by accident, became associated with rock & roll. Yet Charles, like Bland, stuck mostly to what are best described as proto-soul performances. Much of his output prior to 1959 consisted of his own brand of gospel-blues songs like 'Blackjack' (1955), 'Drown In My Own Tears' (1956) and, the flip side of 'I've Got A Woman', 'Lonely Avenue', which was a straight blend of blues pentatonic melody and gospel-tinged, 'crying', vocals.

Though he incorporated a female vocal group, the Raelettes, into his recordings in the mid-fifties, Charles did not adopt the boogie-gospel melodies patronised by other vocalists and groups. Yet his style remained in the rhythm & blues category, with the accent on the *rhythm*, in contrast with, for instance, the blues-gospel fusion of B. B. King.

The production of pop via the secularisation of the lyrics of otherwise straight gospel songs was also a feature of the early and mid-fifties. Vocalists such as Clyde McPhatter, Jackie Wilson and

Sam Cooke, and the vocal groups who developed the 'hot' vocal style which supplanted the earlier 'cool' style of the Ink Spots and the Ravens, usually stuck with the straight, major-key boogie melodies that were popular with the church-based groups. This is particularly true of Cooke's recordings. His final recording sessions with the gospel group, the Soul Stirrers, were not immediately distinguishable from many rock & roll records by vocal groups of that time.

In their respective approaches to melodic structure, Ray Charles and Sam Cooke present an interesting contrast. Cooke's blend of major-key boogie with the gospel beat and vocal techniques differed markedly from Charles's fusion of blues melodies and gospel vocals. The contrast is especially of interest because both of these artists have been proposed, from time to time, as the 'father' of soul music. They also provide a neat exemplification of the variety of blends obtainable from the blues-boogie-gospel complex of musical elements.

A somewhat different contrast is that between Charles and B. B. King. Both began recording blues–gospel pieces in the late forties. They differed mainly in their approaches to rhythm. Charles incorporated New Orleans and jazz, as well as gospel elements, into his piano accompaniments, reflecting both the time he spent in the 'crescent city' and his parallel career as a pianist/composer in jazz (where he was a leading figure in the 'soul' movement of the fifties). His piano style seems to have been as influential in the Nashville-centred country field as it was in rhythm & blues circles, particularly in terms of its rhythmic elements. This is evident if Charles's work from around 1952 is compared with Floyd Cramer's later work (e.g. from 1956 onwards). (This adds to the irony of Charles's eventual rise to the big time via his interpretation of country songs.)

Riley 'Blues Boy' King, on the other hand, achieved prominence by evolving distinctive guitar and vocal styles. His guitar technique was a further development of the line from Charley Patton and Robert Johnson, through to Robert 'Junior' Lockwood and Robert 'Nighthawk' McCullem. His vocal technique, however, owes more to gospel than to blues singing, though it can still be seen as a development of Johnson's approach. Rhythmically King was closer to the Son House to Muddy Waters line (also including Robert Nighthawk). King's popularity among Blacks, which has been unusually large for a modern bluesman, has largely been attributed to his gospel-style vocals. His influence in the white community, particularly amongst musicians, rests, however, on his guitar technique. He together with Otis Rush, Jimmy Rogers and Buddy Guy, defined first modern blues guitar playing, and through the work of musicians like Eric Clapton, Jimmy Page and other disciples, defined blues–rock, 'progressive-rock, and eventually 'hard-rock' guitar techniques, in the sixties and seventies (a tradition carried on by the 'heavy metal' guitarists during the eighties).

In recent years both blues and gospel vocal techniques have been very influential in pop music. The gospel techniques and mannerisms which transformed rhythm & blues in the fifties were also a factor in the development of rock vocal styles in the sixties and seventies. But so also was a modified version of early blues techniques. This tradition appears to have begun with Bob Dylan's solution to his problem of constructing an appropriate singing voice for a young northerner singing southern country music (both black and white) without sounding like a Greenwich Village 'folk-singer'. Though his most obvious model was Elvis Presley, at least the young Presley of Sun Records, Dylan seems to have preferred a more novel solution, that of a synthesis of southern styles which stopped just short of a caricature. The relatively 'flat' delivery of blues vocal styles was accentuated further, bringing it even closer to the intonation of a speaking voice. With it came a modified drawl and what appeared to be a voice 'cracked' by over-use or hard times.

Dylan seems to have been rather proud of the results of his vocal experimentation, for on his 'Talking New York' (1962) there is a passage where he describes an incident in Greenwich Village in which someone, presumably the proprietor of a coffee shop, or a folk club, refuses to give him employment on the grounds that '. . . you sound like a hillbilly – we only have folksingers here'. Dylan recounts the episode with evident satisfaction; what was intended as an insult was treated as a compliment by him. His vocal disguise worked.

The technique was honed during Dylan's first four years of recording. It is particularly noticeable on his reworking of the Charlie Pickett song 'Down The Highway' (1937), on *The Freewheelin' Bob Dylan* (1963), and on 'Chimes of Freedom' and 'It Ain't Me Babe', from *Another Side of Bob Dylan* (1964). But the technique became a new *rock* vocal style with the release of *Bringing It All Back Home* and *Highway 61 Revisited* (both 1965). It quickly became fashionable within what was regarded as rock music's *avant garde* at that time. Jim Morrison of the Doors and, in the long run, more importantly, Lou Reed with the Velvet Underground, adopted the Dylan vocal style. It was imported into Britain, first by David Bowie, in the late sixties, but most notably by Bryan Ferry of Roxy Music at the beginning of the following decade. Roxy Music were generally thought of as little more than a novelty act, by critics of that time. For 'glam. rock', as it was called, seemed to be simply a rather camp revival of fifties rock & roll. Yet both the early albums and the very successful single, 'Virginia Plain' (1972), were a foretaste of things to come; namely, the punk and New Wave movements of the mid-seventies.

The seventies also highlighted a competition between guitar styles at a time when technological developments were providing electronic 'instruments' which could threaten the guitar's domination of pop music for the first time. The 'single-string' blues-rock style which had given guitarists like Eric Clapton first a cult following then the status of prophets of instrumental technique, as is usually the case in musical development, became a cliché as, and partly because, it became the central style in rock music. At the same time increasingly sophisticated electronic hardware made it possible for any sound to be synthesised, allowing records to be produced without, as it were, the benefit of musicians, as, for example, in the case of Jean Michel Jarre's *Oxygene* (1977). Whether such technological innovations will eliminate the imaginative musician from pop altogether is a question which only time will answer.

The string-band tradition in pop

The rise of punk and New Wave guitar styles had been foreshadowed not only by Roxy Music and David Bowie but also by The Band. And as The Band's Robbie Robertson showed, the 'new' guitar styles were neither new nor revamped rock & roll techniques. Robertson showed, as did Billy Gibbons of ZZ Top, that blues, let alone rock, guitar does not have to involve a great deal of staccato passages in the treble register, neither does it necessarily require a large dose of musical and performance histrionics. Robertson's beautifully understated guitar on Dylan's 'Visions Of Johanna' (1966), perhaps even more than his work on The Band's albums, exemplifies this point to perfection. Likewise, Gibbons's guitar work on the Top's masterful 'Jesus Just Left Chicago' (1973) shows the beauty of the 'cool' guitar techniques in the blues tradition.

Throughout the many changes in musical styles of the last sixty years the guitar has remained the core instrument in pop; a status never seriously threatened prior to the development of the modern synthesisers. And the modern pop band of guitar(s), bass-guitar and drums, plus various supplementary instruments, is still recognisably a close relation of the ubiquitous country string-band of the early days of the century.

The original string-band format of banjos and fiddles was to be found all over the country areas of the southern USA around the turn of the present century. Gradually the guitar displaced the banjo, first, according to most historians, among black musicians and lastly among the white musicians of the southern mountains. By the beginning of the pop era the typical country string-band was composed of one or more guitars, possibly a banjo or two, plus fiddles and often washboard and jugs. Malone (1968), in common with most recent country music historians, argues that the white musicians, particularly those of the Piedmont region, also adopted black guitar techniques. And it is certainly true that most of the white pioneers of the instrument, including Maybelle Carter, Sam McGee, Mose Rager, Ike Everly and Jimmie Rodgers, admitted their debts to black guitarists. This seems to have been especially the case with respect to finger-picking styles, as Kienzle (1984) details.

The guitar that gradually displaced the banjo as the pivotal instrument of the string-band was, and is, almost as distinct from the Spanish, or 'classical', guitar as that instrument is from its eastern European and Asian cousins, such as the Russian balalaika, the Greek bouzouki and the Indian tambura. The pop guitar is essentially an American instrument, though adapted from the Spanish model (just as that instrument was, presumably, adapted from earlier instruments). Even the 'acoustic' version of the American guitar differs from its Spanish 'parent' in terms of its size, shape, materials, and perhaps most importantly in terms of the techniques used to play it.

The one instrument that has offered competition to the guitar's central position has been the piano. Yet, largely due to the increased volume available from the American guitar, the two instruments have also been extremely successful working in tandem, particularly in the context of the evolving string-band. In fact the augmentation of the string-band by means of the inclusion of a piano, so popular in blues bands in the thirties and forties, provided most of the prototypes, and eventually the archetype, for the rock & roll band of the fifties.

The evolution of the string-band, both in terms of changes in the

basic lineup and in the supplementary instruments, provides an
important guide to continuity and change in pop music. In
conjunction with developments in song families, musical traditions
and musical families, the changes in pop's basic musical unit provide
historians and critics with a large part of the principal information
required to describe and evaluate the essential processes of pop music
development. For whether changes are precipitated by audience or
financial requirements, or by technological innovations, those
changes are mediated by, and find their manifestations in, songs, or
equivalent musical items, produced by groups of musicians working
within particular musical traditions.

Throughout the history of pop music development has consistently
involved both continuity and change. Each set of performances which
has been perceived, at the time or with hindsight, as crystallising a
new tradition, invariably blends new elements or structures with
recycled ones. Thus the transformation of one or more traditions
typically combines the exploitation of and contributions to existing
traditions. These principles are exemplified by three of the most
important periods of pop development; the crystallisation of rock &
roll in the early to mid-fifties, the beginnings of British rock (or
'British R & B') around ten years later and the development of punk
and New Wave approximately a decade after that. The influence of
certain themes in rhythm & blues in all three 'revolutions' is an
obvious and somewhat crude analysis of the continuities running
through them. A more sensitive analysis follows the realisation that
each development added to the features of rhythm & blues borrowed
by Presley, Buddy Holly, Chuck Berry and the other pioneers, and in
addition that each development was oriented towards the original
rhythm & blues elements partly through the 'veil' of its precursor.
Thus the recordings of sixties bands like the Stones and Cream seem
to affect the way bands such as Dr Feelgood and The Clash perform
rhythm & blues and rock & roll numbers. Close attention, for
instance, to Dr Feelgood's version of 'Rolling And Tumbling' (1975)
shows a heavy debt to the version by Cream (1966). And elements of
sixties rock permeate much of the work of the majority of bands
associated with punk and the New Wave. This filtration obviously
adds to the richness of the traditions in pop music. And it is far from
being a recent phenomenon. As noted above (p. 25). Elvis Presley's
version of Sleepy John Estes's 'Milkcow Blues', called 'Milkcow

Blues-Boogie' by Presley, owed more to versions by Bob Wills, and possibly to other western swing recordings, than to Estes's original.

The process is not merely sequentially additive. With several musical generations of interpretations to choose from it is possible for a new band to choose any one version or, of course, elements from a combination of all those available. Elvis Costello's interpretation (1981) of Joe Turner's 'Honey Hush' (1953), for instance, leans heavily on the Johnny Burnette Trio cut of the song (1956), though the tempo and the rhythm of Costello's version are closer to sixties rock than to the fast and bouncy rockabilly of Burnette. Yet it is certainly not Costello's lack of competence in such areas that produces such results, as he has shown by 'Mystery Dance' (1977) and other rock & roll tracks. The process of extending song families by the addition of new elements and the creation of new songs in the manner of previous traditions as Costello has done with 'Honey Hush' and 'Mystery Dance' is the very heart of pop development. It is a process which has consistently produced exciting new sounds, often at the same time as paying more than adequate tribute to the 'old masters' of pop, and which has consistently, from the twenties to the eighties, produced records of a quality to outlast the marketing excesses and the gossip surrounding their release.

Chapter 2

Back in the early days

Though pop music was undoubtedly a product of the twentieth-century revolution in communications technologies, in particular those of radio and gramophone records, in strict musical terms the changes thus engendered were, at least at first, less than revolutionary. Neither the popular music of the urban areas nor the 'folk', or 'country', music of the rural south underwent an *immediate* transformation upon the appearance of radios and records. But changes already under way were accelerated, at first imperceptibly, and the modification of regional musics, particularly through their cross-fertilisation, quickened.

The most immediate effects were, of course, upon the size, composition and distribution of the audiences that performers could reach via radio broadcasts and/or records. And though in the early twenties the radio stations of the US were, on the whole, ostensibly 'local', often employing transmitters of only 100 watts, they could often be received over very large distances in those days of rather peaceful airwaves. Some of the more powerful stations, such as WBAP in Fort Worth, WSB in Atlanta and WLS in Chicago, reached listeners throughout most of the States. Bill C. Malone reports that in the early twenties, 'WBAP programmes were picked up by listeners as far away as New York, Canada, Hawaii and Haiti . . .' (p. 36). Likewise, Joe Newman, the jazz trumpeter, remembers listening in New Orleans to WLS (Chicago) radio in the twenties (aural communication, 1984).

WBAP and the WLS were among the first radio stations to feature (white) country music in their programmes; WBAP intermittently from early 1923 and WLS, via its 'Barn Dance', consistently from April 1924. And just over a year later, in November 1925, what was to become probably the most famous and the most influential radio 'barn dance' programme, WSM's (Nashville) 'Grand Ole Opry', began broadcasting.

There seems to have been very little rural black music broadcast in the early and mid-twenties. Whether this was due to radio station policy, the location of radio stations (there was only one station in Mississippi by 1922, for instance) or the inability of black families to afford radio receivers, remains unclear and in need of research. Though as it is evident that many Blacks from even the poorest areas managed to buy gramophones and records to play on them poverty seems unlikely to have been the most important factor in this example of media segregation.

It is important to remember at this point that the record companies *also* took a long time to appreciate the market potential of, particularly, black country music. Thus it was 1926 before Paramount recorded Blind Lemon Jefferson. Writing of Jefferson's first two sides, 'Booster Blues'/'Dry Southern Blues', Dixon and Godrich (1970) argue that 'They were unlike anything that had appeared on record before. Blind Lemon's expressive, whining voice and his fluent guitar – complementing and sometimes replacing the voice – were an unbeatable combination' (p. 34). Jefferson went on to become arguably the most important artist on, at least, Paramount's 'race' catalogue, in terms of both sales and musical quality.

Initially the record companies stuck to urban music, including those records they published for black consumers. The extraordinary success of early blues-cum-vaudeville records such as the ubiquitously cited 'Crazy Blues' by Mamie Smith, seemed to suggest that the record companies believed there was only a market for black music of an urban nature. Thus for a few years the 'race catalogues', as they came to be called, consisted mostly of northern, urban, black women, singing to the accompaniment of jazz orchestras or pianos. Though a great deal of wonderful music was thus put on record, particularly after the discovery of singers of the quality of Bessie Smith, Gertrude 'Ma' Rainey, and Trixie Smith, that music, which has often been known as 'the classic blues' in jazz circles, owed almost as much to vaudeville, popular, and jazz traditions as it did to rural black music traditions, from whence arose the extremely dubious opinion that such singers were musically more sophisticated than the rural blues performers (a subject dealt with more fully in Chapter 6).

By 1922 the record companies were going through their first slump.

Titon reports that 'In 1919, Columbia's net income before taxes was $7 million; in 1921 it lost $4.3 million, and its stock dropped from 65 to 1⅝. In 1923 it filed for bankruptcy and went into receivership, while continuing to produce records' (p. 204). Columbia's was not an isolated case; as Godrich & Dixon confirm: 'Eventually even Victor began to feel the squeeze – their sales fell from $51 million in 1921 to $44 million in 1923, and then dropped to $20 million in 1925. Something had to be done . . .' (p. 42).

The slump was widely blamed, then and since, upon the competition from radio, and, certainly, the broadcasting boom in the early twenties must have been a factor in the record market slump. For one thing, in the early twenties radio receivers would usually provide the listener with higher fidelity than could be obtained from the 'acoustically' recorded products of the record companies (the system of 'electrical' recording, which generally improved the sound quality of records, was not in general use before 1926). An additional factor in favour of radio was that it involved just the single purchase, whereas the gramophone required the purchase of records as well, and at 75 cents each in the early twenties records were very expensive items for poor households of that period. For many southern families, particularly those of an agricultural background, the cost of a record could easily represent ten per cent of their weekly income. But there were advantages as well: records could be borrowed from friends and neighbours, and, unlike the radio, they allowed the listener to choose what music was played. Furthermore, when treated with reasonable care even those early shellac '78s' proved to be extremely durable.

As the large sales of records by artists appearing regularly on 'Barn Dance' type radio programmes seem to show, radio and records were not necessarily mutually exclusive in terms of sales. Quite probably then, as now, hearing a song on the radio could prompt listeners to buy it on record.

The obvious answer to the record companies' problems of the early twenties was that of opening up new markets. Those of rural America in general, and of the South in particular, were obvious choices. For though urbanisation had been an accelerating process since the Civil War the US, and particularly the South, was still largely a rural country in the twenties, with almost a third of the population earning its living through agriculture. In addition, most of the transmitters were located in the urban areas of the North, Mid-West and the West Coast.

At first, though, the record companies faced the problem of their lack of experience of the rural markets. On the whole they were managed by northern, middle-class urbanites, more at home in the fields of popular and art musics than in those of folk and country, and this seems to have applied equally to the 'all black' Black Swan label, which, prior to its merger with Paramount in 1924, concentrated upon the urban, female blues singers.

Even the first 'field trips' to the South did little to change the record companies' catalogues. For instance, the pioneering trip by Ralph Peer on behalf of Okeh records in June 1923 produced no recordings of black country singers. What it did produce were recordings of Fannie Goosby and Lucille Bogan, both of whom sang in, more or less, the urban manner, and both were accompanied by a pianist.

Yet that first trip to Atlanta did result in the recording of the first genuine 'hillbilly' sides, according to Malone. And as befits the genesis of country music on record it involves a moral tale which highlights the inexperience of Ralph Peer, and by implication his colleagues, at that time.

At the behest of Polk Brockman, Okeh's talent scout and distributor in the Atlanta area, Peer recorded two songs by Fiddlin' John Carson on that first field trip. The songs were 'The Little Old Cabin in the Lane' and 'The Old Hen Cackled and the Rooster's Going to Crow'. Malone tells us that initially Peer 'responded as one might expect of a northern urbanite upon first being initiated into the exotic world of southern folk music. He thought the singing was awful and insisted that only Carson's fiddle tunes be recorded' (p. 41). Brockman insisted that Peer record and release the vocal and fiddle performances, however, and '. . . offered to buy five hundred copies of Carson's first recorded and unpressed numbers immediately. Unable to conceive of a regional or national market for such items, Peer issued the record uncatalogued, unadvertised, unlabled, and for circulation solely in the Atlanta area' (p. 41). Of course, after little more than a month Brockman had sold that batch of records and had ordered a further five hundred. Peer, realising he had made at least a *commercial* error, put the record into the label's 'popular' catalogue, thus bestowing upon Carson's efforts national publicity and distribution. Malone argues that 'This was the real beginning of the hillbilly music industry' (p. 42), a not unreasonable argument, as the WLS (Chicago) 'Barn Dance' did not begin broadcasting until April 1924 (and did not achieve coast-to-coast networking until 1933), whilst the WSM (Nashville) 'Grand Ole Opry' show did not begin until late 1925.

As the overall sales of records continued to fall in the years between 1920 and 1928, somewhat ironically the number of releases in the 'race' and 'hillbilly' catalogues spiralled. Dixon and Godrich state, for instance, that the number of blues and gospel records released per year jumped from around fifty in 1920 to over *five hundred* in 1928.

Yet despite the many field trips to southern locations during the next three years, at least by Okeh and Columbia, it was not until 1926 that country blues performers of any stature were found and recorded. The first of these, Blind Lemon Jefferson and Blind Blake, were both recorded by Paramount in Chicago. It was Paramount's policy at that time to rely on talent scouts and the public to recommend performers, who were then taken to the company's northern studios to record. This policy certainly did not weaken the company's ability to find adequate blues performers, for their artists' roster eventually included Gertrude 'Ma' Rainey, Charley Patton, Frank Stokes, Son House, Skip James, Roosevelt Graves, and Tommy Johnson, as well as Jefferson and Blake.

Paramount relied heavily upon mail-order sales, whereas their competitors tended to market their products through local distributors in the regions and major cities. And Paramount used the mail-order system to their further advantage by inviting customers in the regions to send in suggestions for the company's artist and repertoire department. But much of Paramount's success in the 'race records' market was owed to their black recording director, Mayo Williams, who not only took charge of producing recordings but also helped with the wording of the label's advertisements. Whether his black identity was the important factor or not, Williams's expertise in the area of black country music appears to have been a priceless asset to Paramount in the 'race' market.

Such expertise was not monopolised by black producers for long. Ralph Peer obviously made the most of his field experience with the Okeh label, for in 1927, when Victor entered the country markets, they put their field operations into his hands. The move paid off in spectacular fashion, for in his first year of field trips Peer found and recorded Blind Willie McTell and Julius Daniels (in Atlanta), Jimmie Rodgers and the Carter Family (in Bristol, Tennessee), plus Cannon's Jug Stompers, the Memphis Jug Band, Tommy Johnson, and Jim Jackson. From that point Victor (from 1929 RCA-Victor) became, arguably, the leading record label in the emerging pop industry.

The Southland gave birth to . . .

Any one of a number of events in the twenties could be taken as marketing the birth of the pop music industry. Ralph Peer's discovery of Jimmie Rodgers in 1927 is an obvious choice, given the immense popularity and influence of Rodgers. On the other hand, blues fans and historians might point to the initial recordings of Blind Lemon Jefferson (1926), those of Bessie Smith (1923), or even the ubiquitously mentioned 'Crazy Blues', by Mamie Smith, in 1920, as the genesis of pop. Those with a hillbilly orientation might stress, as does Malone, the national marketing of Fiddlin' John Carson's first pressings (1923), or the first radio 'plug' of a previously recorded number, which again according to Malone (pp. 39–40) seems to have been the broadcasting, on WBAP (Fort Worth), by the Texas fiddler Eck Robertson, of the songs 'Sally Goodin' and 'Arkansas Traveler'. The broadcast took place in the March of 1923, the recording session in the June of the previous year.

Such arguments, like those surrounding the first rock & roll, soul, etc., record, are better viewed as entertaining games than as serious historical questions. For just as, in the words of the old adage, one swallow does not make a summer, so not one of the events mentioned above can alone be said to have constituted anything so definite as the beginning of the pop industry, if taken in isolation. Together, however, they and similar events did amount to a significant shift in the way that America's country musics were propagated. For very quickly the songs and musical styles of all the regions of the southern states were transmitted, by radio and records, not only throughout the US but also around the world. By the end of the twenties there were collectors of blues and hillbilly records in Canada, Britain, France and Australia, and probably a number of other countries.

The new communications technologies accelerated the musical cross-fertilisation between black and white and between the various regions, which had previously been mediated by means of itinerant musicians and by the succeeding waves of internal migrations by large parts of the population (South and West in the nineteenth century, and North in the early twentieth). Performers like Blind Lemon Jefferson, Gus Cannon, Blind Blake, and Jimmie Rodgers toured extensively, with minstrel or medicine shows, or playing for the

workers in railroad gangs and lumber camps, before they were
recorded. These wandering musicians spread new musical ideas and
techniques, just as their predecessors had introduced first the banjo
and then the guitar, plus the various techniques for playing those
instruments. And though the musical terrain of the rural South in the
thirty or forty year period prior to recording remains in the area of, at
best, educated speculation, it seems safe to assume that by the
beginning of the twenties varieties of ragtime and blues were to be
found in most parts of the South and in many of the northern cities.
These 'new' musics were likely to be found in coexistence with older,
more 'traditional', kinds. And the local string band would usually
play a mixture of each for the Saturday night dance.

In the case of the south-eastern states, the musical 'map' of the
period seems well illustrated by the early records of the Carter Family.
The Carters – A. P. Carter, his wife Sara, and their sister-in-law
Maybelle – have commonly been portrayed as epitomising the musical
traditions of the 'mountain folk'. Their repertoire and musical
techniques were eclectic, however. The guitar style of Maybelle owed
a great deal to black influences. According to Tony Russell, one
particular influence was '. . . one Leslie Riddles, a black singer/
guitarist from Kingsport, Tennessee. His job was to learn the tunes
(the Carters) collected, while A. P. Carter noted the words. Under his
tuition, Maybelle picked up many of her instrumental ideas' (p. 41).
Despite this tuition Maybelle did not become anything more than an
adequate guitarist, and the many claims to the contrary from
members of the country music fraternity are best thought of as
resulting from affection and respect for the Carters' performances as a
whole. When compared with many of her white contemporaries from
the region, for instance Dick Justice, Frank Hutchison, Sam McGee,
or Alfred G. Karnes, she sounds no more than competent
(comparison with virtuosos such as Willie Walker or Willie McTell
would be pointless). She was not particularly influential as an
instrumentalist in the development of white country music either,
even among 'flatpicking' specialists. Eventually the 'choke' style,
seemingly developed in Kentucky by black guitarists such as
Sylvester Weaver and Arnold Shultz, through its adoption by
musicians like Bill Monroe, Merle Travis, and Chet Atkins,
dominated country fingerpicking from the late thirties onwards.

Ironically, perhaps, the most obvious legacy of the Carters'
instrumental techniques was in the 'folk music' movement which

became big business in both the US and Britain during the early and middle sixties. To 'folk' fans of that period the Maybelle Carter guitar style virtually defined the sound one expected to hear in the clubs which mushroomed across Britain from around 1962. In fact the Carter Family vocal sound, and much of their repertoire, were adopted by British 'folkies' during the sixties. Carter numbers like 'Worried Man Blues', Wabash Cannonball', 'I Never Will Marry', and 'Wildwood Flower', with which the Carter Family had a huge hit in 1928, formed the basic materials of a popular and ideologically acceptable repertoire for innumerable 'folk groups' in Britain. The popularity of the Carter Family's repertoire in Britain during the sixties, stimulated by contemporary recordings by Joan Baez and Pete Seeger, probably involved the reintroduction of British songs to their native soil.

The Carter Family were only in part a 'traditional folk music' group. Their music mirrored most of the varied influences on the mountain music of that period. Though their vocal techniques and much of their material preserved an older style of the region, certainly their approach to instrumental techniques was relatively new (at least in 'folk' terms). And the interesting use of 'bottleneck' (or 'steel') guitar accompaniment on a number of their records, including 'Sweet Fern' (19??) and 'Foggy Mountain Top' (1929) sounds like a compromise between the blues style and the supposedly Hawaiian-derived style of 'pedal steel' which is still a major component of country & western music. Aside from their approach to the guitar, the black influences upon the Carters' music seem to have been smaller than might be expected. The song called 'Carters Blues', for instance, sounds more like an old English ballad than a blues. Even in the material most apparently derived from black sources, such as 'The Cannonball' (193?), where the lyrics are typical of those found in blues, the Carters' versions, perhaps due to A. P.'s talent for song arranging, gave the song an almost 'traditional' hillbilly sound.

In the twenties hillbilly music, even that from the south-eastern state (or 'old South' as it was called) had no single identity. Certainly it lacked anything like the 'Nashville sound' developed in the late fifties. Instead, like the others regions of the South, the South-East contained musicians producing a huge array of musical forms and styles, from 'old time' ballads (many of European origin), to the 'common-stock' songs of the 'Stackalee' and 'John Henry' type, to the dance tunes of the string bands. Also black *and* white musicians were performing, and eventually recording blues.

White country music achieved its identity gradually, and through the Nashville-based industry, created by the success of WSM's 'Grand Ole Opry', but stimulated, to an extent that is difficult to overrate, by the career of Jimmie Rodgers. That identity was gained largely at the expense of outlawing the musical experiments, especially those of an inter-racial nature, which were still apparent in the twenties and thirties. The country music industry gradually became the musical equivalent of a Whites-only ghetto. And this development was only disturbed, and then momentarily, by the success of rock & roll, during which Elvis Presley and others restated in performance the blues roots of the hillbillies.

The success of Jimmie Rodgers helped to give hillbilly music a shape, an outline, which his many disciples developed in the years following his death in 1933. Though he is best remembered, at least by those outside the mainstream of country music, for his 'blue yodels', it was probably through his overtly sentimental songs concerning dying hobos, sweethearts, carefree cowboys and the like, that he exerted his most lasting musical influence upon hillbilly music. Also of course, his modest demeanour, which endeared him to the working folk of the southern regions, combined with his huge commercial success, gave would-be successors at least the gist of a formula for hillbilly music stardom. His commercial success was not merely unprecedented in the fledgling pop industry, it was pretty startling by any show-business standards of the time. It should be remembered that the whole of his short career occurred during the depression, which affected his southern, working-class fans harder than most sections of the population. Yet despite the depression, Rodgers could command, in 1929, $600 a week for touring, and by 1931 he was probably earning well over $100,000 a year from record sales alone; he is also said to have owned several guitars worth more than $1,000 apiece.

Rodgers's brand of blues, the 'blue yodels', were a curious hybrid, having the form and mostly the lyrical materials of blues, yet achieving a lighter tone and texture than was common within that genre. He managed this balance, not by using ragtime ingredients, as was common within the South-Eastern region, but by incorporating a lilting boogie structure, and by giving his 'blue yodels' a melancholic tinge which is generally absent from blues.

Such is the weight that Rodgers' memory carries in country music circles that Malone claims Rodgers as 'The white country singer most influenced by Negro music, and the one who perfected the white blues pattern' (p. 83). The evidence on records suggests, however, that Malone's claim rests more on country music legend than on even a reasonable amount of objective analysis. Actually, a significant number of hillbilly musicians of the twenties and early thirties recorded blues performances which were closer to the black model than the records of Jimmie Rodgers. Many of these were from the Piedmont area, including Dick Justice and Frank Hutchison, who were both from West Virginia, Clarence Greene from North Carolina and, of course, Larry Henseley from Kentucky. These white musicians, and possibly a large number of others, were competent enough in the blues idiom to make recordings which compared favourably with many of the performances cut by Blacks from the same area.

A great deal of evidence now exists which points to an appreciable amount of external influence upon the blues of the Piedmont area during and immediately prior to the era of 'field-trip' recording. This evidence is of two types consisting of statements made to researchers by musicians who had been active in the twenties, and in addition the recordings of the same period.

Both types of evidence suggest that the influence of Blind Lemon Jefferson was extremely important in that, as in other, areas. Jefferson toured the area, and his records sold well there (to both black and white record buyers it seems). On the subject of his influence via his personal appearances, Russell quotes two musicians from the area:

'Up 'til then', recalls the Kentucky mountain musician Roscoe Holcomb, 'the blues were only inside me; Blind Lemon was the first to "let out" the blues'. Hobart Smith of Saltville, Virginia, remembers seeing him about the beginning of World War I. 'It was along about that time that Blind Lemon Jefferson came through, and he stayed around there about a month . . . I think that right about there I started on the guitar.' (p. 48)

Jefferson is also thought to have toured after he had begun to record: this makes difficult in many cases to determine whether his influence on a particular performance was via his records or his personal appearances. This difficulty does not arise in the case of Henseley's version of 'Matchbox Blues' (1934). It is not only possible to be fairly certain that Henseley learnt the song from a record but, as Jefferson made three different cuts of the song, two of them quite dissimilar, it is possible to determine which of the Jefferson recordings Henseley used. Jefferson's first recording of 'Matchbox', and the one 'copied' by Henseley, was cut from the Okeh label (during March 1927, in Atlanta). He subsequently cut two more versions for Paramount in Chicago a month later. The first verse of the Okeh version is:

Up on the river mam- walk down by the sea
Up on the river, walk down by the sea
I got those tadpoles and minnows arguing over me.

This is followed by the title verse, familiar to generations of blues, rock & roll, and rock fans:

I just stand here wond'ring would a matchbox hold my clothes (2x)
Ain't got so many matches – got so far to go.

Henseley's first two verses are lyrically indentical to these. And he also repeats Jefferson's guitar part, including the introduction, which differs from the Paramount cuts considerably (on both of the versions for Paramount, Jefferson opened the song with the title verse).

The Henseley recording demonstrates the revolutionary possibilities of commercial recording. They made it possible for musicians to familiarise themselves with a particular song, or performance, at their leisure. A record could be played and replayed until every line of the lyric, and every musical nuance, were memorised. This would have been very difficult, if not downright impossible, for all but the most gifted of musicians, whilst public performances were the only method of musical dissemination.

The 'note-for-note' copying of a recorded performance seems to have been a fairly rare occurrence in the early days of recording. And as it is typical of the genre for blues songs to be put together from stock phrases and/or verses, either completely or in part, the origins, in terms of either the composer or the area of composition, are often a matter of educated guesswork on the part of historians. Yet the available evidence suggests very strongly that, even prior to the beginning of his recording career, Jefferson was influential not only in his native Texas and the Piedmont region, but also in Mississippi. In fact, if any one person deserves the title 'father of the blues' it is Blind Lemon Jefferson.

A series of recordings serve to demonstrate the importance of Jefferson for black and white blues musicians. They are, in order of publication:

Tarter & Gay – 'Brownie Blues' (1928)
Clarence Greene – 'Johnson City Blues' (1928)
Tommy Johnson – 'Lonesome Home Blues' (1928)
Robert Wilkins – 'I Do Blues' (1928)
Dick Justice – 'Brownskin Blues' (*c*. 1028)
Bayless Rose – 'Original Blues' (1930)
Charley Patton – 'Pony Blues' (1930)

The Justice recording has been described by Russell as '. . . a melee of stock phrases and verses from Blind Lemon's 'Black Horse Blues' (1926) and 'Stocking Feet Blues' (1926)' (p. 85). In a strictly lyrical sense this is an adequate description, though it ignores the possibility that Jefferson used 'stock phrases' himself. The lyrics of the Justice recording are as follows:

1. Won't you tell me mama, honey, where did you stay last night (2x)
   With your hair all dirty and your clothes not on you right.

2. Look here mama, honey, what you have done done (2x)
   You done made me love you, now your man done come.

3. Lord I'm leaving you now, to worry you off my mind (2x)
   . . . ? and drinking, and I don't mind dying.

4. When I met you mama you had no hair at all (2x)
   Give me back the wig I bought you
   Let your doggone hair go bald.

5. Won't you tell me what time the train rolls through your town (2x)
   I want to laugh and talk with a long-haired teasing brown.

6. One goes up at eight, honey, one goes down at nine (2x)
   I wanna laugh and talk with that long-haired brown of mine.

Verses 5 and 6 of the Justice recording are virtually the same as Jefferson's verses 1 and 2 in 'Black Horse Blues'; and verse 1 of the Justice number is more or less the same as verse 7 of Jefferson's 'Stocking Feet Blues', which goes:

Little girl, where did you stay last night (2x)
Your hair's all down and you really ain't walking right.

Verses 1 and 4 of the Justice number certainly *became* 'common-stock' blues components. Ralph Willis, a Piedmont musician of a subsequent generation, recorded a piece called 'Tell Me Pretty Baby' (*c*. 1950) based on verse 1 of 'Brownskin Blues', and Sam 'Lightnin'' Hopkins, a Texas bluesman and protegé of Jefferson, cut a version around the same time. He also recorded a number he called 'Give Me Back That Wig' (*c*. 1949) which was based on Justice's verse 4.

Musically, the Justice number seems to be a modification of Jefferson's 'Black Horse Blues' (see Appendix A for transcriptions). Justice may well have merely intended to 'soften' the rather stark music line used by Jefferson. The guitar accompaniment used by Justice is not, however, very close to that on the Jefferson recording.

The recordings by Tarter and Gay and Bayless Rose sound like further modification of the 'Black Horse Blues' components, and unlike the Justice version both Tarter and Gay *and* Rose refer constantly to the 'brown' of the title. Otherwise there are few lyrical connections between the three recordings. Aside from their titles, the important connections between the three recordings are their melodic structures; for they each sound like a (slightly different) variation on the 'Black Horse Blues' melody line.

In contrast, the recordings by Clarence Greene, Tommy Johnson, and Robert Wilkins all have guitar parts based upon that used by Jefferson on 'Stocking Feet Blues'. In particular, it was the introductory figure of the Jefferson number that was taken up by the other three musicians. The recording by Greene, which lyrically consists of a series of stock blues phrases built around the '. . . going back to Johnson City . . .' theme is notable only for the competence with which Greene handles the complex guitar part. (In fact Greene should perhaps be regarded as an early example of that peculiarly 'white' phenomenon of the 'blues *guitarist*', for the vocal part on his recording seems to be of less importance than the guitar part,) Greene's version of the introductory figure involves a rhythmic modification to the Jefferson recording which is echoed by the Johnson and Wilkins versions. Wilkins, in fact, subsequently used the same guitar figure, played with a good deal more fluency, on two numbers, 'Get Away Blues' and 'I'll Go With Her Blues', cut in 1930.

It seems probable that Greene, Johnson, and Wilkins, all took the guitar figure from Jefferson's 'Stocking Feet Blues', which was a very popular record. If that was the case, or even if that particular guitar part was in general currency prior to Jefferson's recording, these records illustrate how 'stock' phrases, of both the lyrical and musical kind, were central to the development of blues as a musical type.

. . . The country blues

The use of stock lyrical and musical phrases as all-purpose 'building-blocks' in blues composition has contributed to one of the more important controversies in blues research, that being the problem, in general, of blues composition. The central question in the controversy is whether blues songs can *ever* be said to have the work of a single identifiable composer. A number of historians and researchers, including Samuel Charters, have argued that blues composition should be thought of as 'folklore'; that is, as of *joint* authorship by all those involved in the blues tradition. Thus Charters (1963) writes in terms of blues singers '. . . creating a verse pattern . . .' rather than in terms of *composing* a song.

The work, and what those unconvinced by the 'blues-as-folklore' argument would call the *legacy*, of Blind Lemon Jefferson is an eminent example of the problem. The question of whether Jefferson was a composer of original songs is made very difficult by the peculiarities of composition and development in the blues. For the compositional method of using stock phrases as general purpose building-blocks not only resulted in the song family tradition of blues development, but also provided that development with a more suitable, and at the same time more fundamental thread. Thus the song family method can be seen as one of the consequences of compositional method in blues, whereby sometimes the modified versions of all the phrases of a blues would be used as the resources for a 'new' song, whilst at other times a song family extension would result.

A further complication in the problem results from the history of early commercial recording. Jefferson, like a number of his contemporaries, had been performing for many years prior to the start of his recording career. Thus an important period of blues development, the formative years in fact, is not documented to an extent necessary for detailed analysis. What evidence there does exist for the period is largely in the form of the memories of the musicians of the period, plus those of their families, friends, and admirers. In addition to this oral documentation there is also the evidence 'buried' in the subsequent recording history, of course. This does show us the 'state of the art', as it were, as it was initially committed to discs. By combining these two kinds of evidence it is possible to make some sense of those formative years. It is therefore possible to make some reasonable deductions from evidence concerning the age of per- formers when they first recorded, plus the *type* of materials they put on record. Jefferson and Charley Patton, who were born before the turn of the century (Patton *c.* 1890 and Jefferson in 1897) both mixed

other materials, including minstrel, ragtime, and vaudeville, in with
their blues repertoire. Though little is known about Jefferson's
antecedents, at least in terms of who actually taught or influenced
him, Patton is widely reported (e.g. by Palmer, p. 51) to have been
taught at least some guitar techniques by an older musician called
Henry Sloan.

If the repertoires of Jefferson and Patton are compared with those
of older musicians who were recorded in the twenties, certain musical
patterns seem to emerge. Two good examples are Henry Thomas,
born c. 1874, from Texas, and Gus Cannon, born around 1885, from
northern Mississippi and, eventually, Memphis. Both Cannon and
Thomas were first recorded in 1927, and on those recordings both
men exhibited an emphatic ragtime element in their approach to
'blues'. This was more pronounced in the work of Thomas, who in
fact was known as 'Ragtime Texas', than in Cannon's, but was
nonetheless present in both. Also, faint echoes of Thomas's rhythms
can be heard in the somewhat younger Blind Lemon Jefferson,
whereas some of the minstrel tunes which had played an important
part in Cannon's early career were still present, though not
prominent, in the recorded work of Charley Patton.

The following 'musical generation', those born around the turn of
the century, tended to record little which showed any traces of
ragtime. In the Delta, 'followers' of Patton, such as Son House (born
1902), Willie Brown (born c. 1900), and Tommy Johnson (born
1896), stuck mainly to the blues for their materials (though most of
them, again, following the example of Patton and Jefferson, would
also play gospel numbers). And the next musical generation,
including Muddy Waters (born 1915), Robert Johnson (born c. 1912)
and Chester 'Howlin' Wolf' Burnett (born 1910) played only the blues
and, in the case of Robert Johnson, prototypical rock & roll.

Thus the hypothesis that, in country areas, the blues gradually
'replaced' ragtime in the years immediately following the turn of the
present century does find some support from the available evidence.
That is, blues as we view them today would probably have been
difficult to find before 1910, even in the Delta, the rich alluvial
country north of where the Yazoo river joins the Mississippi, which
produced the earliest reports of prototype blues. There Charles
Peabody, an archaeologist from Harvard, heard what may have been
the beginnings of the music outside Clarkside, Mississippi. Among
the 'hollers' and 'jump-in' songs he heard refrains which later became

common-stock for blues lyrics, including the refrain.

They arrest me for murder, and I never harmed a man,

a line which was commonly completed, in blues songs, by the stanza

They arrest me for forgery, and I can't sign my name.

Peabody's trip to the Delta was in 1901. Two years later W. C. Handy, whilst waiting at the station in Tutwiler, a few miles from Clarksdale, heard a man playing a guitar with a knife ('bottleneck' style) and singing the refrain:

Going where the Southern cross the Dog.

Though mystified by the strange lyric at the time, Handy found out later that the local name for the Yazoo and Mississippi Valley Railroad was the Yellow Dog, and that a few miles south, at Moorehead, it crossed the tracks of the southern railroad. The man was making up a song about his journey, it would seem, as he waited for his train.

The 'train song' became an important part of the blues, of course. A quarter of a century later Charley Patton and Willie Brown recorded songs about Delta railroads. Patton sang about the Pea Valley, the train which connected Dockery's plantation, where he grew up, with the local towns.

I thought I heard the Pea Vine when she blowed (2x)
Blowed just like my rider getting on board. (1929)

And Willie Brown sang of the M. & O:

When I leave here I'm gonna catch that M. & O. (2x)
I'm going way down south where I ain't never been before. (1930)

Just when and where the term 'blues' was first used to denote a type of music is still unclear. It is significant, though, that both W. C. Handy and Gertrude 'Ma' Rainey were among those who claimed to have started the usage. Certainly the publishing and publicising of the term and the music, albeit his 'tidied up' variety, by Handy did a lot to reinforce the connection of the name and the music. And 'Ma' Rainey spread the news by including the music in her act long before blues were recorded.

As a musical type the blues is not easy to describe. Traditionally, writers on the subject take the other, emotional, meaning of the term too seriously in attempts to delineate the genre. Yet for its fans the music is immediately recognisable, but via its structure rather than through its supposedly 'sorrowful' qualities. In fact, as a music the blues is no more sorrowful than, for instance, popular, art-music, hillbilly, or many 'folk' musics. Hillbilly music in particular, and especially the modern 'country & western' variety, has a far stronger tradition of overt expression of sad and sorrowful themes, in the manner of the 'tear-jerker'. Like most songs, blues reflects human life in general, though concentrating on the experiences relevant to the singer/composer and immediate audience. Blues songs are thus, not surprisingly, concerned with such topics as sexual relations, travelling, drinking, being broke, work and the lack of it, etc., etc. If there is one central emotional attitude typical of the music it is that of *irony*. And whether this represents a cathartic method for overcoming the 'blues', as many writers, including Southern (1983, p. 331), claim, is mere psychological speculation. For the number of psychological states involved in blues singing may well be as many as there are performers. Some undoubtedly did it for the money, a normal motivation for professional entertainers. Still others quite obviously saw themselves as 'artists' with something important to give to the world (among these we would count at least Skip James, Robert Johnson, and Muddy Waters).

The ironic qualities of the music have always been enhanced by the prevailing musical structure of the blues: though this has very often been described as being, wholly or partly, in a 'minor key', that is, really not an adequate representation of the music's structural properties. The melodic patterns of blues very often look like minor tunes, particularly when transcribed. Yet the aural effect, which is far more important, is one closer to harshness than to the traditional minor effect of 'sad' sounds. Thus many European and Anglo-American 'folk' songs which contain minor intervals in their melodies often look, on paper, similar to blues songs, yet when heard they sound very different. In fact many of the musics, including country & western, which do specialise in sorrowful sounds, use certain major key melodic patterns to achieve the required 'sad sound'.

The 'harsh' tonality in blues is particularly apparent in what Robert Palmer, following Muddy Waters, calls the 'deep blues', i.e. those with their roots in the Delta. These have a structure based on the 'blues pentatonic' (see Appendix A). This mode is composed of the first, fourth and fifth tones of the scale plus 'altered' (or 'accidental') thirds and sevenths. The altered thirds and sevenths constitute what have come to be known as the 'bluenotes'. Though the 'bluenote' phenomenon is difficult to describe within the terminology of western musical theory, it constitutes a tone in between minor and major tones. That is, the major tone is 'leant on', flattening it somewhat, or the minor is sharpened in the same manner. On the guitar this can be done by bending the strings with the left hand; and on the piano an equivalent effect can be obtained by means of 'crushing' the notes (that is by playing adjacent notes at the *same time*, so blending them). The techniques required for the vocal expression of the mode are more difficult to master than many people seem to realise, and little more than a handful of those who have been recorded can be considered virtuosos. Prominent among those are Bessie Smith, Robert Johnson, Muddy Waters, Elvis Presley, Ray Charles, and Aretha Franklin.

As these and a few other artists have illustrated, blues singing requires vocal range, intensity and the most delicate control. But it also requires the ability to provide subtle melodic and rhythmic improvisation. Bessie Smith's 'Gulf Coast Blues' (1923) is a wonderful demonstration of these qualities, as is Robert Johnson's 'Come On In My Kitchen' (1936), in which he shows to perfection the technique of using the guitar as a 'second voice' by matching the tones and textures of voice and guitar. And Muddy Waters's recording of 'Long Distance Call' (1951) exhibits beautifully the subtlety of vocal mannerisms involved in all the most accomplished blues singing. This is especially apparent in the first line of the final verse, as he sings

Hear my phone ringing, sounds like a long distance call,

sliding effortlessly between the major and the 'blue' tones, with just the right mixture of hope and bitterness in his voice.

Elvis Presley may seem a surprising, even a perverse, choice to anyone who has yet to listen closely to his best work in the blues field, though few would deny the awesome qualities of his voice. Despite Presley's well-established brilliance on his *Sun* recordings, perhaps his most convincing performance as a blues vocalist is on his version of the Lowell Fulson number 'Reconsider Baby' (1960), cut during the sessions immediately following his army release.

Ray Charles and Aretha Franklin are better known as soul singers. Yet unlike many of the gospel-trained vocalists who stuck closely to the major scale in their secular performances, as in the case of Sam Cooke, Charles and Franklin have often recorded songs with melody lines based upon the blues pentatonic. Charles' 'What'd I Say' (1959) and Franklin's 'I Never Loved A Man' (1967) are perfect examples of this aspect of their work.

The melodic structure is the basic *musical* component of the country blues song. Of the three fundamental song components, *lyrics, melody,* and *harmony,* it is the last named that is of least importance to the genre. For country blues are typically constructed so as to maximise the compatibility of their lyrical and melodic components. Thus the central 'logic' of the music is that of 'horizontal' (i.e. melodic) rather than that of 'vertical' (i.e. harmonic) coherence. It is a particular feature of Delta blues, for instance, that vocal and guitar parts are sung and played in unison, especially in the case of recordings where the vocal part is accompanied by 'bottleneck' style guitar, wherein the voice and guitar 'echo' each other. Harmony in country blues is an embellishment, secondary to the melodic line, which has become more important as blues have increasingly been played in bands.

An all too common method of describing the 'fundamental' musical structure of blues, particularly by writers with a jazz or popular music background, is that proposing a 'typical' chord sequence. It is ubiquitously given as:

1st line	-------- /------- /------- /------- /
chord symbols	I I I I
2nd line	-------- /------- /------- /------- /
chord symbols	IV IV I I
3rd line	-------- / ------- /------- / ------- /
chord symbols V	IV I I

Thus the 'typical, twelve-bar' blues is commonly described, in shorthand, as being of an AAB, I–IV–V–IV–I, form (wherein the AAB shows that the first, lyrical, line of the stanza is repeated)

However, the descriptive outline given above seriously distorts the structure of country blues. For not only does it imply that a particular harmonic progression is a crucial part of the music's structure; it also ignores the phenomenon of 'bluenotes' in the music. The more enlightened commentators at least include in such outlines symbols such as I^{7dim} and IV^{7dim} to denote the use of diminished chords. Without the addition of diminished chords the outline resembles a boogie progression rather than that of a blues. And even as an outline of boogie progressions it is little more than a very basic, practical, guide, providing a simplified 'musical map' for those who wish to strum out a boogie pattern, for instance.

Given the fundamental *melodic* nature of blues structures, the outline does not even give an adequate guide to (chordal) guitar accompaniment. Country blues often begin on the dominant (i.e. Vth) tone of the scale. Furthermore, the actual chord position used to 'cover' the vocal line can be one of several, including that of the Vth chord, confined in the outline to the third stanza. Many Delta and Chicago 'downhome' blues commence with a diminished seventh (^{7dim}) tone. These include the Muddy Waters recording of 'Long Distance Call', in respect of the stanza quoted above (p. 61). A chord progression which conforms to the verbal part, as appearing on the record, could be:

chording: $I^{7dim\ 7maj.}$ IV IV^{7dim} IV   V
vocal: Hear my   phone ring——ing——
chording: V   V   IV IV IV^{7dim} I   I
vocal: Sounds like a   long dis——tance call
(See Appendix A for transcription and analysis.)

Beginning the verse on the diminished seventh, as Muddy Waters does here, is a common feature of Delta, and Delta-derived blues. Moreover, the melodic structure of the whole line is typical of that blues strain. Thus the tune of the first two lines of the verse is noticeably similar to those of, for instance, B. B. King's 'Rock Me Mama' (1961) and Robert Johnson's 'Rambling On My Mind' (1936). The line is composed of two musical phrases, as illustrated above (p. 55), the progressive structure of which conform to typical phrases of Delta blues. And as we have previously noted (p. 56), the construction of blues songs by means of stringing together a number of lyrical and musical phrases has always been the basis of both continuity and change in that music.

Structure, form and development in blues

As part of an attempt to formulate a 'song producing model' (p. 138 *et passim*), Jeff Todd Titon argues that a blues stanza (or 'verse') should be thought of as comprising six phrases (pp. 142–5). From this point of view an outline of a blues stanza would have the following shape:

```
                    phrase a         phrase b
Line 1 / ------- / -------/ ------- / ------- /
                    phrase c         phrase d
Line 2 /------- /------- / ------- / ------- /
                    phrase e         phrase f
Line 3 /------- / ------- / ------- / ------- /
```

This 'phrase structure' operates lyrically as well as melodically. It also provides a structural level allowing compositional choice apart from that involving single words and notes, within the twelve-bar, three-line verse form.

  The phrase structure of blues stanzas allows for subtle variations of lyric and melody in the composition of new songs as well as in the modification of old ones, i.e. in song family development. A number of the songs mentioned above (pp. 54–6) illustrate perfectly phrase structure choice. Stanza 7 of Jefferson's 'Stocking Feet Blues':

```
        a                      b
Little girl   where did you stay last night
        c                      d
Little girl   where where did stay last night
        e                      f
Your hair's all down   and you, ain't walking right.
```

Becomes, in Justice's 'Brownskin Blues':

```
        a                                  b
Won't you tell me mama, honey, where did you stay last night
        c                      d
Won't you tell me mama   where did you stay last night
        e                      f
With your hair all dirty   and your clothes not on you right.
```

Later (c. 1949) Sam Hopkins recorded a song called 'Tell Me Pretty Mama', the first verse of which ran:

Tell me pretty mama / where'd you stay last night
Tell me pretty mama / where'd you stay last night
Your hair's all tangled / and your clothes ain't fitting you right.

  The three recordings show typical variations at what might be called the phrase 'level', but they also show variations of single words and complete lines (bearing in mind, of course, that a variation of one word counts also as a phrase modification).

  There are obviously some problems involved in applying phrase structure analysis to the *lyrics* of blues songs. Some of the problems are of a grammatical nature and some stem from idiomatic usage. The most important consequence of both varieties of problem is that often a phrase will be equal in length to a line (rather than half a line). These considerations do not render the analysis useless, but they do suggest that phrase analysis of the lyrics should not be taken in isolation from the musical structure.

The phrase structure approach does seem to be rather more applicable to the melodic structure of blues songs. As Titon (pp. 142–3) claims, the vocal line in blues songs does commonly involve a pause ('rest') after approximately two bars (half a line), often with a instrumental fill-in of two or three notes. There is also a significant degree of melodic patterning apparent at the phrase structure level. This patterning shows up in what musicologists call 'melodic contours', which are graph-like representations of musical notation showing the changes of pitch in the form of a curve. Below is part of the melody line from verse 3 of Muddy Waters 'Long Distance Call' expressed as a melodic contour.

phrase a   phrase b   phrase c   phrase d

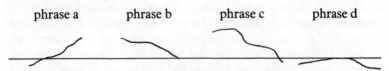

The contour is typical of Delta blues melodic patterns, being particularly close to that of the 'Minglewood Blues/Roll and Tumble' song family.

The logic of phrase structure is a fundamental part of blues song composition, for the mere selection of tonal components, as we have previously noted, does not provide a sufficient basis for a typical blues structure. For the order of occurrence of the selected notes is as important as their individual tonal qualities. Thus the 'rules' (or patterns) of melody construction are similar to those of lyrical composition. Only instead of words being strung together in phrases which are grammatically *and* idiomatically coherent, in melody construction the phrase structures need only be idiomatically coherent (in other words, the resultant tunes must sound like typical blues melodies).

The phrase structure compositional rules allow for a number of variations. Many versions of 'Minglewood Blues', for instance, begin their opening phrase on the fifth note of the scale instead of, as in the quoted verse from 'Long Distance Call', on the diminished seventh, but thereafter follow the same melodic contour. Other songs and performances, notably Robert Johnson's 'Rambling On My Mind', substitute the major sixth, for the diminished seventh on occasion.

The phrase structures are arguably both more fundamental *and* more important components of blues than the twelve-bar AAB format. Modifications and extensions of archetypal phrases (lyrical and melodic) have always been the bases for compositional developments in the music. This is demonstrated by the prevalence of song families in blues recording, which is a typical result of lyrical and melodic phrase modification. And the phrase structures peculiar to blues have been incorporated into songs using the 32-bar from of popular music, for instance in rock & roll, soul, and rock musics, without their being distorted. Ray Charles's 'What'd I Say' and Eric Clapton's 'Layla' (1970) are just two examples of this process.

An important, perhaps crucial, characteristic of blues, in terms of the development of pop music, has been its structural compatibility with boogie. Most of the common phrase structures and many of the melodic contours of boogie are very close to those of blues. In fact many of the available modifications of blues melodic contours, including that of substituting the major sixth for the diminished seventh, result in what we have called 'blues-boogie' structures. A number of songs which were initially recorded in the boogie mode can, with a minimal number of modifications, be played using Delta blues phrasing. An excellent example of these is 'Sitting On Top Of The World'. Compare, for instance, the original version by the Mississippi Sheiks (1930) with that by 'Howlin' Wolf' Burnett (1957), and that of the Robert Johnson reworking of the theme for his 'Come On In My Kitchen' (1936). Between them these versions cover most of the possible gradations from the boogie major scale to the Delta pentatonic.

The legacies of the blues

For those pop fans who view the development of the music as a phenomenon distinct from jazz and popular musics, as is increasingly the case, the country blues are seen as having been a constant source of materials and inspiration for succeeding generations of performers and audiences. The country blues, especially the variety spawned in the Delta by Charley Patton and his disciples, have been the source of vitality and 'earthiness', as well as musical structures, for innovative pop musicians. The feelings for the music inspired by the blues in young and old, black and white, persons throughout the world, during the last twenty to thirty years, amount to a truly extraordinary phenomenon. To most of their American contemporaries the lifestyles of Blind Lemon Jefferson, Charley Patton, and Robert

Johnson must have seemed *anything but* the materials from which heroes are made. For in those days the 'anti-heroes' and 'working class heroes' of today's popular fiction were yet to become the familiar figures they are to us (though a beginning had been made with the 'pulp fiction' devoted to western 'desperadoes'). Patton and Johnson, and for much of his life Jefferson, lived in conditions close to those chosen to depict poverty in the Third World in television documentaries of the 1980s. Many of their friends spent time in county jails or prison farms, on charges ranging from assault to murder, as did Leadbelly and Bukka White. Johnson himself died, according to the most recent reports, from knife wounds administered by a jealous husband.

A few months after Johnson's death John Hammond of Columbia Records was still searching for him for the *Spirituals To Swing* concert he was planning. A quarter of a century later Hammond made up for some of his disappointment by releasing a tribute album of Johnson's recordings. The blurb on the front of the album, heralding Robert Johnson as 'the king of the Delta blues singers', must represent one of the few occasions when record company publicity writers actually managed to *under*state the case. The record enabled Johnson to become a legend, revered by rock fans and performers. And curiously enough, one of Johnson's latter-day disciples, Eric Clapton, led a band (Cream) in the sixties which, though relying heavily on the legacies of Johnson's music, was known as a '*progressive* rock band'.

However, most of the developments involving country blues structures in modern pop music have resulted from blendings of blues structures with those of the other members of the blues-boogie-gospel family, often within the 32-bar framework of popular music. This was especially the case during the fifties, as the musics which came to be known as 'rock & roll' and 'soul' were developed.

Chapter 3

Roll over Beethoven; tell Sinatra the news

That rock & roll involved a revolution within the music world is an assessment few people would quarrel with. The disagreements begin when the nature of that revolution and the dates of its occurrence are under discussion. Though there are many reasons for this state of affairs perhaps the crucial one stems from the difficulties involved in pinning down the musical parameters of rock & roll. There are certain musical featues of the genre which devotees recognise, even when they are encountered in an unexpected context, as in such latter day 'tributes' to rock & roll as the Beatles' 'Lady Madonna' (1968) or Elvis Costello's 'Mystery Dance' (1977). These and many other recordings from the sixties onwards exhibit melodic, harmonic, rhythmic, instrumental and other features which, at least, *remind* the listener of rock & roll from the fifties.

Many fans of rock & roll, including a number of critics and historians of the subject, have preconditions regarding acceptable and unacceptable recording dates built in to their criteria when judging the authenticity of putative rock & roll records. These preconditions are especially apparent with respect to the 'death' of rock & roll. And it is particularly interesting, from the historical point of view, that this is sometimes expressed in terms of a particular year, but often in terms of significant musical or extramusical events. Thus whilst Charlie Gillett (1983) argues that 'The mostly slow and unsympathetic response of the major companies to rock 'n' roll enabled the independent companies to dictate the fate of the music. They brought it to life in 1953, and left it for dead in 1958' (p. 65). Peter Guralnick (1971) gives the following picture: 'But then rock 'n' roll died. It was over before it even had a chance to slyly grin and look around. In its place came a new all-synthetic product . . . we had entered what was then called the Philadelphia era of rock' (p. 20).

In these, and most other definitions we have obtained, the dates and events referred to are commonly linked to each other and to further events and social conditions. In short, it was not sufficient for probably a majority of rock & roll fans for, after a given date, a vocalist or band to produce a record with the correct *musical* ingredients alone. As one British fan told us: 'There were *no* authentic rock & roll records made after 1961.'

Various others gave dates between 1958 and 1963, invariably with reference to preceding and/or accompanying musical and social events they perceived as crucially relevant to the 'death' of rock & roll.

Yet it is not merely the case that rock & roll is generally thought of as simply belonging to a particular time-span, but that as a phenomenon it has dimension other than the purely musical ones. In other words, rock & roll is commonly thought of as a *socio*musical phenomenon, and is therefore closely associated with a specific set of social conditions which occurred during a relatively specific period in time.

It is of course true that all musics are properly treated as sociomusical phenomena. They all occur within some form of social framework, and thus have socially derived limitations imposed upon them, in terms of both their form and content and in relation to how, where, when and by whom they are performed. Usually such social parameters are manifested in both crude and subtle forms, if only in the sense that some are hotly debated and even rejected by some members of society, others are more or less universally regarded as inescapable facts of life. Among the important dimensions of this social framework are those identifiable as aesthetic, moral, political, economic and technological, though on the whole they are usually to be found as compounds of two or more of these.

Thus, whilst for some Americans living in the fifties rock & roll raised aesthetic questions alone, for others it either constituted or highlighted important moral or political dilemmas, whilst a different section of the population saw it as dangerous economic phenomenon. Of course, whichever of these lines was taken, media people found rock & roll good copy.

For some of the more conservative 'moral entrepreneurs' in American society, rock & roll constituted a symptom of moral degeneration. An example of this response was the following:

Asa E. (Ace) Carter of the North Alabama Citizens Council, a group formed to resist court-ordered school desegregation, said in an interview (*Newsweek*, April, 1956) that jazz and rock 'n' roll were a plot by the NAACP (National Association for the Advancement of Coloured People) to 'mongrelize America' by forcing 'Negro culture' on the South; he characterized rock 'n' roll as 'the basic, heavy-beat of the Negroes. It appeals to the base in man, brings out animalism and vulgarity'. (Hamm, pp. 400–401)

To many of the younger fans, particularly those outside the South, this kind of response must have come as something of a shock. Many of them expected their parents, and public figures, to voice aesthetic disapproval, as those VIPs interviewed in the media did, but serious moral and political objections were an altogether different thing.

To the section of American society accused by Asa Carter of instigating the 'plot' of rock & roll, that music and the social movement associated with it must have seemed more than a little ironic. Here were white youths listening to rhythm & blues, using black slang, in some cases copying the dress styles of the young Blacks, in many cases willing to attend concerts with racially-integrated audiences, whilst Southern Blacks strove, throughout most of the rock & roll era, to desegregate Southern schools, buses and restaurants, and generally to obtain *in fact* the civil rights guaranteed them by the US constitution. One of the abiding paradoxes of those times is that of numbers of Whites accusing the black community of forcing upon them what some Blacks were already accusing Whites of stealing.

Large numbers of Americans must have wished the whole thing would disappear before more cans of worms were opened to view. The equation of rock & roll with racial tensions in the South focused more attention on the problem, and provided more television pictures for world consumption, with the attendant probabilities of escalation of demands and resistance to those demands.

Perhaps the NAACP members involved in the Southern struggles saw statements like that by Asa Carter as powerful, if unintentional, advocacy for the integrationist and civil rights causes. Certainly many of the young Whites who supported the civil rights movement during the early sixties are likely to have been nurtured on rock & roll as school and high school students.

Rock & roll was also seen as a threat to the establishment structures of the American music industry, wherein for half a century a few large record companies, together with the American Society of Composers,

Authors and Publishers (ASCAP), had dominated popular music, and therefore virtually commercial music as a whole. In the words of Charles Hamm:

> . . . rock & roll threatened the established popular music industry at almost every level. There was no need for arrangers, orchestrators, or conductors; instrumentalists with standard schooling, who could only play only note for note, could not cope with it; publication of songs as sheet music was incidental and a quite minor part of the process; the singing style appropriate to such music was alien to most of the singers who had made careers as performers of Tin Pan Alley songs. (p. 404)

In this brief passage Hamm captures brilliantly the clash of two fundamentally different approaches to the production of music on a commercial basis, seen from the point of view of the popular music establishment. He describes with obvious sympathy the reactions of unease engendered in that world by the arrival of a music totally 'alien' to it.

The popular music industry of the 1950s was organised still as it had been since the early days of the century. For though gramophone records had gradually gained a larger share of the industry's total revenue since the twenties it was not until the mid fifties that records grossed more than sheet music. So the advent of a music which threatened to make sheet music virtually obsolete, whilst at the same time diverting most of the additional sales of records away from the major companies, was bound to be viewed with alarm by both ASCAP and the major record companies. For until rock & roll disturbed everything, or so it seemed to ASCAP members, the music industry, or the popular market at least, had been organised so as to maximise the benefits to ASCAP members. So by the beginning of the rock & roll era that industry was still organised in a way which reflected its nineteenth-century origins, with sheet music the basic product and with the record industry virtually 'tacked on' to this primary market as, was radio. Thus ASCAP was able, for decades, to guarantee its membership advantageous deals in terms of radio broadcast fees and record sale royalties, due to the monopoly held by its members over popular music copyright.

The popular music industry was cast, as Hamm illustrates, in the image of the art music world. Songs would be written, usually by people who did not perform, then published in sheet music form, for sale to performers, orchestra leaders, artist and repertoire executives of record companies, and similar members of the profession, as well as to ordinary members of the public. Thus the primary manifestation of the product was that of the sheet music publication. Performances, whether recorded or live, also followed closely the procedures in the art music world. The self-styled 'orchestra conductor', and both the musicians and the vocalists would *read* their parts.

Rock & roll, however, was the culmination of a tradition which moved from the folk music methods of aural transmission through live performances to the pop music processes of publication and transmission through the media of radio and records. This direct move skirted the intermediate stage of written publication and transmission. Thus the aural and improvised dimensions of America's Southern folk tradition were preserved in the pop tradition born out of the radio and gramophone industries, and emerging, first on a national scale but soon after on an international one, to challenge not only the ascendancy, but also the fundamental practices of popular music.

The way in which American folk music virtually bypassed an evolutionary stage, that of written publication, as it turned into pop music, parallels, and is a small-scale example of, cases on the wider stage of socio-economic development where societies that began the process of industrialisation later than Britain bypassed one or more of the stages undergone by the 'first industrial Nation'. For some countries, for instance, the modernisation process has *not* included a stage in which steam-engine power and large-scale production of, and construction in cast iron have, in combination, played a crucial role in the growth of the economy, as they did in Victorian Britain.

The bypassing of the 'written publication' stage in the evolution of folk to pop resulted in the idiosyncrasies of rock & roll described above by Hamm. Though mysterious to musicians and executives in the popular music field of the fifties, those peculiarities of rock & roll were largely a result of the distinctive evolution of that music. Of particular importance was the retention of aural methods of transmission. For these included the aural practices whereby songs and performance techniques were learnt by new musicians. And these aural learning methods provided the requirement of, and the ability to produce, improvisations in performance. The two features are often closely linked, in that learning by ear typically involves becoming familiar with musical formulas which generate adequate chord progressions for melodic contours, to take the case of guitar accompanists as an example. Thus the competent pop guitarist will recognise that a particular vocal line has a boogie, a blues-boogie, or some other structure, and therefore that certain chord progressions, and also certain guitar phrases, etc., would constitute adequate accompaniment to it.

These competences and musical formulas were not the result of any mysterious processes; they have always been part and parcel of aural music traditions. In the case of rock & roll, the 'new' music was created by musicians who understood, through their musical *experiences*, the traditions which produced it. Musicians who had grown up with blues, boogie or even a particular hillbilly sub-type, could usually see the musical structures relevant to the rock & roll records they first heard, that is, they could hear the bits of blues, boogie, gospel and hillbilly of which each rock & roll song was a particular blend.

Though there were many styles of rock & roll, they were all blends of blues-boogie-gospel structures, including a number of hillbilly variants. A short, usually rhythmic, step from the music of Hank Williams, Jimmie Rodgers, Robert Johnson and Big Joe Williams, to name just a few of the pioneers, and you had rock & roll. Taking, for instance, the Rodgers recording of 'Blue Yodel No. 1 (T for Texas)' (1927) the lilt of the song inclines towards the off-beat. In many of Robert Johnson's songs the back-beat is even stronger. It is especially evident, for instance, on his 'Ramblin' On My Mind' (1936), 'From Four Until Late' (1937) and 'I Believe I'll Dust My Broom' (1936). Just how small would be the changes required for Johnson's work to become rock & roll in all but name can be appreciated by listening to any of the recordings of 'Dust My Broom' made by Elmore James from 1952 onwards. Big Joe Williams had a very experimental approach to blues, at least during the early part of his long career; in fact some of his very early recordings, especially 'Little Leg Woman' (1935), may well have influenced Johnson. Williams produced particularly interesting recordings from the point of view of rock & roll historians when working with the guitarist Henry Townsend and the pianist Walter Davis. The recording of 'Sweet Sixteen' (1935), with Davis taking the vocal, has melodic, rhythmic and lyrical affinities with rock & roll. The song is in the relatively unusual eight-bar strophe form, made up of two-line, four-bar, verses plus a refrain of the same length. The lyrics are frankly erotic, depicting a woman who is absolutely sure that she continues to look 'sweet sixteen', but also has the maturity to remain in control of her sexual encounters:

Verse 4   She' out there looking like a sugar lump
          She said 'you wanna bump me
          You gotta make me drunk
Refrain   Feeling good, feeling good
          Feeling like I'm ever sweet sixteen.

The tendency, in rock & roll songs using blues-boogie blends was towards the major-scale boogie patterns (in respect of their melodic progressions). A particularly common feature was that of the appropriation of boogie 'walking-bass' patterns as melody (i.e. vocal) lines. This, of course, maintained a tradition in pop which was one of the many legacies of the Southern folk practices of the pre-recording era. It was a tradition which was given additional impetus by the increase in popularity of boogie-woogie piano music during the late thirties and early forties, a period when that particular expression of boogie was fashionable in jazz and popular music circles, partly because it featured in the *Spirituals To Swing* concert (1938) promoted by John Hammond.

Boogie on down the years

During the forties both the term 'boogie' and the music it described finally became the 'in-word'. Just as boogies had been called 'blues' in previous decades, for commercial reasons (e.g. Meade Lux Lewis's 'Honky Tonk Train Blues' (1927)) so even some songs with a blues structure were called 'boogie' in the forties and fifties for similar reasons. But commercial manipulation of descriptors had few ill effects upon the evolution of the music. For in the years following the *Spirituals To Swing* promotion, piano, guitar and vocal boogies, and blues-boogies, provided materials for hillbilly, 'race' and popular hits. The Delmore Brothers had a hillbilly hit with 'Hillbilly Boogie' (1945), and at the same time coined the name for a new white, country style. They followed this in 1946 with 'Freight Train Boogie', and with the slower, differently structured, 'Blues Stay Away From Me' in 1949. Though the term 'hillbilly boogie' was new the music, of course, was not. The white country industry's foundations had been provided by the blues-boogies (the 'blue yodels') of Jimmie Rodgers almost twenty years previously. The new elements in 'Hillbilly Boogie' and 'Freight Train Boogie' were their use of boogie walking-bass and 'eight-to-the-bar' rhythms.

As, around 1946, 'race' records came to be known as 'rhythm &
blues' records, so the experimentation with boogie structures by black
musicians began to produce more and more prototypical 'rock & roll'
records. Along with the rather urbane sound of discs like Louis
Jordan's 1946 hit, 'Choo Choo Ch'Boogie', there appeared records
with the less inhibited country sound, showing the influences of blues
and gospel from the Delta and Texas in their hard, driving rhythms,
guitar and saxophone solos, and that of back-country preachers in
their vocals. Wynonie Harris's 'Good Rocking Tonight', which had
been a hit for Roy Brown the previous year and was later covered in
1954 by Presley, exemplifies this trend. A number of the early
recordings produced by Sam Phillips's *Memphis Recording Service* also
contributed to the new sound. These included 'Rocket 88' (1951), by
Jackie Brenston and the Delta Cats (Ike Turner's Rhythm Aces
renamed for the session) and Rosco Gordon's 'T-Model Boogie'
(1952). Many of the early releases on Phillips's Sun label continued
the new type of boogie sound. Among them were two cuts by Little
Junior (Parker) and his Blue Flames, 'Feelin' Good' and 'Mystery
Train' (both 1953). For the former Parker and the band used a riff
which had served as the basis of John Lee Hooker's 'Boogie Chillen'
(1949), along with lyrics suggestive of the Hooker song. When, in
1955, Presley recorded Parker's 'Mystery Train', he used the guitar
riff from 'Feelin' Good', which could easily be heard as a guitar
impression of a train, as the back-up sound to his vocal.

In the same year as Brenston's 'Rocket 88', Cecil Gant, using the
pseudonym GuntherLee Carr, cut a track called 'We're Gonna Rock'.
This was yet another country-style boogie piece. And its proximity to
rock & roll is evidenced by the fact that many a fan of Jerry Lee Lewis
has mistaken the Gant piano introduction for the work of Lewis.

Piano-led boogies were an early and abiding feature of rock & roll
music, and this tradition was heavily influenced by a number of New
Orleans pianists. The most successful of these, Fats Domino, had his
first rhythm & blues hit with a number he recorded as 'The Fat Man'
(1949). The song, or at least its tune, was a pianist's benchmark in
New Orleans, but was better known in that area as 'Junker's Blues' (as
such it was recorded by Champion Jack Dupree in 1958). A version of
the 'Junker's' theme, 'Lawdy Miss Clawdy' gave Lloyd Price *his* first
hit, in 1952, on which Fats Domino played the piano introduction and
solo, both of which appear, with some modifications, on the Presley
version of the song of 1956 (this time played by Shorty Long).

Presley's approach to the song appears to owe more to the vocal style of Wynonie Harris than to that of Lloyd Price (the latter's singing on 'Lawdy Miss Clawdy' is rather turgid). And in fact Harris cut yet another version of the theme, this time called 'Christina', in 1954, which included an introduction very similar to Domino's, though shared by the piano and guitar.

The doyen of New Orleans pianists, whose real name was Roy Byrd, but who was known as 'Professor Longhair', or 'Fess' in that city, also cut a version of 'Junker's', called 'Tipitina', in 1953 (though without getting the hit his musicianship warranted). This record, perhaps more than any of the few cut by Byrd, shows not only Fess's mastery of the piano, a mastery which probably influenced the playing of Ray Charles, as well as Fats Domino and Allen Toussaint, but also demonstrates his stunning vocal techniques. His approach to the employment of melismatic embellishments made them so acute, in terms of their contours, that often the effect would be close to that of Byrd managing the impossible feat of harmonising with himself. Aural evidence suggests he may well have influenced Joni Mitchell's approach to singing. And though he has seldom admitted to any artistic debts, Little Richard Penniman's vocal gymnastics and piano techniques, at least as evidenced by his rock & roll hits for the Specialty label (most of which were recorded in New Orleans), also owe more than a little to the Professor.

Bill Haley and The Comets, the band that led the assault on the popular music dominated national (then international) charts with rock & roll recordings, relied heavily on the new blues-boogie sound. Their first attempt at achieving a breakthrough with rhythm & blues material, in 1952, was a recording of the Jackie Brenston song 'Rocket 88'. The band's sound, even at the pinnacle of their fame as a rock & roll outfit, resembled a cross between western swing, Memphis rhythm & blues and Kansas City 'jump bands', with perhaps the latter component predominating. The influence of Count Basie is especially obvious in Haley's 'Rock-A-Beatin' Boogie' (1956), which is one of the most straightforward conversions of a boogie walking-bass pattern to a vocal line ever recorded.

For his first major hit, though, Haley used definite blues-boogie progressions. That record was, of course, 'Rock Around the Clock'. It included the classic blues-boogie progression from the diminished seventh to the major sixth, followed by a progression to the major fifth. This progression, together with the parallel one employing the diminished third, the major second, and the tonic, was to become the classic rock & roll figure. Perhaps its most perfect expression within the genre was as the central guitar figure of Bill Doggett's 'Honky Tonk' (1956) (see Appendix A).

Elvis Presley also relied on both boogie and blues-boogie structures for his rock & roll records. His work for Sun Records, which apart from other considerations gave 'rockabilly' its parameters, consisted of a shrewd blend of rhythm & blues, hillbilly boogie, and honky-tonk techniques and materials. It is noteworthy, for instance, that all his Sun records had rhythm & blues materials on one side and hillbilly songs for the other. But though Presley has often been described as a 'country & western' singer who discovered the possibilities of rhythm & blues sang by a white boy, his musicianship was, on the contrary, a hybrid phenomenon, as was that of Chuck Berry. Presley's understanding, in at least a thoroughgoing practical sense, of the musics he drew on for his contributions to rock & roll, is especially apparent when his performances are compared to a random sample of his many imitators, including those from the Sun 'stable'. None came close to his *fluency,* the ease with which he played with complex rhythms and difficult melodic progressions.

Rock & roll music . . . and people

Without the contributions of Elvis Presley and Chuck Berry, rock & roll, as both a music and a socio-economic phenomenon, would have been, at the very least, *very* different. At Sun and, at least during the first few years, at RCA-Victor, Presley laid down definitive characteristics of the music *and* opened the doors to a world of previously unseen possibilities for Southern country musics as commercial resources, with a potential in cultural, as well as ecomomic, terms to do for the South what cotton and tobacco had once done. For a few years, Presley virtually defined not only how white rock & roll should sound, but also how it should look. The number of would-be pop singers who received their chance to grace the spotlights and the recording studios merely on the grounds that they bore a passing resemblance to Presley and could manage an approximation of his stage technique runs into hundreds, at least. It was a phenomenon which affected Britain, and eventually France, as well as the US. Most of these 'Elvis substitutes' faded quickly in to the shadows. Yet some outlived the reason for their start in pop by learning alternative ways of being rock stars. Among the latter were Britain's Cliff Richard and America's Rick Nelson. Probably they were both able to leave behind the origins of their popularity because they both managed to produce at least one or two recordings which were accomplished rock & roll performances without being *directly* connected to the work of Elvis Presley. Cliff Richard's 'Move It' (1958) has the distinction of being the closest thing to the rock & roll of America's South produced in Britain during the fifties. In a country where the techniques of blues-boogie guitar playing were as much a mystery as were the principles underlying Indian and Japanese folk musics, this was something of an achievement.

Chuck Berry was almost certainly rock & roll's foremost lyricist and guitarist. His conception of melody was probably also definitive. Like Presley, Berry combined elements of virtually all the musics of the South, yet his lyrics were simply *American*. The images in songs like 'Schoolday', 'Sweet Little Sixteen' and 'Johnny B. Goode', all from his vintage year of 1957, and many others of his pieces, captured the behaviour and the aspirations of rock & roll fans in America and Europe. The humour in songs such as 'Almost Grown' (1958), 'Reelin' & Rockin' ' (1957), and 'Promised Land' (1964) combined the sharpest of wit with a sympathy for human predicaments found only in the very best lyric writers.

Yet Chuck Berry's lasting influence has been as a master of rock & roll guitar. His combination of rockabilly and electric blues styles, in a blend that was distinctly his own, defined rock & roll guitar for generations of fans and musicians. As Rick Vito wrote in a recent issue of *Guitar Player* (June 1984): 'Probably more rock guitarists around the world have been influenced (either directly or through covers) by Chuck Berry's lead playing than by any other rock guitarist of the '50s. Even today, Chuck's solos sound as exciting and vibrant as they did over 20 years ago – proof of their true classic stature' (p. 72).

Though he used more or less the same scales as other blues-boogie guitarists, Berry found phrases and figures which sounded wholly original.

Presley and Berry, because of their popularity and abilities, were unifying forces. In so far as rock & roll became a distinctive *music* during the fifties it did so largely because of these two. Through their importance in the sociomusical phenomenon that was rock & roll their musical performances became formulas, not only in terms of how to get rich quick from a product resembling rock & roll, but also in terms of the necessary ingredients for a song recognisably in that idiom.

There were, of course, contributors of importance to rock & roll music who owed no debt to either Presley or Berry. One of these was Bo Diddley (Ellas McDaniel). His first single, coupling 'Bo Diddley' with 'I'm a Man' (1955), seemed at first to be an aural tapestry of Afro-American traditions, rather than a contribution to a new musical style. 'Bo Diddley' has lyrical affiliations with traditional black American nursery rhymes and children's games, as well as the 'dirty dozens', which have appeared both as song forms and in the guise of 'ritual insults' amongst urban Blacks. Musically, and especially in terms of its rhythm, the song is probably descended from the 'ring shouts' which the early Afro-American converts to Christianity blended with psalmistry to render their new faith more culturally acceptable. A record called 'Hambone' was cut in 1952 which was attributed on the label to Red Saunders, and featured a vocal group chanting rhymes related to both those in 'Bo Diddley' and those in the Inez and Charlie Foxx hit 'Mockingbird' (1963).

The flip side, 'I'm a Man' is a straightforward 'Downhome' Chicago blues, including the archetypal Chicago blues riff of the first – fourth – third diminished – first progression. Muddy Waters also recorded the song in 1955, though his version was entitled 'Mannish Boy', and credited to bassist Willie Dixon (though in aural appearance it is the same song as 'I'm A Man').

Bo Diddley recorded a string of rhythm & blues hits throughout the mid to late fifties, and though only 'Say Man' got into the American pop charts (none reaching the British charts) he was influential among rock & roll musicians during the fifties, directly and via Buddy Holly, and as a 'rhythm & blues' artist in Britain, where bands like the Animals and the Rolling Stones relied heavily on his songs for their repertoires. Ironically, Bo Diddley stated (personal communication, March 1982) that he has always seen himself as a rock & roll musician, always disliking the 'rhythm & blues artist' label. (He has certainly always done his best to reach integrated audiences, a policy he refuses to view as anything but radical.)

Both Fats Domino and Little Richard, as we have indicated, brought musical dimensions to rock & roll which derived from traditions complimentary to those drawn on by Presley and Berry. Fats played almost pure New Orleans boogie throughout the fifties. His piano introductions and solos were often elegant, and on occasion, as for instance on the 'fade-out' piece concluding his 'Natural Born Lover' (1959), unbelievably beautiful. But they were never frantic, or even born of *any* undue excitement on the part of Fats; he relied on his band, and particularly Lee Allen and Herb Hardesty on tenor saxophones, Cornelius Coleman on drums and Harrison Verrett or Walter Nelson on guitar, to supply the rock & roll sounds. Domino's ability as a pianist was seldom tested on record, but in concert he has usually give glimpses of his virtuosity. If anything his proficiency on the piano seems to have improved over the years, for in June 1983 he gave a concert to a packed Festival Hall on London's South Bank, which had the audience not just enraptured but on its collective feet dancing in the aisles and stomping to the beat.

Little Richard's first recordings, cut in Atlanta in 1951 and 1952 for RCA-Victor, were close to the Texan-cum-West-Coast styles of Roy Brown and Charles Brown. But his move to the Specialty label, and recording studios in New Orleans, showed a completely different musician. The controlled hysteria on records like 'Tutti Frutti' (1956) and 'Lucille' (1957), veiled, for many listeners, impressive vocal and pianistic abilities. The complex cross-rhythms of 'Slippin' and Slidin' ' (1956) would have been too complex for many rock & roll (*and* popular music) vocalists.

Like that of Fats Domino, Little Richard's best work is shot through with an innocent pleasure. And in the case of Little Richard this seems to include a sheer delight engendered merely by the availability of a recording studio and a band affording him the opportunity to sing.

The term 'innocence' is often used by critics to describe the prevailing mood of the Everly Brothers' records. This is an appropriate label for not only the Everlys but most rock & roll records. The Everlys brought the hillbilly tradition of harmony groups to the rock & roll scene, a tradition stretching back to before the early pop music. Earlier acts like the Delmore Brothers had taken the style through to the 'hillbilly boogie' fashion of the forties. The Everlys changed the style very little in order to sell it as rock & roll, even adapting Little Richard's 'Lucille' to what was very close to a hillbilly boogie with rather more accentuation of the off-beat than had previously been common, and sung without any of the urgency of the Little Richard version.

The terms 'innocence' and 'naivety' successfully describe the apparent demeanour of most rock & roll, in terms of both material as well as performance. And though much of that demeanour was in fact contrived by record producers, publicists, managers, and the performers themselves, a great deal of it was genuine. Often this was a kind of failed sophistication, but then a great deal of the innocence in the world is just that. The behaviour of the adolescents depicted in many of Chuck Berry's songs, including 'Sweet Little Sixteen' and 'Sweet Little Rock & Roller' (1958) are of the 'failed sophistication' kind, whereas their composition may well be described as contrived innocence, in as much as Berry artfully exposed his subjects' attempts of sophisticated behaviour. Presley's 'sexual gyrations', as they were called, and Buddy Holly's lyrics, may both have been the result of naivety. Certainly Presley's stage act was an unlikely outcome of someone having both the intention and the capability of showing their sophistication and worldliness. Holly's lyrics, on the other hand, were, if contrived, the work of a very talented writer.

The innocence in rock & roll was probably most evident in the movement's most ostentatiously dedicated followers, the Teddy Boys, the rockers that most of the Teds became, the rockabillies. One rocker interviewed by us summed up the naivety we associate with the rock & roll movement by first answering a question, of some pomposity, concerning the 'essentials of rock & roll' by stating simply 'Well, it's just effing beautiful innit', then explaining that he had modified the swearword because he was being tape recorded, and thought it might appear in print. In his heyday he had been famous in his (small) home town as one of the Teddy Boys who dressed outrageously – in drape suits, fluorescent pink or lime green socks and 'brothel-creeper' shoes – slouching around the town centre, leering at the girls and fighting with his friends. Yet in all the leering and the strutting, as well as the astonishing sense of dress, there was a tongue-in-cheek element, mirroring that in the lyrics of, particularly, Chuck Berry and Buddy Holly.

The rockabilly rebels

Rockabilly music was probably exhausted as an evolving form by 1957 or 1958. As Peter Guralnick put it, rockabilly was '. . . the purest of all rock & roll . . . a music of almost classical purity and definition . . . It was, to begin with, Southern music, blues-inspired and bluegrass-based, in Carl Perkins' definition, "blues with a country beat" ' (in Miller (ed.) 1981: p. 61). It was a music of a new generation of poor

Southern Whites, singing the blues without the self-consciousness of
their musical ancestors, and, with no consideration for the feelings of
Opry purists, coming out of their honky-tonk closets and rocking the
blues in public.

The honky-tonk music tradition had been something of an
underground movement for years before the rockabilly explosion,
shunned by the Opry establishment and the more straight-laced of
'country music' fans, though, legend has it, providing the venues for
performers like Hank Williams to let their hair down and play heavy,
rhythmic dance music.

By the early fifties hillbilly music had acquired a new name,
'country and western', and had lost much of its freshness in its rise to
prominence in the entertainment industry. As Bill C. Malone argues:

> By 1950 many of the features that had been in only embryonic form during
> early periods now had become stereotyped. Some type of western clothing,
> regardless of the singer's origin, had become the accepted form of stage
> costume. The steel guitar, with a variety of instrumental techniques, had
> become the dominant instrument. (pp. 228–9)

Or, as expressed by Waylon Jennings:

> Lord, it's the same old tune, fiddle and guitar
> Where do we take it from here
> Rhinestone suits and new shiny cars
> It's been the same way for years
> We need a change.
> ('Are You Sure Hank Done It This Way', 1975)

Also in 1975, Robert Altman's movie *Nashville* was released. As a
picture of the country & western scene it was less than
complimentary. In fact, many country fans described it as a
'caricature': yet many more accepted the movie as providing a fairly
accurate account of an industry which had come very close to being a
caricature of itself. *Nashville* pictured country & western as an
enterprise which exploited, much of the time in a cynical fashion, its
origins in folk culture: in the way of life, including the attitudes and
values, of the rural, Southern, working family. The central characters
in the movie are portrayed as either hypocritically feigning
attachment to the prescribed values, presumed to be an inherent
component of the hillbilly tradition, *or else,* as being inescapably
enmeshed in the mythical roots of the music. For the features
highlighted by both Malone and Jennings were, and continued to be,
the more apparent symptoms of an inherent set of contradictory

conditions in the hillbilly music industry.

Ironically, those conditions were already apparent in the career of Jimmie Rodgers. As we have noted, the 'singing brakeman' was, for much of his short career, a *very* wealthy man by any contemporary standards, let alone those the working folk whose situation was most affected by the depression, and who, at least in hillbilly mythology, were Rodgers's most important audience. Thus as the 'folk-culture' became an industry so the paradox, exemplified for many hillbilly 'constituents' by the biblical comparisons between rich men expecting to enter heaven and camels negotiating the eyes of needles, became more acute and more difficult to escape. Yet it was not simply that country music stars were rich. Southern Americans could admire such people. The problem was, and is one of performing songs depicting a simple, if not humble, way of life, in such a way as to *glorify* that simplicity, and decry the effects of affluence, urban lifestyles, and similar alternatives to the cultural values enshrined in the hillbilly tradition. The problem is not peculiar to country & western music. It is also present when rock stars, with million-dollar incomes and the material trappings to match, feel the need nonetheless to convey an image incorporating 'street credibility'. Yet the effects upon the products of the country & western music industry were the resultant stereotypical songs and performances, noted by Malone and Jennings and portrayed in great detail by Altman. The practical problem for the music makers of Nashville was, and is, that the 'folk-culture' of their mythology became, by the fifties, little more than a stereotype: the world had changed a great deal since the death of Jimmie Rodgers. Unfortunately, the commitment in any branch of the music industry, as in many others, to stereotypical ideals and models tends to that stereotyping in the resultant products.

The rockabilly explosion of the fifties was thus able to compete with country & western on favourable terms, just as rock & roll as a whole was able to offer a viable alternative to popular music.

Rockabilly thus derived much of its vigour from the fact of its liberation from stereotypical values, a liberation resting firmly on aesthetic foundations. The epithet 'rebels without a cause' fits the rockabillies perfectly. At its best the music had something approaching fury in it, but a fury born more of ecstasy and hope than of anger. As an aesthetic rather than a moral or political rebellion it encapsulated the rocker's fantasies of indulging in a constant series of escapades involving great cunning and daring, and the contravention of all the laws pertaining to drinking, driving, fornication, and the like, whilst constantly outwitting the local sheriff. The spirit of the rockabilly movement is captured perfectly in the lyrics of the Carl Perkins record 'Dixie Fried' (1956):

Well on the outskirts of town there's a little night-spot
Dan dropped in about five o'clock
Pulled off his coat, said the night is short
Reached in his pocket and he flashed a quart
And hollered 'Rave on children I'm with ya,
Rave on cats', he cried
'It's almost dawn and the cops are gone,
Let's all get dixie fried!'

The song captures not only the vigour but also the naivety of rock & roll. The music was never overly complex, and its message was simply 'life is for fun'.

But the impact of the rock & roll movement belied its simplicity; its message underlined, and thus magnified, by the moral, political and commercial rejections of that movement. The legend of its birth in the face of adversity, in the form of racial and regional prejudices and the requirements of the popular music establishment, its qualities of sheer, unadultarated fun combined with brash commercialism, and its supposed 'death' at the hands of its political and commercial 'enemies' became, in the end, a powerful mythology.

Unlike the mythology prevailing in country & western circles in the early fifties, and even later, the mythology that was the legacy of rock & roll encouraged, rather than inhibited, creativity and imagination. It reinforced those socio-economic and cultural factors which promoted the 'do-it-yourself' tendencies of a generation. Thus the generation nurtured on rock & roll music and the things they associated with produced a significant number of people who eventually recreated parts of the world they inherited according to the spirit of rock & roll. Most obviously, people like Bob Dylan, John Lennon and Paul McCartney laid the foundations for the rebirth of the pop industry in rock music. Meanwhile, Bery Gordy, Jerry Wexler, and many others put together alternative foundations in soul music. Other rock & roll refugees transformed the fashion business, the newspaper business, and the production and marketing of cosmetics.

The mythology of rock & roll, particularly those parts of it relating to the 'death' of the music, acts, as do all myths, as both a veil and a spotlight. The sociomusical phenomena known as rock & roll was one of the many symptoms of change which appeared in post-war America, and then spread to Europe. The United States changed from a country in the midst of a severe depression to one in which the wealth of the average citizen was many times greater than in any previous society, all in the space of a few years. And the depression had been partly responsible for the fact that by 1950 a great deal of country & western music and most rhythm & blues available in recorded form were by new, independent, and often tiny, record companies. For the state of those markets during the depression was probably the most important factor in the decisions taken by the major record companies to withdraw from, or neglect, the Southern, country, markets. Thus the commercial, as well as the musical, seeds were sown at least as early as the late thirties.

In 1939 an alternative to ASCAP, the Broadcast Music Incorporated organisation, was set up. As hillbilly and blues writers and publishers had never felt welcome in ASCAP, the new organisation had a ready source of new markets. And when, in 1941, a dispute arose between ASCAP and the association of radio broadcasters over fees for broadcasting rights, BMI were given an opportunity to, among other things, push country musics, but also gain more new members, for the dispute included a ban on the broadcasting of all ASCAP material.

The ban, imposed by the American musicians' union, on all recording with those companies unwilling to contribute to an unemployment fund in 1941, gave a boost to those small record companies which had the sense to reach agreement with the union.

These two factors, leading as they did to new outlets for the products of those publishing and record companies that specialised in country musics (black *and* white), were probably pivotal in bringing about the conditions suitable for the emergence of rock & roll, or at least some new musical form. The growth of BMI and the new record companies was also stimulated by the growth of the consumer market during the forties and fifties, as it was by changing taste in music, a phenomenon not exclusive to the young.

Revolutions are usually dated from the time their momentum renders them almost immune from counter-measures. Thus the popular music industry woke up to the fact that times were changing long after companies like Chess, Sun, Atlantic, and King had established themselves and, whether by accident or design, had established rock & roll as, at least a temporary, fact of life for companies like RCA-Victor, Decca, and Columbia.

The major record companies and the Tin Pan Alley publishing houses did, eventually, recover from the shock of rock & roll's emergence. RCA-Victor found that it could buy, and by its own standards very cheaply, the contract of Elvis Presley, and sign people like Sam Cooke. Publishing houses found rock & roll fans who could also write songs, in the persons of Neil Sedaka, Carole King, and others.

Whether factors like the incorporation of Presley into RCA-Victor and Hollywood, the death of Buddy Holly, the 'Payola scandal', and similar events 'killed' rock & roll as a creative force, is a question which will never receive a definitive answer. More research may well produce better answers than are now available, by answering some of the outstanding questions.

It is possible, for instance, that rock & roll, like forms before and since, exhausted the possibilities of, its evolution, at least in the climate of the fifties. Alternatively, it may have been the case that the rock music which emerged in the sixties, together with soul music, were exactly where the dominant strains of rock & roll were leading. Some scholars of the genre would cite the Presley recordings from around 1958 and the work of people like Sam Cooke, Jackie Wilson, and James Brown, as evidence for this view.

Certainly, the later work, in what can be seen as rock & roll idiom, by the Band, T. Rex, Elvis Costello, and others, benefited from the musical and temporal distance between them and the 'classic' period of rock & roll music.

Chapter 4

Across the great divide

Just as it is a matter of some debate as to when rock & roll began, so the precise moment of its death is equally contentious. Most observers would, however, seem to settle for the late 1950s. Peter Guralnick (1971) sums up the general feeling neatly: 'When the treacle period of the late fifties and early sixties engulfed us we recited the familiar litany, by now grown stale from repetition: Elvis in the Army, Buddy Holly dead, Little Richard in the ministry, Jerry Lee Lewis in disgrace and Chuck Berry in jail' (p. 16).

With the Beatles not due to emerge until 1963, the consequence of this kind of thinking is that the late fifties/early sixties have come to be regarded as a fallow period, an unfortunate interval between rock & roll and rock. The issue is further obscured by the predominance in popular music during those years of bland white singers whose 'boy-next-door' good looks and carefully-tailored image proved to be as widely acceptable as their trite, Tin Pan Alley material.

The problem with this kind of assumption is that subsequent developments such as soul and rock must then be seen to have appeared instantaneously, as in a miracle. There is, furthermore, an implicit denial of the experimental nature of much of the music from that period. Rhythm & blues musicians had always been inclined to take a pragmatic approach to whatever material came their way, resulting frequently in innovation. Between 1959 and 1963 this tradition continued in the work of both established performers and younger singers and musicians who had grown up with the music of the fifties and who were now initiating careers in their own right. Similarly, the music of certain rock & roll stars was developing and changing with, in some cases, important consequences for what was to happen later. Above all, to deny the worth of these years is to disregard a genuine fusion of black and white music on a level of intimacy not encountered since the early 1950s or, arguably, the mid-1920s.

Much of the music of this period cannot be categorised as rock & roll, soul, or rock, though elements of all three are present. It is more instructive to consider what progress was being made within pop music as a whole, however, than to become preoccupied with what had ceased to exist. It is easy to sympathise with Peter Guralnick's reaction as a contemporary teenager ('What we did at the age of fifteen was to retreat into the past. The past year or two', *ibid.*, p. 20), but – admittedly with the advantage of hindsight – it is now possible to view the years 1959–63 in a new light, that is as a period of transition.

Solomon Burke was not the first black singer to make use of a white musical idiom. We have already seen, in Chapter 3, how Chuck Berry's 'Maybellene' bore a closer resemblance to rockabilly than to rhythm & blues. As early as 1951, Wynonie Harris had had an R. & B. hit with Hank Penny's 'Bloodshot Eyes'. Yet when he recorded the country ballad 'Just Out Of Reach' in December 1960, Burke achieved an almost seamless blend of black and white. Where Harris had obscured the origins of a song by making it entirely his own in arrangement and delivery and Berry's treatment was not followed up by other rock & roll singers, Burke's recording proved to be the first in a pattern which was to have important implications for soul music and, it will be argued, for early rock. 'Just Out Of Reach' (recorded for Atlantic at the suggestion of Paul Ackerman of *Billboard* magazine and at the request of Jerry Wexler) has many of the characteristics prevalent in the country music of the time. It opens with, and continues to feature, a somewhat unctuous white vocal group; it is set at a lilting tempo; and its lyrics tell the familiar tale of a suitor pining for an unattainable, idealised lover. Burke, a former gospel singer, sounds entirely comfortable, his almost exaggeratedly clear vocal articulation seeming to indicate respect for the idiom rather than unfamiliarity.

Other contemporary recordings by Burke display similar features. 'I'm Hanging Up My Heart For You' (1962) and 'Yes I Do' (1964) include a piano accompaniment which recalls the work of the Nashville session musician, Floyd Cramer. 'Goodbye Baby' (1963) is another country-style song, but this time the general content is more marked, with the presence of a black vocal group and Burke's uninhibited lead. He also continued to record gospel-flavoured rhythm & blues numbers such as 'Everybody Needs Somebody To Love' (1964) – covered subsequently by the Rolling Stones – in which the chorus breaks into applause at Burke's vocal intensity, thus recalling the fervour of the black church. But it was the country/ gospel blend, featuring the authoritative black vocal over a prominent, if relaxed, rhythm section and – above all – the distinctive *lilt*, which prefigured soul so clearly.

Although 'Just Out Of Reach' sold a million copies, it was the experiments with country music of the more established Ray Charles which attracted widespread attention. Charles must have posed record store managers with some terrible categorisation problems during the 1950s. An accomplished jazz pianist and alto saxophonist, an early Atlantic album, *The Great Ray Charles* (1956), consists of instrumentals only. He came to prominence, however, in the West Coast R. & B. scene, clearly influenced by Nat 'King' Cole and Charles Brown. On the other hand, few would deny his claims to rock & roll credibility through such recordings as 'I've Got A Woman' in 1954 (covered by Elvis Presley) and 'Hallelujah I Love Her So' (1955). The truth was that he was equally adept at all black music idioms, a fact reinforced by the pronounced gospel character in his vocal style. (This versatility was not quite as rare as has sometimes been maintained. The parallel examples of Dinah Washington and Big Joe Turner can be cited, although in both cases, changes were of musical environment rather than conscious policy.) Given Charles's eclecticism, therefore, it should have come as no surprise when he chose to tackle country music on his move from Atlantic to ABC-Paramount in 1959. In fact, he had begun the process just before he changed companies with the release of Hank Snow's 'I'm Movin' On', but rather like case of Wynonie Harris's 'Bloodshot Eyes' cited above, Charles's treatment was such to render the original unrecognisable.

Although he had two early R. & B. hits with ABC-Paramount – 'Sticks And Stones' (1960) and 'Hit The Road Jack' (1961) – it was with his renditions of pure contemporary country material, arranged and orchestrated in appropriate manner with choir and strings, that Charles found unprecedented popular success. 'I Can't Stop Loving You' was number one on the *Billboard* chart for five weeks in the summer of 1962, while 'You Are My Sunshine'/'Your Cheating Heart' (also 1962) and 'Take These Chains From My Heart' (1963) were Top Ten successes. The reasons for the popularity of these records are numerous: Charles was already an established artist with

R. & B. fans – he was now acceptable to country music followers and large numbers of the white adult record-buyers, some of whom may have remembered him from his jazz days, but many of whom would have been reassured by his 'genius' title and were thus happy to welcome him to the popular music fold.

Critical opinion has not been quite as well-disposed. Charlie Gillett has written that 'From 1962, Ray Charles degenerated, a musical decline matching that of Elvis Presley' (p. 203), a statement with which few of Charles's 1950s fans would disagree. However, it is hard to imagine that the significance of his success would have been lost on young black singers and would-be recording stars. Not only had Charles augmented the profile of the black artist in the white-administered entertainment world, but by recording the previously alien country music he had created a climate where virtually any blend might be possible.

Sam Cooke was already an established gospel star by 1956. It was in the year that he began to record some secular material, including the subsequent hit 'I'll Come Running To You' (Specialty). That he was self-conscious about breaking with gospel music is illustrated by the fact that he used the pseudonym Dale Cook for his first secular release, 'Lovable'. However, there was no hint of any discomfort in his handling of these songs, or for that matter any other material he recorded for Keen and ultimately RCA.

Admittedly, he possessed a beautiful voice, but that alone would not have carried him through the frequently trite songs he had to perform. What is remarkable is that he invested Tin Pan Alley tunes with a dignity they scarcely deserved and even managed to incorporate vocal improvisations so familiar from his days with the Soul Stirrers. Naturally he excelled on strong rhythm & blues material such as 'Bring It On Home To Me' (1962) and 'Little Red Rooster' (1963), but he also handled novelty items like 'Everybody Likes To Cha Cha Cha' (1959) without any difficulty. Additionally, he recorded superior versions of standards from the popular ('Summertime', 1957) and country ('Tennessee Waltz', 1964) fields.

Cooke produced an almost unbroken sequence of hits from 1957 to 1964, the year of his death; there were three posthumous hit records in late 1964 and 1965. (The 'B' side of one these, 'Shake', was the prophetic 'A Change Is Gonna Come' which will be discussed in its political context in Chapter 5.) His music is proof of the feeling in the late fifties/early sixties that anything *was* possible, for he absorbed without effort the complete range of contemporary pop. Neither was there the suggestion that he might be merely dabbling: material of contrasting origin was recorded within the same time-period, and in any case was unified by Cooke's graceful vocal style, itself an influence on many subsequent soul artists. As the anonymous author of the section on Cooke in *The Encyclopedia Of Rock Volume Two* (1967) has it: 'He stands at the head of the entire sweet soul ballad tradition . . . he demonstrated that an R & B artist could still retain a vital relationship with the black audience while surviving in the teenage pop market and in a Las Vegas night-club context as a performer of standards' (p. 103).

A variety of male and female singers and vocal groups around the USA were adapting quickly to the changes brought about by such pioneers as Burke, Charles, and Cooke, blending the gospel/R. & B. tradition which had infiltrated rock & roll so thoroughly with previously alien musical forms and studio arrangements. One thinks not only of established stars such as the Drifters (in particular, 'There Goes My Baby' from 1959) and Fats Domino (whose remarkable 'Natural Born Lover' of 1960 incorporated dazzling blues piano-playing, lush tenor saxophone, and strings), but also of a generation of young newcomers. In 1964, for example, Irma Thomas imbued 'Time Is On My Side' with a gospel feel not normally associated with her nor with her New Orleans origins. The Impressions, from Chicago, turned the potential encumbrance of an orchestra into a positive asset, enhancing the lilting tempos of many hits, culminating in 'People Get Ready' (1965), which used the traditional gospel metaphor of the train as a means of deliverance from (in this case) political and social oppression. But it is in the work of Arthur Alexander that we may find an unprecedented mixture of styles and relentless experimentation.

Alexander has been ignored by critics, and one can only speculate on the reasons for this. His voice certainly lacked the purity of Sam Cooke and the authority of Ray Charles; his chart success was also minimal. Furthermore, his music is impossible to categorise. Yet the recordings he made for Dot between 1960 and 1964 had clear implications both for the development of soul and for the birth of rock.

To start with, Alexander was backed by white musicians David Briggs (piano), Norbert Putnam (bass), and Jerry Carrigan (drums). This established a tradition both at Fame Studios, Muscle Shoals,

Alabama – where most of Alexander's early recordings were made –
and at Stax, in Memphis. This apparently simple fact was of extreme
importance. It was not just that the musicians were white and from the
South (thus guaranteeing a background in country music). They were
also new to session work and thus not 'schooled' to reproduce an
idiom, yet their understanding of the discipline of rhythm & blues is
clearly evident. The result is a combination of energy and restraint
and this, added to the prominence given to the rhythm section in the
arrangements, defined the epithet 'tight' – so frequently applied to the
musicianship of 1960s soul records. Furthermore, it helps to
challenge the common assumption that soul was by definition a 'black'
music. Briggs Putnam, and Carrigan (all of whom moved on to
successful careers as Nashville session men) were succeeded at Fame
by white players such as Tommy Cogbill, Roger Hawkins, Jimmy
Johnson, and David Hood who variously appeared on hit records by
Aretha Franklin, Wilson Pickett, and Percy Sledge. At Stax, white
musicians 'Duck' Dunn (bass) and Steve Cropper (guitar) were
present on numerous soul recordings by artists such as Otis Redding,
Sam and Dave, and Eddie Floyd, as well as Wilson Pickett before his
move to Muscle Shoals. They also constituted one half of the racially-
integrated working band, Booker T and the MGs. Cropper was also a
soul music composer, a counterpart to the white Dan Penn at Muscle
Shoals; additionally, both Fame and Stax were owned by white
entrepreneurs: Rick Hall and Jim Stewart respectively.

As to Alexander himself, he made a rather unconventional start to
his songwriting career. Bill Millar, in his sleeve-note to the collection
of Alexander's early recordings (*A Shot Of Rhythm And Soul*, Ace,
1982), relates how 'She Wanna Rock', composed by Alexander and
Henry Lee Bennett, was recorded in Nashville by the country singer
Arnie Derksen in April 1959. It was shortly after this that Alexander
began to make his own records, beginning with 'Sally Sue Brown'
(1960) which, although it resembles a blues in melody and vocal
delivery as well as in its piano accompaniment, possesses a loping
rhythmic gait more akin to a medium-tempo country piece. In
subsequent recordings, a country music influence was almost always
present, usually, however, as just one element in an otherwise eclectic
mixture.

'You Better Move On' (1961) is one of Alexander's best-known
compositions, largely due to the fact that it was recorded three years
later by the Rolling Stones. It is set, as were at least four other

Alexander songs of the period, to a shuffle beat punctuated by clipped guitar chords redolent of Ben E. King's contemporary hit 'Stand By Me'. Yet the melodrama of King's record is replaced by a feeling of melancholy on Alexander's, a typically country music characteristic, emphasised by the nature of the piano backing. Similar remarks apply to 'Anna' (1962) which in addition includes strings and a white vocal chorus. It is interesting to compare Alexander's recordings with the Beatles' version made a few months later for their first album *Please Please Me* (1963). Taken at a slightly slower pace and featuring John Lennon's relatively uninhibited vocals, the Beatles' rendering seems to reintroduce the more characteristically 'black' elements avoided by Alexander. Further correspondence between the work of Alexander and that of the Beatles may be seen in the former's recordings of 'Where Have You Been' (1962) and 'You Don't Care' (1965), neither of which was covered by the British group, yet show a resemblance to early compositions by Lennon and McCartney.

'You Don't Care' has Alexander venturing into country music vocal mannerisms to a greater extent than he had done previously, even when tackling straight country material such as 'I Wonder Where You Are Tonight' (1963) or the Gene Autry-Fred Rose-Ray Whiteley composition 'I Hang My Head And Cry' (1962). Yet there is interest to be found in the contrast between these two recordings. Whereas the former amounts to a conventional country rendition, the latter, while set at a typically cantering pace, includes not only a blues-influenced piano accompaniment but a riffing horn section encountered more usually in rhythm & blues and which became widespread in soul music.

Alexander continued to experiment, even when he did not incorporate the country influence into his music. His version of Charles Brown's 1950 hit 'Black Night', for example, made in 1964, is arranged and delivered in the manner of Tommy Tucker's 'Hi-Heel Sneakers', issued on Checker in the same year; it also contrives to include Chicago-style harmonica. 'A Shot Of Rhythm And Blues' (1961), though recalling both R. & B. and rock & roll in its sentiments and exuberance, places the emphasis firmly on the on-beat: it re-emerged as a common item in the repertoires of numerous British 'beat' groups of the early 1960s.

The fact that Arthur Alexander mixed apparently disparate musical elements so relentlessly may have contributed to his lack of large-scale popular acceptance. Unlike Sam Cooke, who synthesised contrasting forms into a homogeneous style, or Ray Charles, whose deliberate assimilation of country music established him as a celebrity in the popular music field, Alexander may also be seen as commercially rather naïve. Yet the environment in which he worked and the results he produced constitute soul music to a degree only equalled by his influence upon early rock performers. Solomon Burke, on the other hand, stayed closer to his blend of gospel and country music, a fact which eased his transition to success as an early soul star. The work of all of these artists can be regarded as soul music before that label came to be applied. As such, it predates the 'black music' ideology associated with soul, the accuracy of which has already been shown to be questionable: these issues will be discussed further in Chapter 5.

If the period 1959–63 was seen only as a time when black and white musical traditions were converging to produce soul, this would be sufficient to destroy the assumption that these years represent a fallow period for pop music. There were, however, contemporary developments in the work of white artists which had clear implications for the music we recognise as rock.

During the early 1960s the majority of white pop singers had no commercial reason to turn to black musical styles for their material or inspiration. Indeed it made rather good sense not to. For one thing, chart success tended to be proportional to musical banality and innocuous romanticism. For another, there was a ready-made source of appropriate songs in the output of numerous young popular music writers, many of whom would be on hand to participate in the arrangements, production or marketing of the material. It would be overstating the case, however, to apply this judgement to all the white performers of the day. Dion and the Belmonts, for example, brought to some of their work together the characteristically black vocal group sound of the 1950s. Even when Dion went on to pursue a solo career he retained some contact with rhythm & blues, most notably in 'Ruby Baby' (1963) and 'The Wanderer' (1961), the opening of which suggests an affinity with urban blues.

In addition, the music of certain established white rock & roll stars was developing. Jerry Lee Lewis had recorded rhythm & blues material earlier in his career, but it was a direct result of his 1961 hit version of Ray Charles's 'What'd I Say' that he made a series of R. & B. covers for Sun in June 1962 which were subsequently included on the album *Rockin' Rhythm And Blues*. However, Lewis chose not to repeat the experiment, and began to concentrate instead on country music.

In the meantime Elvis Presley had returned from his stint in the US Army to record the album *Elvis Is Back* (1960). By this stage Presley's voice had acquired a deeper, harder quality than is to be found on his earlier records: it was yet to display what Escott and Hawkins describe as a 'plummy vibrato'. While the album contains a number of lightweight, overtly commercial items such as 'Make Me Know It' and 'Soldier Boy', it is Presley's handling of the blues/R. & B. material that is of most importance. Firstly, there are versions of Clyde McPhatter and the Drifters' 1954 R. & B. hit 'Such A Night' (a very close rendition) and Little Willie John's 'Fever' of 1956 (although Presley's version bears a greater resemblance of Peggy Lee's 1958 cover). He also tackles two songs from the blues end of the R. & B. spectrum – 'Like A Baby' and 'It Feels So Right' – in an idiomatic fashion, the presence of tenor saxophone on the former lending a further authenticity.

But it is in Presley's rendition of Lowell Fulson's 'Reconsider Baby' that we can observe an unprecedently close relationship to Chicago blues by a white singer. Most notable in Presley's authentic vocal inflection and timing, allowing for a power of expression not even possessed by the original recording (compare his version of Junior Parker's 'Mystery Train' discussed earlier). The accompaniment, by white studio musicians, is similarly faithful to the black tradition and includes an extended tenor saxophone solo; aural evidence suggests that Presley himself plays acoustic rhythm guitar, the simple but effective blues riff resembling as it does his playing in the television special of 1968. One can only speculate as to the results that would have been produced had Presley recorded at this time at Chess Studios in Chicago.

The significance of these sessions (which also yielded 'Mess Of Blues', the 'B' side of the 1960 hit 'It's Now Or Never') is that they initiated the white blues style so crucial in the development of rock. We might characterise this as the use of the urban blues stock to produce pop music with the rhythmic emphasis on the on-beat. Fundamental, too, was to be the introduction of the blues guitar sound, the importation of which into Britain should be credited to another white rock & roll star, Eddie Cochran.

In 1960, Cochran embarked on an extensive British tour and it was during this period that he recorded 'Milkcow Blues'. What made his

version different from others within this song family (see Chapter 1)
was that it made use of the archetypal Chicago blues guitar riff, an
even without precedent in white pop music. Furthermore, we know
that Cochran provided tuition, before his death in April 1960, to at
least one British guitarist, Joe Brown. Brown has related, in a
television tribute to the American (1983), how Cochran demonstrated
to him the techniques of playing on the bass strings and of 'bending' a
string, both of which feature prominently in the urban blues guitar
style. Brown also states that these methods were unknown in Britain
at the time, a fact which enhanced Brown's own career in session
work. We may be confident that, given Cochran's widespread
exposure during his visit both on stage and on television, that Brown
was not the only British musician to take note of Cochran's technique.
Previous knowledge of American guitar styles would have inevitably
have been based on jazz or the loose approximation of rock & roll
purveyed by local tutors such as Bert Weedon: there is no aural
evidence to the contrary.

  British musicians certainly had some catching-up to do. Prior to
1960, very little had been produced in the way of worthwhile
imitations of American pop music. Singers and musicians with no
previous grounding in the idiom had been rushed into the studio by
impresarios anxious to capitalise on the increasing popularity of rock
& roll. There was a suspicion that certain singers were selected more
for their physical resemblance to white American stars than for their
vocal abilities. Any creditable treatment of US music was confined to
the field of jazz, where musicians such as Ken Colyer, Humphrey
Lyttelton, and Chris Barber approached their source material with
scholarship and respect. Yet these musicians had been working on
their styles for over ten years by 1960: American traditional jazz can
fairly be said to have been assimilated into a British environment at
that stage. While the innovations of Presley and Cochran can be seen
to have contributed to the birth of rock, its further development lay in
the hands of the generation of British musicians who had been
studying and playing rock & roll during their formative years and who
were now ready to put their experience to good use.

  John Lennon was infatuated with rock & roll as a teenager. He
became particularly obsessed by Elvis Presley: his Aunt Mimi
recalled, in an interview quoted by Philip Norman (1981), 'I never got
a minute's peace. It was Elvis Presley, Elvis Presley, Elvis Presley. In

the end I said, "Elvis Presley's all very well, John, but I don't want
him for breakfast, dinner *and* tea." ' (p. 21). His interest in the music
never really left him. His first studio album after the demise of the
Beatles, *John Lennon/Plastic Ono Band,* included three items with a
heavy back-beat ('Remember', 'Well, Well Well', and 'I Found Out')
and featured throughout pronounced echo on the vocal track, a device
which was to become a distinctive characteristic of his solo work. In
1975, Lennon released *Rock 'N' Roll* which consisted in the main of
the 1950s material of such artists as Chuck Berry, Little Richard, and
Fats Domino.

Paul McCartney was accepted as a member of the Quarry Men (the
earliest incarnation of the Beatles) only because he knew the chords to
Eddie Cochran's 'Twenty Flight Rock'. Although his music no longer
bears any resemblance to rock & roll, his affection for the music is still
apparent. On the BBC Radio Programme 'Desert Island Discs',
broadcast in the early 1980s, McCartney chose five rock & roll records
in his allocation of eight selections.

It is not surprising, therefore, to learn that the Beatles concentrated
on rock & roll material during their residencies in Hamburg, which
commenced in the summer of 1960. Included in their repertoire were
such items as Carl Perkins's 'Honey Don't' and Chuck Berry's 'Too
Much Monkey Business' as well as latter day Presley hits such as
'Love Me Tender'. Yet at their first recording sessions for
Parlophone, in September 1962 and February 1963, which yielded
their first two hit singles and the whole of their first album (*Please
Please Me*), the emphasis was upon contemporary rhythm & blues
and the compositions of Lennon and McCartney. This formula was
repeated for their second album, *With The Beatles.* In fact, the only
incontestably rock & roll song appeared on that second LP release,
namely Chuck Berry's 'Roll Over Beethoven'.

It could be argued that by that stage the rock & roll of the 1950s was
no longer a commercial proposition, and that the Beatles chose instead
to turn their attention to what might be regarded as 'underground'
music as yet unfamiliar to most British record-buyers. However, the
Beatles' apprenticeship in rock & roll informed their work on the early
albums in certain crucial respects.

Most notably, the singing of McCartney and, in particular,
Lennon, brought a rock & roll character to both their own originals
and the R. & B. material they took on. Lennon, for example, did not
attempt to copy the vocal styles of Smokey Robinson and Barrett

Strong in the versions of, respectively, 'You Really Gotta Hold On Me' and 'Money'. His own methods were already developed by then, namely the rasping delivery and uninhibited approach of his mentors. In this way, Lennon and McCartney were free to handle what was largely obscure material in any case in an essentially personal fashion. This process was complemented by the fact that the Beatles tended to slow down the tempos of the original recordings for greater effect, examples of which include their treatment of Arthur Alexander's 'Anna' and the Shirelles' 'Baby It's You'.

Similarly, their instrumental work, while perhaps lacking the fluency and timing of the American product, compensates by supplying an attack and intensity clearly derived from prolonged exposure to rock & roll. In this respect, their version of 'Money' can almost be said to prefigure the 'heavy rock' methods of several years later.

The result of such processes was a music which sounded distinctive *and* authentic. On hearing 'Love Me Do' for the first time, many listeners assumed that it was the work of a black group or, at the very least, that it was American in origin. Of course Lennon and McCartney also discovered that they had the ability to compose commerically successful pop tunes, a fact which has tended to obscure their efforts in other directions. Their involvement with rock & roll cannot be said to have influenced these songs, with the possible exception of such early efforts as 'I Saw Her Standing There'. While it is true that an R. & B. influence is apparent in certain originals, for example, 'All I've Go To Do', 'Little Child', and 'Not A Second Time', these compositions can hardly be counted as being among their most popular. Yet at least the overtly commercial material the Beatles produced *was* their own: antipathy to Tin Pan Alley is illustrated by the fact that they withstood pressure to record 'How Do You Do It' (composed by the professional writer Mitch Murray) at their first session. The song was subsequently a number one hit in Britain for Gerry and the Pacemakers.

Rock & roll songs such as 'Long Tall Sally' and 'Honey Don't' continued to appear occasionally on Beatles releases and in their stage-act, culminating in their version of Larry Williams's 'Dizzy Miss Lizzy' on the *Help!* album of 1965. This, and 'Act Naturally' from the same LP, were to be the last items not to be composed by members of the band until the 39-second fragment of the Liverpool folk-song, 'Maggie Mae', appeared on the Beatles' final album release

Let It Be. In December 1965, they issued the LP *Rubber Soul*, and the transition to wholly original material was completed. This now bore little relation to their early recordings. The songs were more personal in content, making use of lyrical conceits and instrumental arrangements, the nature of which was entirely individual. (George Harrison was reportedly outraged at the Hollies' cover version of his 'If I Needed Someone'.) The subject matter of many of the compositions was certainly striking and completely foreign to the British pop music of the period, especially in the songs on which Lennon seemed to be the dominant influence, for example 'Nowhere Man', 'Norwegian Wood', and 'In My Life'. Furthermore, the Beatles were beginning to discover the possibilities opened up by four-track recording – principally the way in which sound could be 'layered' over a period of time to create something aurally distinctive.

Links with American rhythm & blues and rock & roll were now severed. The Beatles had established a tradition of British pop music, a development totally without precedent. Other artists, most notably The Who, now concerned themselves with reflecting their own environment, rather than borrowing images and inspiration from elsewhere. It should be reiterated, however, that this state of affairs was not created in a vacuum. The Beatles' assimilation of rock & roll into their music was crucial in providing for the conditions under which further development could take place. Additionally, their work heralded a new competence among British musicians, a vital factor in the formation of rock. The relationship between American and British music was destined to continue, resulting in further important changes during the mid-1960s.

While the Beatles stopped playing rock & roll in 1965, the Rolling Stones never started. Though often considered peers in the forefront of the growth of British pop music of the 1960s, the background, experience, and methods of the two bands were quite dissimilar. To start with, there was an important age difference between their leading members. John Lennon, for example, was almost four years older than Mick Jagger and over three years older than Keith Richard. Paul McCartney (born in 1942) was senior to Jagger by two years. Although these variations would seem insignificant in other contexts, they were vital in the degree to which rock & roll, with a duration of prominence in Britain scarcely spanning five years, could be understood and absorbed. In 1956, for example, the year in which

Elvis Presley had hits on both sides of the Atlantic with 'Heartbreak Hotel' and 'Hound Dog', Lennon was sixteen years of age, Jagger twelve.

Their comparative lack of involvement with rock & roll was not a matter of concern for the Stones, however. In a much-quoted interview with *Jazz News* conducted prior to their debut at the Marquee on 21 July 1962 Jagger stated, 'I hope they don't think we're a rock 'n' roll outfit.' One imagines that the Beatles, who were yet to make their first recordings for Parlophone, would have expressed no such fears about that response to their music. On the contrary, the Beatles had existed as a unit for some seven years by then, with rock & roll constituting the staple element in their repertoire. The Stones, in contrast, were in the recording studios within a year of that first club appearance.

The question must therefore be posed: what *did* the Rolling Stones regard themselves as? It could hardly have been as a jazz band, although the group's drummer, Charlie Watts, had previously worked in a traditional jazz context. More likely it would have been as an outfit comparable with Blues Incorporated, with whom Jagger had occasionally sung and for whom the Stones were substituting at the Marquee gig.

The mainstays of Blues Incorporated, Alexis Korner and Cyril Davies, had been playing blues and R. & B. material for many years by that point, a fact that was almost entirely unknown in Britain, and even in London itself until they formed the band in 1961 and a club, in Ealing, at which to feature their music more regularly than they were able to do at the Marquee. Korner and Davies had both begun as traditional jazz musicians but – possibly as a result of the influence of the jazz musician, Chris Barber – had become interested in blues during the early 1950s, leading to their formation of the London Blues and Barrelhouse Club in 1955. Barber himself was instrumental in bringing to Britain blues performers such as Sonny Terry and Brownie McGhee, Otis Spann, and Muddy Waters during the 1950s, a fact which may unwittingly have compounded the critical view that blues was to be regarded as an adjunct of jazz.

These matters, however, did not concern the young audiences at the Marquee and Ealing clubs. They regarded traditional jazz as old-fashioned and the commercial American Pop of the period as too tame; blues and R. & B. represented a radical and exciting alternative. The Stones profited from this state of affairs and it was not long before their potential as a business proposition was recognised by the management team of Andrew Oldham and Eric Easton.

Possibly in order to enhance their commercial prospects, the Rolling Stones drew on a relatively wide range of black music styles on their early recordings. On the whole, however, they chose material by artists whose talents had scarcely been recognised, especially in Britain. Contrary to belief, Chuck Berry's records had not made much of an impact in Britain during the 1950s; his biggest British hit prior to the 1970s was 'No Particular Place To Go' in 1964, *after* the Stones had enjoyed success with his 'Come On', their first single release. A large number of record-buyers became aware of the existence of Jimmy Reed and Slim Harpo only because of the inclusion of their songs ('Honest I Do' and 'I'm A King Bee' respectively) on the Stones' first album *The Rolling Stones* (1964). Likewise, there were adaptations of the contemporary rhythm & blues material of Marvin Gaye ('Can I Get A Witness') and Irma Thomas ('Time Is On My Side').

One might occasionally be critical of the Rolling Stones' methods. They take Muddy Waters's 'I Just Want To Make Love To You', for example, at an impossibly fast pace, thus emasculating the strength and threatening undertone of the slow and relentless original rendition. Tempo acceleration, presumably to create an exciting effect, was to become a common error among British bands covering black American material; in this case it may have been a result of sheer lack of experience: compare, for instance, the Beatles' treatment of 'Anna' and 'Baby It's You' discussed above. Yet on other occasions, the Stones' treatment of their source material displays an original and perceptive approach. By handling Buddy Holly's 'Not Fade Away' in Bo Diddley's characteristic style, they effectively drew attention to Holly's debt to Diddley. (Holly had admitted this influence both verbally and musically, as indicated by his recordings of 'Bo Diddley' and related original compositions such as 'Peggy Sue'.) The Stones also completely transformed the Staple Singers' original for 'The Last Time' (1965), converting it into a near-rock & roll rendition through the pronounced emphasis on the off-beat.

The compositions of Jagger and Richard were undistinguished and few in number at this stage. What was important was that they made use of strong material from the black tradition, and brought what was previously largely unfamiliar to a new generation of record-buyers and, by implication, would-be performers who set up their own groups based on the Stones' example. They also epitomised the new-found competence and confidence among British instrumentalists. Their version of the Valentinos' 'It's All Over Now' (1964) is arguably of at least equal quality to the original in terms of the instrumental accompaniment. Jagger's singing, too, compares favourably here with Bobby Womack's: it was only when tackling the more demanding Chicago blues material such as Muddy Waters's 'I Just Want To Make Love To You' or 'I Can't Be Satisfied' (from *The Rolling Stones No. 2*) (1964) that he came to grief.

The Stones' desire for authenticity was paralleled in the work of the Animals, who came to similar prominence during 1964. The Animals were greatly assisted by the accomplished piano-playing of Alan Price, a definite advantage when reproducing blues and R. & B. It was this, together with a general concern for accuracy, which gave the Animals' early recordings their authentic sound. Their first single 'Baby Let Me Take You Home' (1964) was the latest example of a song family which had it roots in the New Orleans tradition. We may be sure that the Animals were conscious of Bob Dylan's version, 'Baby Let Me Follow You Down', contained on his first album, *Bob Dylan* (1962). After all, the song they chose for their second single, 'The House Of The Rising Sun' (also 1964), appears on the same Dylan LP. Yet there had been earlier readings by Professor Longhair (as 'Baby Let Me Hold Your Hand' in 1957) and Snooks Eaglin (as 'Mama Don't You Tear My Clothes' in 1958). The Animals' version does not resemble Dylan's and this fact, together with the knowledge that their singer, Eric Burdon, possessed an enormous collection of blues and R. & B. records, suggests at least an awareness of the song's New Orleans provenance as evidenced by the Longhair and Eaglin recordings. Similarly, 'House Of The Rising Sun', though adapted by Dylan, is a song of indeterminate origin, encountered in the repertoires of black folk performers such as Josh White.

Such considerations are reflected by the manner in which the Animals approached their work. While Price's abilities as a boogie pianist were their best asset, Burdon's voice, though occasionally strained and hoarse, often displayed an unselfconscious aggression. Their guitarist, Hilton Valentine, was seldom called upon to produce solos of any length or intensity, but still fulfilled his role with a technique which was more than adequate. Their version of Chuck Berry's 'How You've Changed' (1964) is a good example of their talents – it is a convincing reworking of a song otherwise ignored by

British bands, and while Burdon's vocal does not attempt to recreate Berry's wry approach, the group's performance as a whole would have done justice to an aggregation of Chicago session-men.

In 1963 Muddy Waters made his third visit to Britain. He had experienced difficulties on his previous two trips, initially because local audiences were unprepared for his amplified sound, and subsequently because he had reverted to the country blues in his effort to please them: there were now complaints from those expecting him to play Chicago-style. This in itself illustrates the change in approach that had taken place between 1958 and 1962: there was now an awareness of blues as a music quite separate from jazz, and this, together with fact that young musicians were beginning to turn to urban blues for their inspiration, improved the standing of such artists as Waters among the music's new audiences. The 1963 visit was part of an American Folk Blues Festival package which also included post-war stylists such as John Lee Hooker, Otis Spann, and Sonny Boy Williamson. Williamson, who stayed on in Europe after the AFBF tour was over, made a particularly favourable impression. Both he and Waters came to be celebrated by audiences *and* musicians, who were quick to acknowledge their influence, conferring upon them an honorary membership of the British pop elite. Musical forerunners of rock, these Chicago bluesmen now also amounted to rock stars. This arrangement worked to mutual benefit. Not only did the Americans achieve greater commercial success (Muddy Waters often admitted how sales of his records increased as a direct result of his acceptance in this country) but they also extended the appreciation of the blues beyond its previous narrow confines.

Yet the lure of chart success was still strong among many British bands. Largely through the efforts of the Beatles and the other Mersey groups, 1964 became a year of plenty for local acts, both at home and in the USA, where between February and October twenty British singles sold over a million copies. The Yardbirds, who had accompanied Sonny Boy Williamson on several occasions at his appearances around the country, experienced the dilemma of whether to continue to play their rhythm and blues style rock, which was not proving to be commercially successful, or whether to record material with a greater potential for reaching the chart. They chose the latter course of action with the result that 'For Your Love' (1965) made number two in Britain and number six in the USA. Disillusioned by this decision, their lead guitarist, Eric Clapton, left the group and joined John Mayall's Bluesbreakers.

Clapton's career with the Yardbirds, Mayall, and shortly afterwards with Cream epitomises the transition from R. & B. rock to blues-rock to rock. An awareness of Chicago blues, fostered – as we have seen – by visits to Britain by the originators and the recording of their compositions by groups such as the Rolling Stones, led inevitably to the discovery of the music's source, the blues of the Mississippi Delta. Closely linked to this investigation was the yearning to sound as authentic as possible and to reject compromise in favour of credibility. Concomitant with the acquisition of the technique necessary to handle such demanding music (or, in some cases, as a result of the frustration at not being able to do so) came the realisation of the powerful effect – essentially in the hands of a guitarist – that this might have upon an audience. Clapton himself stated, in an interview published in *Melody Maker* on 15 October 1966 (and quoted by John Pidgeon in *Eric Clapton*, 1976, p. 65), 'My whole musical attitude has changed. I listen to the same sounds but with a different ear. I'm no longer trying to play anything but like a white man.' We might regard this statement as a definition of rock music philosophy.

Mayall and Clapton released only one album together, but it was an influential one. *Blues Breakers* (1966) contained items from what was by now a familiar origin – Little Walter, Ray Charles, and so on – but, significantly, included two songs one step removed from the more widely-known material being attempted by contemporary British outfits. These were 'All Your Love' by Otis Rush (an artist then obscure to many in this country, but whose Chicago blues retained a strong affinity with its Mississippi roots) and 'Ramblin' On My Mind' by the Delta bluesman, Robert Johnson – an early (if not the first) attempt by a British band at music from this source. While the latter, Clapton's debut as a vocalist on record, was a routine copy, 'All Your Love' contained a Clapton solo, which, though superficially similar to the work of the Chicago blues stylists, exaggerated and distorted their phrasing and tone. Clapton's playing on two originals, 'Double Crossing Time' and 'Have You Heard' was, if anything, even more remarkable, and created the impression that he was making use of all the knowledge and energy he possessed to produce as intense an effect as possible. Whether or not Clapton's growing legion of followers would have experienced as much, or more, satisfaction by listening to the work of such contemporary Chicago blues guitarists as Buddy Guy is not known. The point was that Clapton was young, talented, available, and, as the graffiti on walls all over London had it, 'God'.

These two tendencies – that is, to delve deeper in the search for source material and to place more emphasis upon instrumental prowess – were developed still further with the formation of Cream, which comprised Clapton, drummer Ginger Baker, and Jack Bruce on bass guitar, harmonica, and vocals. Their first album, *Fresh Cream*, released by Reaction late in 1966, lacked any attempt to recreate Chuck Berry and Jimmy Reed hits. Included instead were 'Rollin' And Tumblin' ' (from the extensive blues song family also comprising 'Minglewood Blues' – see Chapter 1), 'Spoonful' (credited to Willie Dixon, but seeming to have its provenance in Charley Patton's 'A Spoonful Blues' of 1929), 'I'm So Glad' and 'Four Until Late', both originating from 1930s recordings by the Delta blues artists Skip James and Robert Johnson respectively. With the exception of the latter item, this material was arranged to accommodate the band-members' individual abilities as instrumentalists, as were their own compositions. In live performance this was taken to further extremes, the songs acting merely as a framework for extended improvisations in the manner more commonly found in contemporary jazz.

Cream's music was quickly labelled 'progressive', a somewhat ironic description given that much of their source material was at least thirty years old, and that their methods were equally well-established. Paradoxically, there was also something of a controversy as to whether the work of Mayall, Cream, and those who followed them could be regarded as blues. The editorial staff of the influential magazine *Blues Unlimited* (based in Bexhill, Sussex) felt that it could not. Retrospective evidence – together with Clapton's statement of intent quoted above – shows that they were right: this was rock.

As if to prove the point, Cream's next album, *Disraeli Gears* (released in November 1967) was dominated by their own compositions, and the mood was more akin to psychedelia than to Chicago or the Mississippi Delta, the single exception being 'Outside Woman Blues' written by Blind Joe Reynolds. Yet on stage Cream continued to use blues material as a basis for improvisation and in particular for lengthy guitar solos by Clapton. This tension was resolved by the issue of *Wheels Of Fire* (1968) which comprised one studio and one live album. The combination proved commercially irresistible: the set reached number one on both the British and American album charts. In October, however, the band broke up, making their last appearance at London's Albert Hall on the 26th.

By that stage, Cream had exerted two crucial influences upon the development of rock. Firstly, they had brought into popular currency hardcore Delta and Chicago blues material. This not only contrasted with the rock & roll and rhythm & blues source employed by the Beatles, Rolling Stones and others; it also inspired curiosity as to the music's origins, leading to an enhanced knowledge of the history of the blues. Many British blues authorities first discovered the music in such a manner though some subsequently rejected Cream's work, purging it from their collections and claiming they had been familiar with the form all along. In the United States, Cream's success represented the second wave of reimportation into that country of its own music. From a musical point of view Cream consolidated the assimilation of black American styles into British pop, a continuity best illustrated by the prevalence of the characteristic blues on-beat rhythmic emphasis in the resultant rock music form.

Secondly, the success of Cream brought about a preoccupation with instrumental skill as an end in itself. Hordes of young musicians looked up to the band with reverence and sought to emulate their technical proficiency. Although it was the guitar solo which became ubiquitous in rock, drummers were also permitted full rein; even bass-players, hitherto obscure and unloved, became celebrities in their own right. The implications of such a situation for the development of rock will be discussed later on in this chapter and in Chapter 7.

As many observers have remarked, Led Zeppelin were ideally placed to fill the vacuum created by the demise of Cream. While they initially made use of a similar source, their approach was, if anything, more uninhibited than that of their predecessors, at times displaying a vocal and instrumental frenzy which won them many admirers. Their first album (*Led Zeppelin*, 1968) included the Willie Dixon compositions 'You Shook Me' and 'I Can't Quit You Babe' (originally recorded by Otis Rush), yet the principal influence on their treatment would seem to be the singing of Jack Bruce and the guitar-playing of Eric Clapton, rather than any Chicago provenance. With the band's second LP release (*Led Zeppelin II*, 1969), links with the blues were formally severed, even though 'Whole Lotta Love' appears to be based on the Muddy Waters recording 'You Need Love', and Robert

Johnson is not credited for the lyrical idea of 'The Lemon Song'. There was, in fact, little need to refer to the blues any more: rock music could sustain itself quite easily through its own standards of songwriting and musicianship, a fact reinforced by the enormous commercial success of Led Zeppelin, especially in the United States. Of their first seven LP releases, five reached number one on the American album chart.

It is perhaps not surprising that the reworking of blues material by white American performers of the early 1960s remained faithful to its source. Musicians such as Mike Bloomfield and Paul Butterfield not only lived in close proximity to the originators but accompanied them in live appearances in front of black audiences. It was therefore essential that they kept their music conventional. In fact, when Butterfield made his first album, *The Paul Butterfield Blues Band* (1965), he employed black musicians Jerome Arnold and Billy Davenport on bass and drums respectively. Tracks such as the band's version of Little Walter's 'Off The Wall' illustrate the resultant authenticity. Although Bloomfield and Butterfield achieved a degree of success, it scarcely equated with that of their British counterparts. This was no doubt because they were *too* concerned with the accurate reproduction of an idiom which lacked universal acceptance in the first place; even the fact that they possessed the distinct commercial advantage of being young and white was insufficient to make them stars.

It is clear that a measure of geographical and environmental separation was necessary in order for blues to exert an influence upon the development of rock music and provide the basis of its widespread popularity. There were no constraints on British musicians to respect the blues tradition and it is arguable that such a lack of inhibition contributed crucially to their success. In America, it was the bands of the West Coast who used the blues most profitably during the mid-1960s, rather than the musicians from Chicago or the South.

Both the Doors and Jefferson Airplane, the first two California bands of the period to rise to national prominence, recorded blues material on their early albums. Jim Morrison invested Howlin' Wolf's 'Back Door Man' (*The Doors*, 1967) with characteristic menace, and returned to the source four years later (*LA Woman*) with a similar rendition of 'Crawling King Snake', a song credited to John Lee Hooker but related to the 1941 Big Joe Williams recording of the same name. Jefferson Airplane included 'Me And My Chauffeur' (a song normally attributed to Memphis Minnie, but part of a wider song family which includes 'Good Morning Little Schoolgirl') on their second album, *Surrealistic Pillow* (1967). Though originally from Texas, Janis Joplin moved to the West Coast early in her career. She often acknowledged her debt to the blues, both in interview and, implicitly, in her singing style: one of her most celebrated recordings was her version of Big Mama Thornton's 'Ball And Chain' (*Cheap Thrills*, 1968). The Grateful Dead began as a jug band and subsequently incorporated R. & B., country, soul, and blues into their performances. Their 1967 recording, 'New, New Minglewood Blues' is of particular interest, being an example of the large song family referred to in Chapter 1 and elsewhere – a fact reflected by the Dead's sardonic title. Captain Beefheart possessed the advantages of both sounding like a black singer and being able to compose what amounted to original blues material. Though following tradition in the use of harmonica and slide guitar, Beefheart evolved an idiosyncratic method of syncopation which seems to enhance the impression of authenticity rather than detract from it. A good example is 'Gimme Dat Harp Boy' from the album *Strictly Personal* (1968).

Large-scale popular acceptance was slow to arrive for the majority of these artists, especially in Britain, where the native product was all-pervasive. One California-based band who did break through were Canned Heat – their first two singles, 'On The Road Again' and 'Going Up The Country' (both 1968) were hits in the United States *and* in Britain. Certain features distingished Canned Heat from contemporary bands operating in a superficially similar area. To start with, they were students of the blues for some time before they arrived in the recording studio. Both Bob Hite and Al Wilson owned comprehensive collections of blues records from all periods of the music's history. Secondly, they concentrated initially on country blues as their source. 'On The Road Again' is, furthermore, anything but a routine copy of a single earlier rendition. Wilson's vocal seems most closely to resemble that found on the Mississippi Sheiks' 'Stop And Listen Blues' of 1930, although there is also a close correspondence with Willie Lofton's 'Dark Road Blues' (1935) and Mississippi Mudder's 'Going Back Home' (1934). To add to the complexity, there are clear links with Tommy Johnson's 'Big Road Blues' of 1928, itself related to 'Dark Road' (1951) by Floyd Jones, whom Canned Heat credit as a composer of 'On The Road Again'; Jones did record a song of that name with connections to the Canned Heat version, though in *Rock File 3* (p. 160) Gillett and Frith give the source as the Memphis Jug Band!

This apparent tangle not only illustrates how the origins of common stock country blues songs are often impossible to discover. It also demonstrates that Canned Heat, through their obvious awareness of at least two earlier renditions, were *themselves* participants in the history of the song's development.

The popularity of 'On The Road Again', not surprisingly, did not tempt Canned Heat away from the country blues, although they continued to use conventional rock instrumentation. 'Going Up The Country' was a version of Henry Thomas's 'Bull Doze Blues' (1928), while their predilection for Delta material was reflected in such recordings as Charley Patton's 'Pony Blues' of 1929 (from the album *Living The Blues*, (1969). There was a slight shift of emphasis in 1970, when the band had a hit with Wilbert Harrison's 'Let's Work Together', possibly accelerated by the death of Al Wilson in September of that year. Canned Heat went on to record with John Lee Hooker (*Hooker 'n' Heat*, 1971), but that stage popular interest in the blues was beginning to wane.

The West Coast was the natural centre for the incorporation of the blues into the emerging white rock genre. It had few cultural ties with the traditions of either the South or North. Black people were permitted to exist in comparative freedom, a state of emancipation most had hoped for in their migration earlier in the century from the southern states to the northern cities. That this had frequently led to disappointment resulted in the preoccupation with California as the preferred destination, exemplified by the sentiments of the protagonist in Chuck Berry's 'Promised Land'. It was therefore inevitable that black and white cultures would integrate – just as they had done in 1940s West Coast R. & B. (which developed in the Los Angeles lounges and supper-clubs owned and patronised by Whites) and in 1950s West Coast Jazz (when young white musicians worked on the principles of bebop, a style initiated in New York by their black contemporaries).

Yet the Californian rock bands were also influenced by the enormous success that British performers were experiencing by the assimilation into their music of black styles. Throughout the United States, in fact, audiences were being reintroduced to the origins of their native pop music, and the significance of this was not lost on established white artists, the most eminent of which was Bob Dylan.

Peter Guralnick (1971) has related how, disillusioned with what he perceived as the decline of rock & roll in the late 1950s/early 1960s, he turned to the blues, which he came upon through folk music (pp. 21—2). Though Bob Dylan had been interested in the blues before he benefited from the resurgence of interest in folk, it is not difficult to see how he began to operate in the context suggested by Guralnick. Like John Lennon (of whom he was a close contemporary), Dylan had been a rock & roll enthusiast during his teenage years, being especially attracted to the music of Little Richard and Chuck Berry; he also played in a rock & roll band when at high school at Hibbing, Minnesota. Quite why Dylan did not continue in this vein is a matter of speculation. Wilfred Mellers (1984) states that 'his opting out of college after six months was not merely a negative rejection of the American Way of Life but also a positive return to an older, more basic American culture' (p. 112). It may also have been that he found his talents unsuited to rock & roll, or that he anticipated its demise as a means of individual expression.

Whatever the case, his affinity with the blues is clearly demonstrated by the content and delivery of his first album, *Bob Dylan* (1962). At least five tracks have their origin in the work of blues artists, most dating back to the 1920s/1930s. 'In My Time Of Dyin' ' is based on Blind Willie Johnson's 'Jesus Make Up My Dyin' Bed' (1927) and also related to 'Jesus Is A Dying Bed-Maker' by Charley Patton (1929). 'Fixin' To Die' was composed and recorded (in 1940) by the Delta blues singer Bukka White, while 'See That My Grave Is Kept Clean' originates from Blind Lemon Jefferson who first recorded it in 1927. 'Highway 51' is credited to Curtis Jones whose version was made in 1938, though the song resembles certain compositions by Big Joe Williams; in any event, Dylan's rendition makes use of the basic blues riff. The song also contributes to the general impression created by the album of travel, loneliness, and disorientation (Highway 51 runs from New Orleans via Memphis to the shores of Lake Superior, Dylan's own birthplace), a central concern in both black and white traditions (see Introduction). 'You're No Good' was written by R. & B. singer Jesse Fuller, while the New Orleans origins of 'Baby, Let Me Follow You Down' have been discussed earlier in this chapter.

It would have been remarkable enough that a while singer of twenty
years of age was recording such material as early as 1961 (the album
was made at two sessions in November of that year). Yet what was
equally notable was that Dylan's vocal delivery showed such a close
relationship with that of the blues singers whose work he was
reproducing. His flat, clipped technique at times amounts to talking
rather than singing, in a manner redolent of Jefferson, White, and
Patton. He actually includes a 'talking blues' ('Talkin' New York'), a
form commonly thought of as originating with Woody Guthrie (from
whom Dylan no doubt derived it) but corresponding clearly with
black vocal mannerisms, as illustrated by Bukka White's recording of
'The Panama Limited' (1930). The influence that Dylan's singing
style was to have upon subsequent rock vocalists has already been
referred to (see Chapter 1, pp. 39–40).

On *The Freewheelin' Bob Dylan* (1963) blues material is still
present, but subject to rearrangement. Thus we find 'Corinna,
Corinna' transformed to great effect, almost as if Dylan had written
the song himself. According to Mellers (p. 128), 'Down The
Highway' 'pays homage' to Big Joe Williams, though the song would
seem to originate with Charlie Pickett's version of 1937; in any case,
Dylan reshapes it in his own way. Also included is the talking blues,
'Talkin' World War III'. Although national acceptance was some way
away (of Dylan's first four LP releases, only *The Times They Are
A-Changin'* reached the Top Twenty on the American album chart:
Bob Dylan did not feature at all), demands were now being made by
the newly reconstituted folk lobby based in New York's Greenwich
Village.

Dylan has often indicated his antipathy for this group of custodians
– indeed, he satirised their purist tendencies in 'Talkin' New York'.
Yet we might assume that he was gratified to gain recognition in some
circles, and he was certainly not slow to realise the commercial
possibilities of his suddenly fashionable protest songs. Though
initially composed of enthusiasts dedicated to preserving what they
regarded as the American Folk Tradition, the Greenwich Village
circle seized on the anthem-like character of Dylan's anti-war
compositions with alacrity. For a time they wielded considerable
influence which was not confined to the United States; in Britain
during the early 1960s there was a considerable growth in scope and in
number within the folk-club network. It is not surprising, therefore,
that Dylan was accused of abdicating his responsibilities when he

appeared at the 1965 Newport Folk Festival backed by the Paul Butterfield Blues Band, and subsequently toured Britain accompanied by a former rock & roll outfit, The Band.

Dylan had been observing the progress of the successful British groups with some interest. Anthony Scaduto (1972) quotes him as recalling

We were driving through Colorado . . . we had the radio on and eight of the Top Ten songs were Beatles songs. . . . They were doing things nobody was doing. Their chords were outrageous, just outrageous, and their harmonies made it all valid. . . . Everybody else thought they were for the teenyboppers, that they were gonna pass right away. But it was obvious to me that they had staying power. I knew they were pointing the direction music had to go . . . in my head, the Beatles were *it*. (p. 175)

We may surmise that such a belief, together with the influence that members of The Band had upon him, caused Dylan to reinvestigate his roots and those of the emerging rock music.

With *Bringing It All Back Home* (1965), Dylan's deliberations came to fruition. The very title of the album indicates a fresh attitude, a fact reinforced by the appearance on the front of the sleeve of LPs by the Impressions and Robert Johnson. Of the seven items on side one, four are distinguished by the pronouned off-beat characteristics of rock & roll. In addition, 'Subterranean Homesick Blues' has strong thematic connections with Chuck Berry's 'Too Much Monkey Business' (Chess, 1956), and 'Outlaw Blues' follows the twelve-bar blues structure. Dylan is clearly comfortable with the material and his frequently gleeful vocal delivery is complemented by a suitably energetic band accompaniment.

Side Two is more sombre in mood, and confirms that Dylan was not yet quite ready to renounce his accomplishments of the early 1960s. This tension between old and new approaches is resolved on the succeeding albums *Highway 61 Revisited* (1965) and *Blonde On Blonde* (1966). The latter album, in particular, represents a resolution of all previous conflicts and draws together all musical and lyrical strands to create an original and distinctive work, ensuring Dylan's pre-eminence in contemporary rock music. Unfortunately, he rather lost momentum as a result of a motorcycle accident in August 1966, and failed to recapture it for *John Wesley Harding* (1968); he then, as many rock & roll stars had done before him, turned to country music with the release of the 1969 album *Nashville Skyline*.

The group that had influenced Dylan and accompanied him so

effectively, The Band, began to make their own records in 1968. In their previous incarnation as the Hawks, they had spent much of their time backing the white rock & roll singer, Ronnie Hawkins, commencing in the late 1950s. Hawkins specialised in the blacker strains of rock & roll, and the Hawks themselves were blues enthusiasts, but at this time, North American audiences were not yet ready to accept their efforts – hardcore rock & roll was out of fashion and the reawakening of interest in the blues, stemming to a great degree from the second phase of the British 'invasion', had not begun.

The Band, therefore, were willing participants in the reinvestigation being undertaken by such an established artist as Dylan. That they themselves began to re-examine and re-evaluate both musical and cultural traditions now seems a natural extension of this process. As Greil Marcus (1977) has written:

> Against a cult of youth they felt for a continuity of generations; against the instant America of the sixties they looked for the traditions that made new things not only possible, but valuable; against a flight from the roots they set a sense of place. Against the pop scene, all flux and novelty, they set themselves: a band with years behind it, and meant to last. (p. 50)

Just as it had taken musicians from an alien environment and culture – specifically, Britain and the American West Coat – to make the most of the possibilities offered by blues and R. & B., so it took The Band (all Canadians, with the exception of Levon Helm, who was from Arkansas) to produce the first popular celebration of White Southern culture. Their first two albums, *Music From Big Pink* (1968) and *The Band* (1969) represent the values and traditions of the South in a personal yet non-pejorative way. Thus the mistress-hired hand relationship described in 'The Weight' is taken for granted and is extended in 'The Unfaithful Servant' where the prevailing emotion is of regret rather than recrimination. There is, too, an empathy with the fundamental concerns of rural existence, essentially work ('King Harvest') and leisure ('Up On Cripple Creek'). While *Music From Big Pink* operates in general in a non-specific environment (what Marcus describes as 'the timeless and mythical American town'), *The Band* reveals an attention to detail which further authenticates the subject matter. This is predicted by the opening track, 'Across The Great Divide', and reaches fulfilment in 'The Night They Drove Old Dixie Down' where the personal implications for the protagonist of the defeat of the Confederate army are presented in characteriscally sympathetic fashion, the thorough knowledge of historical events allowing for the possibility of factual accuracy and thereby impartiality on the listener's behalf.

Although they were all individually versatile musicians and incorporated a wide variety of native forms and styles into their work, The Band rejected the prevailing fashion of overt instrumental virtuosity and fused their musical influences into a uniform yet distinctive sound. Lengthy guitar solos were dispensed with and ostentatious drumming displays were replaced by a precise yet full percussive base. The piano, so important in the conventions of blues, country music, and rock & roll, was reintroduced; the use of a horn section was sparing and appropriate. In short, The Band's sound mirrored their investigation of the Southern white rural tradition.

Established rock stars such as George Harrison and Eric Clapton were quick to draw attention to The Band's virtues, and in time their influence began to permeate a rock scene which was rapidly becoming stagnant. Ths process was accelerated by the commercial success of Creedence Clearwater Revival, the only contemporary outfit operating in a similar area to The Band. Though less specific in their references, Creedence also dealt with typically Southern traditional themes and concerns, in particular the role of the river as both a means of transportation and as a location for settlement – examples include 'Proud Mary'/'Born On The Bayou' and 'Green River' (both 1969). Like The Band, Creedence approached their subject matter from an external viewpoint (they were from San Francisco), such a separation again enhancing the effect. They also avoided instrumental excess and remained faithful to the basic format of two guitars, bass, and drums. This return to fundamentals was reflected in their predisposition to rock & roll, often employing its back-beat rhythmic emphasis, most notably in 'Bad Moon Rising' (1969).

The music of Creedence Clearwater Revival and in particular that of The Band can be seen, in retrospect, to have anticipated what came to be known as the 'New Wave' of the late 1970s. By returning to the traditions established and developed decades earlier they were able to preserve continuity while creating the conditions under which change might take place.

The belief that mainstream rock was degenerating into inert and artistically unprofitable areas had spread to Britain, resulting in a revival of musical activity in pubs and small clubs. Bands such as Dire Straits, Dr Feelgood, and Eddie and the Hot Rods flourished in this environment during the mid-1970s. *The NME Book Of Rock 2* (1977) noted this turn of events, and in an attempt to anticipate new trends, included a section on Punk Rock (p. 405). It explained that the term should now encompass 'U.S. acts like Bruce Springsteen, Patti Smith and particularly, Nils Lofgren'. Though we may now fault the terminology, there was undoubted prescience in the choice of this particular trio: Springsteen wrote for Smith and later included Lofgren in his backing band. He had also begun the process of reworking the music of his youth, the American pop of the late 1950s and early 1960s. It would not be long before it was once again agreeable to be called a rock & roll singer.

Chapter 5

What is black music?

The concept of black music has become something of a shibboleth, to the extent that even to question its pre-eminence amounts to heresy. This state of affairs is typified by the fact that white contributions to blues and even rock & roll are often ignored or grossly undervalued. For instance, in the standard discographies of blues – Dixon and Godrich (1982) and Leadbitter and Slaven (1968) – white musicians are only included either by mistake or as incidentals. In Dixon and Godrich, many of the talented white blues artists are omitted, for example, Jimmie Rodgers, Frank Hutchison, and Dick Justice. Furthermore, Jimmy Davis, the eventual Governor of Louisiana, is included only on the grounds that he accompanied the black guitarist Oscar Woods in certain recording sessions. Similarly, Leadbitter and Slaven, in their Introduction, imply that blues records made by white artists would be of no interest to collectors and scholars. The white one-man band, Harmonica Frank Floyd, achieved his listing in error, owing principally to his authentic 'black sound'. Leadbitter and Slaven had, however, planned to produce a rock & roll discography which, we may be sure, would have included at least the major white performers.

In some measure these attitudes were reinforced in the first instance by all of us who collected blues records and wrote on the subject in the early 1960s. However, few of those individuals would have either anticipated or remained sanguine about the present position.

We are still of the opinion, of course, that those designated as black have made the major contributions to the development of pop music from its earliest origins. Nevertheless this view does not necessarily support the rejection of all white achievements nor the reification of all black performances. Inverted racism is no less patronising than other forms of discrimination.

As any student of American history will know, delineation of people in terms of black and white has always been enormously complex in both theoretical and practical terms. The traditional dichotomous distinction in fact belies these complexities. In dividing persons into those who are black and those who are white we are merely distinguishing between those who are completely white and those who are not. Any such rigid distinction ignores not only the legal but the social realities in the United States.

The whole basis of racial segregation is undermined in terms of fact, if not in terms of consequence, by the phenomenon of 'passing for white'. Though official figures cannot, by definition, be available, Stetson Kennedy (1959) reported at that time an estimate of between five to eight million persons as having successfully passed for white in the USA (p. 52). Obviously many of these people will have had both children and grandchildren by now. Otis M. Walton (1972) refers to an assessment made by Robert Stuckert that in 1960 twenty-one per cent of 'white Americans' were of partially black descent (p. 47).

Legally speaking, the definition as to what constituted a black person varied from state to state under the 'Jim Crow' laws. In Alabama, Arkansas, and Mississippi, anyone with a 'visible' and/or 'appreciable' degree of 'Negro blood' was subject to segregational laws as a black person whereas in Indiana and Louisiana the colour line was drawn at one-eighth and one-sixteenth Negro blood respectively. Clearly, then, it was possible to change one's status – and therefore legal rights – by moving from one state to another.

Such factors render particularly nonsensical any equation of race with musical (or any other) ability. The logic of this kind of racial distinction would lead us to expect that all of the greatest musicians in the blues, soul, and rhythm & blues fields would be those most obviously black in appearance. In fact this is demonstrably not the case: many of the most eminent artists in 'black music' would not correspond to this classification, for example Charley Patton, Robert Johnson, Chuck Berry, Little Richard, and Sam Cooke.

The rigid distinction between 'black' and 'white' is however, despite its illogicality, a fact of life and has led, throughout the history of the United States, to degradation and suffering for those classed as black. In the pop business, until very recently, it has always been the white musicians and entrepreneurs who have most clearly profited.

Jimmie Rodgers, as we have already noted, became extremely wealthy whereas artists such as Charley Patton, Willie Johnson, and Willie McTell died in relative poverty and obscurity. A comparison between the earnings and acclaim achieved by, on the one hand, Elvis Presley and, on the other, Chuck Berry further demonstrates the continuing discrepancy in financial reward and popular acceptance. This disparity is typified by what is perhaps an apocryphal story of how the Rolling Stones arrived for a recording session at Chess to find Muddy Waters painting the studio.

These inequalities were not, however, always a matter of racial division, for not only were middle-class blacks generally contemptuous of rural Southern music but at the same time there had also been a tradition – from W. C. Handy to Berry Gordy – of successfully exploiting that 'commodity'.

In recent times it has often been the case that the fact of racial segregation has blurred other divisions in American society. At least as important, from a strictly musical point of view, have been regional and class distinctions. The promotion of the concept of black music which has been motivated largely by non-musical factors might be described as the marketing of a heritage.

Perhaps the greatest musical asset for this exercise was what came to be known as soul music. For many of those to whom blues represented the degradation of Southern rural life, soul was an acceptable metamorphosis. Many soul recordings were overtly political in terms of their rejection of the notion of Blacks as second-class citizens. Many writers associated with the 'black consciousness' movement of the 1960s, particularly Eldridge Cleaver, objected to country blues on the grounds that it was insufficiently outspoken against the 'black condition'. Whereas much early soul music was produced and recorded in the South, it is nevertheless true that the music did not reflect specifically regional concerns. On the contrary, soul was accepted as an expression of black solidarity, cutting across geographical and class boundaries.

The term 'soul' both delineated a music and constituted the realisation of a new-found pride in a racial identity. It was originally used as a label for a jazz style of the late 1950s which incorporated gospel music and blues, thus acknowledging the roots of 'contemporary black music'. A distinct political character was evident in the work of leading artists operating in this field, culminating in the work of Oscar Brown Jr. whose 1961 album *Sin And Soul* included explicit comments on the oppression of Blacks such as 'Work Song' and 'Bid 'Em In'. Established modern jazz musicians were influenced by the new climate: Charles Mingus issued such items as 'Fables of Faubus' – Orval Faubus was a segregationist Governor of Arkansas – on his album *Mingus Ah Um* (1959), while Max Roach recorded a political statement of LP length, *We Insist! Freedom Now Suite* (1960).

By the early 1960s there was a general sense of disillusionment with the strategy of the Civil Rights movement. Many felt that the death of Martin Luther King in 1968 symbolised the impotence of that philosophy. As far as many young Blacks were concerned the modest, even subservient, requests for what were already their constitutional rights were viewed as indicative of an 'Uncle Tom' approach. Following the adoption of Sam Cooke's 'A Change Is Gonna Come' (1965) as a black anthem, soul music was increasingly used as a vehicle for a more forceful expression of political statements and demands. Instances included 'Say It Loud – I'm Black And I'm Proud' (James Brown, 1968), 'Give More Power To The People' (the Chi-Lites, 1971), and 'Young, Gifted And Black', a Nina Simone song dating from 1968, which seemed to amount to a statement of triumph by 1972 when Aretha Franklin's version was released.

As we have seen in Chapter 4, early soul singers such as Solomon Burke and Arthur Alexander employed aspects of country music in their work. While we may regard such experiments as resulting from conscious decisions on the part of the artists, we must recognise that – given the fact that the power-base of the pop music industry, especially in the South, was still under white control – involvement by white songwriters, musicians, producers, and entrepreneurs in the development of soul was almost inevitable. Though there was an apparent increase in the participation by Blacks in the music that they now regarded as their own property, the relationship between soul (and its successors) and white pop music was to continue.

This may be illustrated by the importance to soul of essentially white guitar styles. Steve Cropper, who appeared on innumerable soul recordings made in the city of Memphis, played in a style much closer to that of other white musicians such as Chet Atkins and Scotty Moore than to the leading blues and R. & B. guitarists of the period. Cropper became so influential that for a time his was *the* guitar sound in soul music, avoiding almost entirely the use of vibrato so common amongst his black counterparts. The use of the wah-wah pedal was crucial to the success of the records of Isaac Hayes, commencing with

'Shaft' in 1971; by then this techique was well established in rock music, having been originally introduced by such players as Frank Zappa and Eric Clapton. It remained a feature of soul recordings for many years, most obviously in the work of the Isley Brothers, as on the album *3+3* (1973) and many others.

In jazz, Miles Davis incorporated selected elements of rock for his album *In A Silent Way* (1969). On this, and successive releases, he employed the white guitarist John McLaughlin. Davis's influence was such that other jazz musicians began use the rock beat as a foundation for their own improvisations; most dispensed with the conventional jazz guitar style in favour of a more rock-oriented sound. Thus 'fusion' or 'jazz-rock' came to depend heavily on rock guitar, both in terms of style and, in some cases, rock musicians themselves, an example being the use of former James Gang and Deep Purple guitarist Tommy Bolin by jazz drummer Billy Cobham for his album *Spectrum* (1974). Jazz-funk, a direct descendant both of soul and jazz-rock, has continued this tradition to the extent that rock guitar is now an inseparable component of the music.

As Michael Bane (1982) and Bruce Cook (1975) have previously argued, pop music has always depended upon the interaction between white and black traditions. For example, Cook states that there has been 'a vast complex of musical borrowing, trades, and thefts that went back and forth between white and black over a couple of centuries' (p. 15). These mutual borrowings go back at least as far as the first Great Awakening of the 1730s. According to Bane,

The Great Revival, as it came to be known, spread from the South throughout the nation, sweeping the country into a religious fervor and, incidentally, spreading revivalist songs to every corner. For the first time white Americans found a way and a place to let go, 'to act like a nigger' with impunity. They had a sanction to touch their senses, to discover their bodies, without risking eternal damnation and a whiff of the brimstone – and *that* was a lesson that white America would *never* forget!   (p. 36)

The Great Awakenings were two successive waves of religious revival which also deeply affected American music. The first Revival coincided with the spread of hymnody and therefore the decline of psalmody. An important influence on this process was the publication of *Hymns And Spirituals* in London (1701) by an Englishman, Dr Isaac Watts. This hymnody was introduced to American congregations by the English Revivalist preachers, and a Boston edition was published in 1739. This new music greatly accelerated the dissemination of harmony, and thus the diatonic scale, throughout rural America, and so inevitably affected the folk musics of the South.

The Second Awakening, *c.* 1780–1830, was renowned for its camp meetings, at which whole communities would worship and sleep in what amounted to tent cities. As Eileen Southern (1983) puts it, 'the camp meeting was primarily an interracial institution' (p. 83). Perhaps more importantly, it seems to have been a fairly *informal* institution with a great deal of spontaneity in both musical and non-musical forms of worship. Because of this, the music of the camp meetings was considerably more lively than earlier American religious musics. Viv Broughton (1985) states that

. . . there is also much evidence that some of the rituals of Africa re-emerged at the camp meetings. Surreptitiously of course and suitably Christianised, but quite definitely African in origin. Like the shouts and the ring-shouts – circles of chanting singers, half-dancing, half marching, stamping out the beats on each word of a drawn out chorus, sometimes complementing the rhythm with hand claps or thigh claps. The first morning of the camp meetings often featured the 'weird spectacle' of an enormous ring-shout completely encircling the whole camp. All the black campers, having sung and worshipped throughout the previous night, now shuffled, chanted, danced and shouted in a spectacular sunrise farewell march. (p. 23)

Many historians, including Southern and Broughton, have argued that camp meetings marked the beginning of what are now known as spirituals and that 'gospel music' was a product of the city environment. The evidence for this kind of spiritual/gospel and rural/urban distinction is minimal, as prior to the early twentieth century no gramophone records were available of either type. Furthermore, just as in blues recording history, the first religious music records were made by urban-located performers.

Evidence provided by early recordings of hillbilly music in the 1920s suggests at least a rhythmic link with both the music of the camp meetings and modern gospel. The predilection for off-beat emphasis can be seen to characterise at least hillbilly and gospel musics.

At the end of this process of musical integration – in other words, by the time of commercial recording – it was impossible to distinguish not only what was rural and what urban in source, but also what came from black and what from white.

The commercial recordings of 'gospel' music during the 1920s and

1930s show little apparent corroboration for any theory relating to its evolution. There was a wealth of styles and types of gospel recorded by black and white, and rural and urban, performers. Much of the work of the black solo artists – for example, Blind Lemon Jefferson, Charley Patton, and Blind Willie Johnson – was musically indistinguishable from country blues. Furthermore it seemed to become standard practice for these artists merely to change the lyrics of a blues in order to offer it as a religious item. Probably the most famous example of this approach was that of Robert Wilkins, who recorded 'That's No Way To Get Along' in 1929 as a blues song and subsequently used the same tune and lyrical theme to create a gospel piece called 'Prodigal Son' (1964).

During this period a wide range of religious music was recorded: much of it occupied a position somewhere between spiritual and gospel forms. The Fisk University Jubilee Quartet's rendition of 'Roll, Jordan Roll' (1913) epitomises the spiritual form. It is striking in terms of its sedate and restrained delivery and its sparing use of harmony. The Fisk Singers seemed concerned to preserve what they saw as a tradition of jubilee singing and also to stress the more dignified elements in black religious music. In many respects their approach was close to that of folklorists and their efforts anticipated those of John and Alan Lomax on behalf of the Library of Congress. The Fisk Singers' methods probably appealed to those middle-class Blacks who found the more uninhibited gospel music unpalatable.

Other gospel recordings made between ten and twenty years later show an eclectic approach to harmony, melody, instrumentation, and rhythm. Washington Phillips, for example, recorded a number of beautifully lilting songs to the accompaniment of a dulceola, which seems to have been a cross between a zither and a dulcimer. By aural evidence alone it is difficult to determine whether Phillips was a black or a white musician. The great Alfred G. Karnes built up a complex relationship between the vocal and guitar parts on performances such as 'I'm Bound For The Promised Land' (1928). This piece has an authentic gospel sound at least in terms of its accentuation of the off-beat and its lively tempo. Its religious message is somewhat understated, which may have shown a desire to increase its potential for secular sales. Despite his hillbilly origins, Karnes manages to approximate a black sound in both vocal delivery and guitar work where his percussive use of the bass strings recalls the techniques of Delta guitarists such as Charley Patton and Tommy Johnson.

The recordings two years later of 'Memphis Flu' by the Elder Curry congregation exhibits all the characteristics of gospel, from the lead vocal of Joanne Williams to the handclapping and vocal interjections by the assembly. The piano playing of Elder Charles Beck is properly described as an off-beat boogie and anticipates the work of many rock & roll pianists, in particular that of Lafayette Leake and Johnny Johnson in their accompaniments to Chuck Berry.

The recordings of Roosevelt and Uaroy Graves in 1929 and 1936 demonstrate some aspects of the evolution of country gospel. In fact the Graves brothers may well have been pioneers in this field. Although they came from Mississippi, they certainly were not innovators in blues, where they merely aped the less imaginative female vaudeville singers. Their religious material, however, developed from the proto-gospel of 'Take Your Burdens To The Lord' (1929) – which had certain features in common with the work of Alfred G. Karnes – to the polyrhythmic performance of 'Woke Up This Morning' and 'I'll Be Rested' (both 1936). On the later sessions the gospel beat is particularly apparent, with prominent piano accompaniment. The Graves brothers are evidence for the view that at least by the 1930s gospel was developing musically in a way that distanced it from country blues.

It was the rhythmic structure of gospel music that later found large-scale commercial expression in rock & roll. This was especially true in the case of Elvis Presley, who was quick to acknowledge the influence of religious music upon his style. Peter Guralnick (1979) quotes an interview with Presley in which he recalls:

We were a religious family, going around together to sing at camp meetings and revivals. Since I was two years old, all I knew was gospel music, that was music to me. We borrowed the style of our psalm singing from the early Negroes. We used to go to these religious singings all the time. The preachers cut up all over the place, jumping on the piano, moving every which way. The audience liked them. I guess I learned from them. I loved the music. It became such a part of my life it was natural as dancing, a way to escape from the problems and my way of release. (pp. 120–21)

Such a background helps to account for Presley's imaginative use of cross-rhythms: his mastery of gospel technique enabled him to vary his rhythmic relationship with the instrumental accompaniment. This is illustrated by his ability to delay his response to the beginning of a guitar or piano phrase, or at other times to anticipate it.

The off-beat syncopation universally associated with rock & roll is obviously a contribution from the gospel side of the blues-boogie-gospel family. Presley's use of syncopated rhythms – particularly evident on Sun recordings such as 'That's All Right' (1954) and 'Mystery Train' (1955) – exemplify this. In neither blues nor boogie is the off-beat syncopation an essential component.

Another well-publicised connection between gospel and rock & roll was the emergence and subsequent importance of the vocal groups, who produced secularised gospel music in the rhythm & blues field during the mid to late 1940s. The vocal group style developed as a consequence of both the increased numbers of urban Blacks and the growing influence of gospel music upon them: this coincided with a decline in the vitality of urban blues as evidenced by the stereotyped and one-dimensional sounds of the Chicago scene. The rising gospel style was at least vital. This new medium allowed young urban Blacks the possibility of a cheap and fashionable outlet for their musical ambitions. The purchase of expensive instruments was unnecessary; rehearsals and performances could be carried out in any location. The traditional picture of vocal groups rehearsing whilst walking home from school is probably quite an accurate one. Contemporary recordings demonstrate, however, that this movement produced a great deal of innovatory work in the areas of harmony and rhythm. The best vocal groups could – in ths manner of jazz artists such as Lester Young and Billie Holiday – transcend the most inane material by the use of imaginative phrasing. An excellent example of this is the Flamingos' 'I'll Be Home' (1956).

There is a danger, however, of overestimating the *musical* contribution of the vocal groups to rock & roll. More important is their role as originators of soul music. The fact that the vocal group style coincided with the emergence of rock & roll – and preceded the public recognition of 'soul' by at least a decade – tends to obscure the nature of that contribution.

As a socio-musical movement, rock & roll seemed to disturb the segregational norm in the United States – it included both black *and* white performers. This aspect of the music was, as far as the American media were concerned, most worthy of attention. The occasional mixed audiences and the adoption by young Whites of black cultural traits were among the features which led many conservative Whites to see rock & roll as a threat to the racial status quo. At least one leading rock and roll group, the Del-Vikings, were integrated. There were

certainly as many important white rock & roll artists as there were
black: alongside Chuck Berry, Little Richard, and Fats Domino
stood Elvis Presley, Jerry Lee Lewis, and Buddy Holly. It is
interesting to note that the integrationist fashion in music soon
disappeared – a good illustration of this was the fact that a few black
rock & rollers were reclassified as rhythm and blues performers
during the 1960s. The records of Chuck Berry and Bo Diddley, for
example, appeared on the British Pye International 'R & B' series. On
the whole, the white rockers were consigned to either country and
western music or to professional/critical oblivion.

Arguably, most of the musical innovations associated with soul took
place during the rock & roll era; these can be observed in the work of
Roy Brown and Bobby Bland in the late 1940s, B. B. King and Clyde
McPhatter (from the early 1950s), Ray Charles and James Brown
(from 1956), Jerry Butler and the Impressions (from 1958), the
Falcons – including Eddie Floyd and later Wilson Pickett (from
1959), and the Drifters (also from 1959). In contrast, the artists who
recorded for Stax and what was to become the Tamla Motown label
were still performing straightforward rhythm & blues prior to 1963.
Booker T and the MGs, who were to become the house band on the
Stax soul recordings, had a hit in 1962 with 'Green Onions' – a record
which at that time was considered to be rock & roll.

Motown is often thought of as the archetypal black music label and
is particularly associated with soul. The reasons for this stem from the
fact that the founder/owner of the company, Berry Gordy, and the
overwhelming majority of its roster of artists and session musicians,
were black. This had been true of no other leading record company for
well over thirty years. The period from late 1963 to early 1965
produced a succession of distinctive and musically superior
recordings on the Motown label, including Martha and the Vandellas'
'Heat Wave' (August 1963), Marvin Gaye's 'Can I Get A Witness'
(November 1963), 'My Guy' (Mary Wells: April 1964), Brenda
Holloway's 'Every Little Bit Hurts' (May 1964), the Supremes'
'Where Did Our Love Go' (July 1964), 'Baby I Need Your Loving'
(the Four Tops: August 1964), Martha and the Vandellas' 'Dancing
In The Street' (September 1964), the Supremes' 'Come See About
Me' (December 1964), and 'Nowhere To Run' (Martha and the
Vandellas: March 1965). Such was the quality and popularity of these
records that they would have assured the artistic reputation of any

small independent record company: in Motown's case, aesthetic success led to financial prosperity and laid the foundation for the growth of the Motown Corporation.

It is, however, difficult to see how Gordy's policy could be regarded as one of producing records solely for the black American audience. Apart from one or two of the company's very early issues, such as Barrett Strong's 'Money' (1960), the bulk of releases were apparently geared to a *national* audience. In style and presentation, company policy could reasonably be described as an up-to-date version of the Nat 'King' Cole formula. This may be illustrated by Marvin Gaye's album *Hello Broadway* (1965) which included such songs as 'People', 'On The Street Where You Live', and 'Hello Dolly'. Furthermore, the stage acts of the Motown artists resembled those of cabaret performers, especially as far as the dance routines were concerned. Often, British fans of the music reacted to televised or live performances with horror, distaste, or puzzled amusement, equating the visual aspects with fallen rock & roll heroes such as Elvis Presley, the sanitised 'rock & rollers' such as Bobby Vee or Frankie Avalon, or popular music artists such as Barbra Streisand or Shirley Bassey. Clearly, for these fans, the stage presentation of the Motown acts belied the music. It should be remembered that in mid-1960s Britain Motown was regarded as 'hip'; a significant percentage of those who collected the records also bought the releases of the Rolling Stones, the Who, and Jimi Hendrix.

It may well be, however, that the Motown stage presentation was a result of Gordy's correct assessment of the company's appeal in the USA, amongst Whites as well as Blacks. Whatever the actual mix of the American audience, it has to be the case that from 1963 onwards Blacks were only a minority of Motown record buyers: this is an inescapable deduction given the records' national and international chart positions.

Perhaps it is inevitable that any label or musical centre which uses a somewhat rigid formula in order to create a distinctive sound will eventually produce static and stereotyped examples of its earlier successes. As we have already noted, this occurred in the Chicago blues of the 1940s (particularly among the Bluebird artists) and also in the Nashville sound of the 1960s. Motown was still able to produce the occasional outstanding item in the late 1960s – for example, Junior Walker's 'Roadrunner' (1966) and Marvin Gaye's 'I Heard It Through The Grapevine' (1967), but these appeared with diminishing frequency.

During the late 1960s and early 1970s the Motown product was increasingly subject to adverse criticism in the music press. Simon Frith (1975) has argued that some of this criticism was racist:

. . . what is under attack is . . . the Motown Corporation, which has, in its iron-fisted pursuit of safe profits, suppressed its singers' natural funk while refusing to allow them to develop and progress. 'Tom travesties' is how *Rolling Stone* described one batch of Motown LPs, 'opportunistic commercial album making of the worst sort'. 'The decline of Motown' was *NME*'s opinion; 'What happened to the days when black music was black and not this mush of vacuous muzak and pretentious drivel?'
Partly this venom is racist. White record labels are equally profit minded, put out an equal amount of pop filler, but Motown is especially evil because its groups are black and therefore naturally tasteful: if they turn out crap it's because they're being made to, if white groups do it's because they want to or can't do anything else. (p. 56)

This is a good example of how some promoters of the 'black music' ethos misrepresent any assessment that is less than favourable as being ideologically motivated. To sustain his argument, Frith would have to demonstrate that such publications had not routinely denigrated white record labels and artists in similar fashion. Actually, the adverse criticism of later Motown recordings never reached the heights of invective poured on, for example, Elvis Presley (from the early 1960s onwards) and Bob Dylan (at various stages in his career), as well as many others. Frith would also have to prove that his interpretation of the real meaning of the *Rolling Stone* and *NME* quotes was the only one possible. These quotes, as given by Frith, could equally well be read as applying to the artists, their management, or both. An illustration of *Rolling Stone*'s catholic prejudice is to be found in the following two extracts from record reviews, by Alan Niester and Paul Gambaccini respectively, published in its edition of 30 August 1973:

Larks' Tongue In Aspic – King Crimson. Remember art rock? Well, it still lives. Every year or so Robert Fripp claws his way from a graveyard of past musical fads, emerging like something out of a Weird Tales Comic book to snivel in an educated English accent that classicism in rock music lives on . . . After a hastily conceived tour and small flurry of attention, he disappears for another year so.
Uriah Heep Live – Uriah Heep. . . . Perhaps if in their tenure at Warner Brothers they strike a better balance between the tastefully heavy and the clumsily overdone the critical abuse will cease. One prays so. Three years of slagging is more than enough to read about anybody.

It should be stressed that both Uriah Heep and King Crimson consisted exclusively of white musicians.

Both Motown and the music of King Crimson or Uriah Heep exemplify the fact that there is not always a positive relationship between critical opinion and popularity. In the pop business musical qualities and fashion trends are often irretrievably interwoven. Popular success can lead record companies and artists down a number of possible roads: *financial* success can, for example, become the only criterion by which excellence is measured. Alternatively, an organisation or institution can exploit the public conscience as a means of selling records. This appears to be the central theme of Robert Altman's film *Nashville* (1975). Altman satirises the assumption that the film's 'heroes' personify the virtues of American life – the music they perform seems to embody the values appropriate to the model American to the extent that the two become inseparable. To dislike country music becomes tantamount to being un-American.

Such areas of social life where fundamental sentiments, moral principles, and political ideals are intertwined are prone to all kinds of exploitation. For many people, country music has come to represent America to the same extent as apple pie and the Constitution. It is only to be expected that any institution that seems to epitomise an ideology in this way will have an in-built resistance to change, including that which might result from any adverse criticism. Thus in *Nashville* the institution of country music is portrayed as exploiting the complex relationships between music as an industry and as an expression of a cultural identity. One may well maintain, as Altman seems to do so implicitly, that such an institution must stand guilty of both misrepresentation and moral blackmail. It is clearly the case that many patriotic Americans cannot reconcile themselves to country music as a package.

Just as detractors of country music, as portrayed by Altman, are liable to be accused of being unpatriotic, so objectors to black music in any form will be charged with racism. One consequence of Frith's line of argument is that the black opponent of Motown, or any similar institution, would be taking exactly the same position as Altman, and would therefore be guilty of cultural disloyalty. Otherwise, we must infer from Frith's reasoning that all critics of black music must themselves be black. This segregation is certainly not implicit in the available literature on the subject.

The music made and consumed by black Americans has always

been extremely diverse. Even within the field of pop music their contributions have been anything but homogeneous. Such considerations have not, however, silenced the competing claims made for individual forms – whether blues, disco, Motown, or jazz-funk – as constituting the only *real* black music. Advocates of a particular musical category will justify their argument by resorting to terms like '*passé*', 'primitive', and 'degenerate' when denouncing rival types. Viv Broughton, for example, states that 'The forms of gospel . . . are evident in soul music, but the incredible passion and power is watered down to facilitate the cross-over' (p. 93). For many fans, the contribution of black musicians to pop is so overwhelmingly important as to be self-evident: this legacy therefore requires no defence. Notions such as 'black music' may thus be seen to be counterproductive in that they call such a conclusion into question.

Chapter 6

Pop music as history and ideology

As the history of criticism and research in all music clearly shows, conceptions of a music can crucially affect its very form and substance. This process includes the rather obvious ways in which the peripheral parts of the industry, such as the music press, radio and television, ensure that there is a constant change in what constitutes fashion. This applies not only to the continual promotion of chart 'sounds' in pop music but also to the changes in the accepted interpretation of the great composers of the classical world. The fashionable aspects of music have always benefited from the evolution of the relevant hardware. One consequence of this evolution has been that even the works of Bach and Beethoven have been repeatedly made available in what has usually been claimed to be a more perfectly audible form: just as 78 r.p.m. records gave way to albums, so mono was succeeded by stereo, etc. Thus the music industry, like most others, employs technological change to build obsolescence into its products.

Yet the manner in which music is perceived and classified can shape its development in less obvious, though very profound, ways. For, as we have previously noted, rhythm & blues was known, euphemistically, as rock & roll during the 1950s, but then recategorised as R. & B. in the early 1960s. This reclassification enable the first British rock bands to distance their music from that of predecessors such as Tommy Steele and Billy Fury and contemporaries in Philadelphia and New York. A certain amount of irony was involved here: both Chuck Berry and Bo Diddley, two self-proclaimed rock & rollers, were regarded as cornerstones of the new music. To some extent this concentration on the Chicago and Detroit R. & B. scenes was related to the fact that two of the most fashionable British labels of the period, Pye International and Stateside, drew mostly on the music of those cities via the products of the Chess, Vee-Jay, and Motown labels. This reaffirmation of musical segregation was extremely consequential. As the self-consciously black soul movement gathered momentum, white rock musicians found themselves excluded by their own prior agreement: this gave impetus to the exploration of earlier types of rhythm & blues. The resultant discovery of the music of Muddy Waters, Howling Wolf, and Sonny Boy Williamson II had a profound effect on the way in which rock music subsequently evolved in Britain. It also had a significant influence upon blues research and scholarship over the next decade.

This reversion to *musical* segregation on ethnic lines recalled the way that the pop music industry was conceived and marketed during the 1920s so as to conform to the prevailing *social* segregationist mores. Thus, in the early days, the distinctions 'race' and 'hillbilly' were necessary guides to the nature of the music produced. For it was not until the aftermath of Jimmie Rodgers's career that the term hillbilly adequately described a musical movement. Following the death of Rodgers the parameters of white country music were established and the original conception of segregated musics thereby given substance. This would account for the decline, during the 1930s and 1940s, in the numbers of white blues musicians recorded. Consequently the second great country star, Hank Williams, was created in the image of Jimmie Rodgers, at least in terms of his recorded work. It has often been suggested, however, that Williams's recordings did not give an adequate picture of his musical range, and his performances on the road, in the honky-tonks, were frequently closer to rhythm & blues. Michael Bane quotes Chet Flippo, a Hank Williams authority, as saying: 'His music was a lot closer to the blues, a lot closer to a swing beat, than the music he recorded later. . . . The music was definitely funkier – he even took horns on the road with him. It was all dance music' (p. 87). Those who search for the 'missing link' between Larry Henseley and Elvis Presley may well owe their frustration to the fact that Williams was not recorded by someone with the musical tastes of Sam Phillips.

Hindsight is least effective in dealing with questions concerning the mental attitudes of previous generations: thus it is difficult to determine whether the initial division of pop music into the categories of race and hillbilly stemmed from culturally conditioned expectations of racial differences in music rather than from a cynical attempt to exploit the prevailing social facts. Given the existing social patterns in the Southern states, it could well be the case that the architects of the pop music industry firmly believed in racially inherited musical abilities and predilections. Certainly it is true that one's perceptions of such phenomena as music are limited, or at the very least coloured, by one's perspectives. For this particular purpose the American expression 'where you're coming from' encapsulates neatly the literal sense in which we use the term 'perspective'.

For example, the pervasive concept of 'progress' which was fundamental to the climate of early twentieth-century America seems to have conditioned the way that the early country and urban blues were perceived. Despite a complete lack of evidence, the first country blues recordings, such as those of Blind Lemon Jefferson, were described as 'old-fashioned', whereas publicity for vaudeville blues vocalists stressed the 'modern' and 'sophisticated' aspects of that style. An instance may be found in this 1926 Paramount advertisement published in the *Chicago Defender* which states: 'Here is a real, old-fashioned blues by a real, old-fashioned blues singer – Blind Lemon Jefferson from Dallas. This "Booster Blues" and "Dry Southern Blues" on the reverse side are two of Blind Lemon's old-time tunes. With his singing, he strums his guitar in real southern style – makes it talk, in fact.' This may be compared with an advertisement (*c*. 1924) by the same record company for releases by Faye Barnes which declares:

> Everybody who has heard the winsome Faye has predicted a wonderful future for her. No less a personage than Tony Langston, musical critic of the *Chicago Defender*, has praised her singing and predicted a brilliant career for her. Faye Barnes is another new Paramount Blues star, formerly Black Swan star, and in just the few months that her records have been sold under the Paramount label, she has become one of the most popular artists in the catalogue.

The contrast in terms of tone and language between the two extracts clearly illustrates the disparity in status, as far as Paramount were concerned, between the two artists. The advertisement for Jefferson's record is at the very least patronising, and also erroneous in its assumption that his music was outmoded. The impression given is that this kind of music was an endangered species – whereas vaudeville is portrayed as the music of the future. Furthermore, in the second extract the music is described with some reverence and the weighty opinion of a *Chicago Defender* critic invoked. It is highly likely that Langston would normally have reserved his acclaim for black concert performers such as Marian Anderson and Lillian Evanti. It is interesting and informative to note that of those individuals mentioned in the two advertisements, the least obscure today is Jefferson.

Presumably Jefferson's records seemed archaic because they were Southern and rural – he also lacked a 'modern' jazz band to accompany him. At that particular time, progress was seen as necessarily linked to technology and urbanisation. This attitude has persisted to the extent that it has become standard practice to refer to urban blues performers as more sophisticated than country blues artists. Even Robert Palmer, when discussing Leroy Carr and Scrapper Blackwell, argues that 'theirs was a more urban, sophisticated sound' (p. 110).

This conception of progress has traditionally permeated the perceptions of blues held by jazz critics and historians. Writers from Iain Lang (*c.* 1942) to Eileen Southern (1983) have described blues as one of the 'precursors of jazz'. Lang also states: 'The blues is not the whole of jazz, but the whole of the blues is jazz. It has no existence apart from this idiom' (p. 30). Like much of the writing on blues from the jazz point of view, these arguments end up by presenting the case in a manner which lies somewhere between paradox and contradiction. It is as if blues has fulfilled its function by providing the foundations for jazz, but unfortunately has continued to exist rather than dying gracefully. The jazz perspective on the role of blues can be compared analogously with crude and distorted versions of the Darwinian Theory of Evolution, which portrays humans as the descendants of apes. A more accurate picture in terms of both human and musical evolution is that humans and apes on the one hand, and jazz and blues on the other, had ancestors in common. In fact, as we have previously noted (in Chapter 2), it is probable that country blues emerged slightly *later* than jazz: whether this was also true of apes is a question we leave to physical anthropologists.

Jazz writers persistently produce misleading descriptions of country blues performers and performances. James Lincoln Collier (1981) observes, for example, that 'Of the men who were playing these primitive country blues, two stand out: Blind Lemon Jefferson and Huddie Ledbetter, otherwise known as Leadbelly' (p. 40). Joachim Berendt (1976) describes 'Mississippi blues' as 'rough, archaic'

(p. 142). Any competent analysis of Jefferson as a guitarist would reveal that he was anything but primitive: rhythmically and melodically, his guitar-playing is extremely imaginative, complex, and dextrous. As a country musician, he should be regarded as far superior to, for instance, the much-vaunted Lonnie Johnson who, despite Collier's assertion to the contrary (p. 324) should be seen as a jazz guitarist who occasionally recorded country blues efforts. These recordings demonstrate that Johnson had an unsure grasp of country blues phrasing (see Chapter 2 and Appendix).

Similarly, Berendt's description of 'Mississippi blues' as 'rough' and 'archaic' not only lumps together the music from the whole of that state, but belittles the only contemporaries of Jefferson who might reasonably be considered his equals. That Mississippi blues was homogeneous can only be an opinion held by someone unfamiliar with the country blues idiom. The state produced styles as varied as those of John Hurt, Charley Patton, Skip James, Roosevelt Graves, Robert Johnson, Willie Brown, and Tommy Johnson. There were in Mississippi a number of country blues schools that arose in the 1920s, the most famous of which is normally described as the Delta blues. It was composed of a group of musicians associated with Charley Patton, his collaborators and disciples. Others schools had as their 'masters' Tommy Johnson (in the Jackson area) and Skip James (around Bentonia, Yazoo County). John Hurt, who was from the hill country to the east of the state, had a style radically different from most of the other Mississippi musicians: he was possibly closer in approach to that peculiar category known as folk blues than any other performer from the region. Hurt generally used, for example, the technique of an alternating bass which can otherwise be heard in the work of 'songsters' and 'folk' artists such as Leadbelly and Mance Lipscomb.

Even though it is difficult to determine exactly what Berendt might mean by 'rough', it seems safe to assume that he is using it as a synonym for unsophisticated. On the whole, the music produced by all of these schools was far from unsophisticated, in terms either of musicianship or lyrical composition. For instance, Skip James's recording of 'I'm So Glad' (1931) is described by Stephen Calt and John Miller (sleeve-note to Yazoo album L 1038) as

. . . a brilliant re-working of a schmaltzy, insipid melody previously recorded by artists like Lonnie Johnson. James merely considered it a 'two-step' piece suitable for fast dances but proudly prophesized after hearing the Cream's hit rock version that no-one would ever copy it successfully. The speed, clarity, and subtlety of touch he attains (partly through using an unorthodox, semi-classical picking position) on 'I'm So Glad' have never been surpassed by any bluesman on any song.

It is the complexity, and unbelievably fast tempo, of the guitar part that gave James every right to feel proud. The performance can reasonably be compared to John Coltrane's 1963 version of 'My Favourite Things' in that both musicians seize upon with savagery the inherent sentimentality of the original and in effect create a caricature of it.

A peculiarity of country blues which is especially evident in many of the Mississippi schools is the interdependence of voice, instrument, lyrics, and melody. Therefore even the most 'poetic' of lyrics lose a great deal of their force when divorced from the total context of the performance. Nevertheless, the imagery employed by such artists as Skip James, Charley Patton, Tommy Johnson, Son House, and Robert Johnson is frequently startling in its originality.

The development of the Delta blues represented in the work of Robert Johnson shows that this music, far from being 'archaic', was in fact rapidly evolving more complex forms. Johnson has been recognised as perhaps *the* genius of the blues by connoisseurs and prominent musicians in the pop world, and it is hard to overestimate his musical abilities. His importance in blues history parallels that of Charlie Parker in jazz. As Berendt says of Parker, ' "Bird lives!" This is still true today and especially today again . . . and Bird's greatness is shown in that this influence lives on in the playing of so many musicians who vary greatly from each other – and this influence will continue to live' (p. 92). Like Parker, Johnson still sounds modern and original today. Since his death no single artist has come close to duplicating, let alone improving upon, his performances. A number of later bluesmen have been able to approximate one or more aspects of his work: thus Elmore James made a career out of one or two of Johnson's guitar phrases and rhythms, Johnny Shines and Muddy Waters have perpetuated his vocal techniques, and Robert Jr Lockwood comes closest to reproducing his instrumental mastery. Many enthusiasts believe that, had he lived, Johnson's post-war style would have resembled that of Otis Rush. His legacy directly, and indirectly – via the influence of James, Rush, and Muddy Waters – upon the work of the Rolling Stones and Eric Clapton was certainly crucial to the development of rock.

As Gunther Schuller correctly argues (for instance, 1968, p. ix) with regard to jazz scholarship, it is important for researchers analysing any music to be familiar with an adequately representative sample of the available materials. In the field of blues, as in that of jazz, this means a familiarity with a large cross-section of recordings. This should involve years of careful listening to a large number of blues records and some attempt to appreciate the qualities contained in them. We feel sure that all the jazz authors under discussion have followed these principles with regard to jazz before writing on that subject. Unfortunately, none of them appears to have given the same consideration to the subject matter before publishing their views on blues. We are certain that such authors would be properly outraged if a country blues expert were to write a treatise on the contribution of jazz to the blues based on a correspondingly scant amount of knowledge on the subject. If, for example, he or she mentioned only Louis Armstrong, Sidney Bechet, Benny Goodman, and Dave Brubeck the response would rightly be one of contempt.

Though there were possibly some valid grounds, prior to the 1960s, for the jazz writers' approach to the blues, since then a large body of research has been produced on every aspect of that music, including that of its relationship to the rest of pop. It is probably significant that most of those involved in this research – with the exception of Paul Oliver and Sam Charters – grew up with rock & roll. This background provided a very different perspective. In particular the work of Mike Leadbitter and Simon Napier, and others, for the British journal *Blues Unlimited* supplied a new approach to the subject, treating blues as a music to be approached on its own terms, distinct from any other. *Blues Unlimited*, and other subsequent specialist publications in Europe and the USA, helped those who had been introduced to blues through 1960s rock to expand their knowledge and enjoyment of the music. Thus they probably had a beneficial effect on the careers of a number of leading blues artists during the 1960s and 1970s, a fact acknowledged by both B. B. King and Muddy Waters.

The interest in blues research in Britain had been initially inspired by the publication of two books at the turn of the 1950s: *The Country Blues* by Sam Charters (1959) and *Blues Fell This Morning* by Paul Oliver (1960). An important feature of these books was that each was accompanied by an illustrative long-playing record. These albums included artists whose work had not previously been widely available

in Britain such as Willie McTell, Memphis Minnie, Bu
and Barbecue Bob.

The emergence in 1963 of *Blues Unlimited* as the journal
Blues Appreciation Society provided a forum for those
oriented interest in blues to express their views. This new approach
was reinforced by the appearance of *R. & B. Monthly* (from 1964) and
Blues World (1965). It soon became clear that the pop-oriented
approach to blues clashed at various points with the perspectives of
jazz writers and folklorists: this involved disagreements concerning
both the nature and the importance of the music. These
disagreements were typified by the conflicting reactions to visiting
American blues artists. For example, the British tours made by
Muddy Waters in 1958 and 1962 were the source of contradictory
responses.

On his first visit, Muddy played his normal amplified Chicago blues
which created a clear contrast not only with the music of the Chris
Barber Jazz Band who were on the same bill, but also with such
performers as Big Bill Broonzy, Sonny Terry and Brownie McGhee,
who had recently appeared in Britain with Barber. As Bob Groom
(1971) recalls: 'Unfortunately, some people, used to acoustic blues,
took exception to Muddy's electric guitar and ferocious singing . . .'
(p. 14). Considering the fact that this occurred at the height of the
rock & roll era, this reaction may seem to be somewhat strange. How
could a British audience of 1958, the year of Chuck Berry's 'Sweet
Little Sixteen', find such a sound so unusual? The answer probably
lies in the fact that at that time the written accounts, and promotion,
of blues were monopolised by persons with a jazz and/or folklore
perspective, and that previous British tours during the 1940s and
1950s had featured artists guaranteed to conform to the blues-as-folk-
music stereotype.

Four years later, on Muddy's next visit, he kept to an acoustic
sound in deference to his previous detractors; however, he was again,
criticised, this time for not being sufficiently modern. The
intervening four years had seen a significant change in the make-up of
the blues audience in Britain. Many of those who formed this new
audience were more familiar with rhythm & blues and would
constitute the potential readership of *Blues Unlimited* and similar
publications. Indicative of the new perspective was an editorial in
Issue 21 of *Blues Unlimited* (April 1965) which under the general
sub-heading of 'Progress' declared: 'At last! Buddy Guy has brought

us the real modern blues to Europe. After failures by both Muddy and Hooker to really show us Guy has won acclaim from dozens of our readers. Thank you Buddy!' In the same issue, a review of Guy's first appearance in Britain described him as performing '. . . with the self-confidence and showmanship so far seen in few visiting bluesmen. Unlike Muddy or Hubert Sumlin, he is not afraid of making a noise, and playing his guitar turned up to full volume, he illustrated to advantage his mean, biting style.'

It should be emphasised that this new perspective was not limited to the advocacy of 'modern' blues but also viewed blues as a tradition separate from those of folk and jazz. This included a novel distinction between black American folk singers who occasionally performed blues songs, such as Leadbelly and Josh White, and those artists who were considered to have originated and/or developed country blues as a musical form.

An expression of the new perspective was the release, in 1962, of an album entitled *Really! The Country Blues* on the mistitled Origin Jazz Library label. This record was intended as a corrective to the Sam Charters compilation *The Country Blues* referred to above. The O.J.L. album included less well-known Delta performers and did not feature any urban artists such as Leroy Carr, Big Bill Broonzy, and Washboard Sam, who had all appeared on the Charters record.

These two albums, the record released in conjunction with Paul Oliver's book *Blues Fell This Morning,* and the O.J.L. issues 1 (Charley Patton), 3 (Henry Thomas), and 5 (*The Mississippi Blues*) had an enormous impact, not least in terms of material, upon the development of rock. Several of the songs contained on them were later to be recorded by major rock performers – in addition, the blues artists featured became legends among rock stars and fans. This is evidenced by the 1978 Yazoo compilation *Roots Of Rock* on which no fewer than six tracks were first reissued on the albums listed above, including Henry Thomas's 'Bull Doze Blues' of 1928 (recorded by Canned Heat in 1968 as 'Going Up The Country'), Willie McTell's 'Statesboro' Blues' of 1928 (recorded by Taj Mahal in 1967 and the Allman Brothers Band in 1971), Kansas Joe and Memphis Minnie's 'When The Levee Breaks' of 1929 (recorded by Led Zeppelin in 1971), and Cannon's Jug Stompers' 'Walk Right In' of 1929 which became an international hit for the Rooftop Singers in 1963.

Of the final two examples one, Robert Wilkins's 1929 'That's No Way To Get Along', was transformed by him in 1964 into a religious song, 'Prodigal Son' – the Rolling Stones 'covered' this second rendition on their 1968 album *Beggar's Banquet*. 'A Spoonful Blues' by Charley Patton (1929) has a more complex history. The versions by the Paul Butterfield Blues Band (1965) and Cream (1966), both entitled 'Spoonful', were obviously derived from the 1960 Howlin' Wolf recording of the same name. Howlin' Wolf appears to have conflated two songs by Charley Patton, 'A Spoonful Blues' and 'Jesus Is A Dying-Bedmaker' (also 1929). The tune of the latter resembles a song recorded by Blind Wille Johnson in 1927, 'Jesus Make Up My Dying Bed'. This again was recorded later by Bob Dylan on his first album (1962) as 'In My Time Of Dyin' '.

Thus Dylan may be seen as a mediator between these early blues LP collections and later rock versions of the material they contained. Also on *Bob Dylan* was 'Fixin' To Die', taken from the Bukka White original of 1940 which appeared on *The Country Blues*. On *The Freewheelin' Bob Dylan* (1963) he included a reworking of Henry Thomas's 'Honey Just Allow Me One More Chance' (1927), featured on O.J.L. 3.

Two further reissue collections from this period also provided material for Dylan, as well as later performers. These were a follow-up compilation by Sam Charters, *The Rural Blues* (1960), and the CBS release of *Robert Johnson: King Of The Delta Blues Singers* (1961). *The Rural Blues* supplied Dylan with the Blind Lemon Jefferson classic of 1928, 'See That My Grave Is Kept Clean' (included on *Bob Dylan*), and Charlie Pickett's 'Down The Highway' of 1937 (on *Freewheelin'*). Dylan was the first, but certainly not the last, modern white singer to take any material directly from Robert Johnson. For his highly original reworking of 'Corrina, Corrina' (*Freewheelin'*), he incorporated the phrase

Got a bird to whistle, I got a bird to sing (2x)

from Johnson's 'Stones In My Passway' (1937).

Therefore the Yazoo album title *Roots Of Rock* was, for a change, rather more than a marketing ploy. It draws attention to how the first few generally available collections of country blues played an important part in shaping the rock music of the 1960s and 1970s. In the process whereby pop fans came to discover their musical roots in the pre-war blues, magazines like *Blues Unlimited* and this first batch of country blues compilations played mutually reinforcing roles. The emerging rock movement in Britain and the USA thus became acquainted with an immediately recognisable history, as many fans have testified. Musicians such as Son House, Willie McTell, and even Jimmie Rodgers were readily identifiable as precursors in a way that Bing Crosby and Al Jolson, for instance, could never be.

As we have already indicated, the new movement recognised as its founding fathers a totally different set of artists from those seen as important by jazz writers and folklorists. This resulted in the rejection, often amounting to denigration, of jazz/folk 'heroes' such as Lonnie Johnson, Big Bill Broonzy, and Brownie McGhee. Unfortunately even Blind Lemon Jefferson suffered by association, to the extent that David Hatch, in a 1965 *Blues Unlimited* record review, felt the need to decry the recent downgrading of Jefferson as a bona fide country blues artist. It should perhaps be noted that the unease Bob Dylan inadvertently exhibited at being classed with the Greenwich Village folk singers was partly expressed in terms of his choice of country blues material, especially 'Fixin' To Die' and 'In My Time Of Dyin' '. His dilemma at this stage of his career was largely explained by the subsequently revealed story of his affinity with rock & roll during his formative years.

Folklorists have traditionally seen their role as one of collection, and therefore preservation, of the musical expressions of folk communities. A common justification for such activities has been the need to rescue musics threatened with extinction. As Fred Woods (1980) has observed, this approach was prominent at least as early as the mid-nineteenth century. He quotes an early Victorian collector, Revd John Broadwood of Sussex, who explains his motives as follows: 'The airs are set to music exactly as they are now sung, to rescue them from oblivion, and afford a specimen of genuine old English Melody, and the words are given in their original rough state with an occasional slight alteration to render the sense intelligible' p. 17). Woods goes on to declare that 'Here, in microcosm, are most of the faults . . . of Victorian and Edwardian collectors. There is, for a start, the assumption that folk song is dead or dying . . . There is also the slight air of patronisation, coupled with the compulsion to "improve" ' (p. 17). What Woods describes as the 'faults' of earlier generations have unfortunately persisted up to recent times. In fact, this position has been compounded by additional misconceptions concerning those musical strains which are part neither of the popular nor of the art fields. This has led to contorted attempts to produce definitions and assessments of both black and white country musics.

The emergence of the pop industry brought a new dimension to 'aural transmission' which had previously been, by definition, a folk medium. This complicated, in particular, the traditional view of commercialisation as a threat, not only to the folk character of the music but also to the continued requirement for collecting as a means of preservation: from the time of large-scale commercial recordings in the South it could be argued that not merely folk *songs* but folk *performances* were captured perfectly on gramophone records. For folklorists, however, the consequential commercialisation of the music could be seen as outweighing the benefits of preservation.

A particularly worrying aspect for some was the likelihood that the performer's role – as opposed to that of the song – would be accentuated. This often led to the stated position noted above (Chapter 2) that the song belonged to the folk culture and not to the individual performers, who at best could be regarded as improving upon traditional material.

Consequently artists like the Carter Family could be seen as using records and radio programmes merely as media for perpetuating the songs they collected, thus encouraging others to maintain the folk tradition. On the other hand, neither Jimmie Rodgers nor his fans perceived his role in quite the same way. Most of his songs were presented as original compositions, written by him and/or his collaborators. Though Rodgers maintained a 'folksy' demeanour throughout his career, the earnings guaranteed by his great popularity among the folk of the southern states – and perhaps the way he spent his money, on, for instance, a mansion and expensive guitars – might well have alienated many folklorists.

It would seem, however, that Rodgers was at least as successful as the Carter Family at perpetuating the folk traditions of the South. Malone observes that the folk musicians of that region who were the traditional source of materials for folk song collectors

... heard his songs, accepted them, and eventually gave them back to folklorists who travelled through the South in search of materials. Rodgers' songs can be found listed in Library of Congress checklists and in the published compilations of a number of folklorists. Among the folklorists, however, only Vance Randolph mentions Rodgers' name. He misspells it, and refers to the 'Blue Yodeller' simply as a 'popular radio entertainer in the 1930s'. Perhaps the other folklorists believed that anonymity lent authenticity to the songs they were presenting, or perhaps they had never heard of Jimmie Rodgers. (p. 94)

As already noted, however (Chapter 2, pp. 50–1), the Carter

Family also had their innovative side. It would seem, from the available evidence, that they often adapted the songs they collected in order to render them compatible with the Carter Family approach to harmony and instrumentation.

With regard to blues, the folklorists' dilemma was made more acute by the fact that the country blues continued to develop during the early period of commerical recordings, and there is a great deal of evidence to suggest that commercial recordings played an important part in that development. The non-commercial recording of blues, though commencing at about the same time as the commercial initiative in the country areas, never offered serious competition in terms of quantity. Many writers continue to argue that the commerical exploitation of country blues led to a distortion of black folk music in general, and country blues in particular, and prefer the body of materials collected for the Library of Congress and similar organisations and individuals.

One individual collector who recorded black folk music, including country blues, during the early period was Lawrence Gellert. Many of these recordings have recently been issued on albums by Rounder Records and on the Heritage label. These collections have been the subject of a great deal of discussion amongst blues *aficionados*, students of guitar technique, and folklorists. The degree of interest surrounding them partly stems from the amount of 'protest' material included, which far surpasses that of any other similar collection, and partly from the apparently innovative character of the blues recordings. The Heritage album (released in 1984) consists mainly of blues by anonymous musicians and is thus aptly titled *Nobody Knows My Name*.

In his review of the album for the British magazine *Blues And Rhythm* (July 1984), Richard Metson argues that 'They are important recordings because Gellert has captured black folk blues as it really was at the time, free from commercial interference and without outside considerations of whether it would sell or not.' This writer makes explicit a view which is often implied in reviews and histories of the music. By using the term 'commercial interference' he in effect assumes that a degree of distortion of the music is an inevitable consequence of commerical recording. He therefore must also assume the existence of something equivalent to a body of materials that could be described as pure folk art.

Metson refers to one aspect of said 'interference', this being the requirement on the part of commercial record companies that the 'product' would be financially viable. This has important implications with regard to the careers of, for instance, Blind Lemon Jefferson and Charley Patton prior to their commercial recordings. For unless the people who made up the audiences for their live appearances were very different from those who bought their records, then it would seem to follow that Jefferson and Patton were required to make similar decisions concerning materials and performance techniques to those made by record company producers and marketing executives. This seems to reinforce the suspicion that folklorists assume that, like themselves, folk audiences put a higher value on preservation than enjoyment of the music.

Metson goes on to say:

. . . the result is surprising on two counts. Firstly, the music is not so far removed from that which was eventually produced in the recording studios, and secondly, but more importantly, the styles utilised pre-date the accepted beginnings and show that blues in its most popular form was already in existence before the intervention of the gramophone record spreading the word.

By 'the styles utilised' he seems to be referring to the unusual guitar techniques used on some of the recordings. Much of the guitar accompaniment employs chord progressions normally thought of as characteristic of a later period. In fact, a number of students of the history of guitar techniques have taken the view that the dates given for the recordings (1924–32) are therefore suspect. More to the point is the fact that, irrespective of any questions of authenticity of date, the recordings do not exhibit evidence of developments in country blues we would expect to find in performances of that period, in spite of Metson's suggestion to the contrary. It should be remembered that a number of country bluesmen had recorded by 1927 – just three years after the alleged date of the earliest Gellert items – and in the case of Blind Lemon Jefferson and Freddie Spruell at least, recording commenced in 1926. It seems, therefore, reasonable to assume that the materials and techniques evident on these commercial recordings had previously existed for a number of years. Thus the mere existence of hitherto unknown country blues performances in that music's 'most popular form' should really not come as a surprise to anyone.

Unfortunately, the anonymity of Gellert's musicians makes it impossible to compare the items under discussion with any commerically recorded sides they may have made. This is not the case, however, with respect to all of the recordings made on behalf of the Library of Congress. Son House, Willie Brown, and Muddy Waters, for example, all recorded for both the Library of Congress *and* the commercial labels. As previously noted (Introduction, p. 0), recordings made for the Library of Congress by Son House and Willie Brown differ substantially in both style and content from their earlier commercial sides.

This disparity is particularly noticeable in the case of Brown. Of his four commercial sides, only two – 'Future Blues' and 'M. & O. Blues' (both 1930) – are extant. Both of these, but especially 'M. & O. Blues', show a degree of realisation in performance of country blues techniques seldom heard before or since. Brown was one of the very few country bluesmen with the ability to conceive and execute a complex *harmonic* accompaniment on guitar to his vocal. In fact his guitar work on 'M. & O. Blues' could be regarded as an example of counterpoint. However on his single recording for the Library of Congress, 'Make Me A Pallet On The Floor' (1941), Brown shows little of the flair, originality of approach, and technical mastery apparent on the earlier recordings: in fact his performance of the old standard is most kindly described as run-of-the-mill. He sounds listless, and also vocally uncomfortable in the key he has chosen to *play* in.

Even Brown's commercial recordings lack the drive of Son House's best work; yet House also lost a great deal of his 'bite' when recorded at the same Library of Congress session. Charters (1967) has argued that on these recordings House displayed a virtuosity lacking on his earlier commercial sides. It is certainly true that the Library of Congress cuts include songs requiring slightly more complex chord progressions than those necessary for 'My Black Mama' and 'Preachin' The Blues' (both 1930), for example. Yet the later sides do not possess the vocal aggression and insistent rhythms of his 1930 work and are often very undisciplined in terms of delivery. Echoing Metson's position with regard to commercial organisations, we might wonder if the House and Brown Library of Congress recordings may have been affected by 'non-commercial interference' from Alan Lomax, John Work, and Lewis Jones, the Library of Congress officials. We might also speculate as to whether their lacklustre performances on this occasion were related to the remuneration obtained which was, according to Son House, a bottle of Coke. Even by the standards of *commercial* exploitation this was somewhat less than generous. We invite the reader to make similar comparisons between the Library of Congress and commercial recordings of Muddy Waters.

Most folklorist positions seem to ignore the effects of factors other than the gramophone record and radio upon the 'folk musics' of early twentieth-century America. Also, it is often the case that they downgrade the role of the innovative musician in folk traditions. The notion of a 'traditional', that is, an unchanging, culture is properly used by social anthropologists as an ideal typical concept. Few social scientists would expect to find any single example in even the most remote and neglected group of human beings. It is therefore verging on the ludicrous to apply such notions to the 'folk cultures' of a large industrial society such as the United States of the 1920s. It should be remembered that *living* folk musics had always been regarded primarily as entertainment, and thus the correct setting for such cultural phenomena would be the Marquee or Max's Kansas City rather than the Victoria and Albert Museum or the Museum of National History.

As we have argued throughout this book (see especially Introduction and Chapter 3), distinctions between American folk and pop musics tend to be the result of rigid presumptions and inflexible definitions of folk music in terms of its methods of transmission. Thus for many folklorists a performance of a song from the folk tradition – using the medium of the gramophone record, 'modern' instruments, etc. – will often be regarded as beyond the boundaries of folk music. For example, Chuck Willis's 1958 hit 'Betty And Dupree' closely resembled, as already noted (Chapter 3), Willie Walker's 1930 version, called 'Dupree Blues', and might well have been the kind of rendition often heard in the Piedmont area during the 1920s and 1930s. The puzzle for folklorists raised by the Willis and Walker recordings is that either *both* or *neither* are folk performances. The obvious way out of the dilemma in which folklorists find themselves in the case of pop music developments from the folk tradition is that of seeing folk and pop musics in terms of a continuum rather than as dichotomous.

An interesting argument which attempts to equate pop (or, as he defines it, 'rock') with folk music is that put forward by Steve Belz. However, as we have already pointed out (see Introduction), his argument rests precariously on putative social-psychological distinctions concerning audience reaction, a particularly weak distinction.

The frequency with which statements, apparently intended as historical and analytical, depend upon notions such as technology and audience response as explaining musical continuity and change is regrettable and somewhat mystifying. We feel that potential readers of musical histories would expect such works to explain evolutionary factors in terms of *musical* phenomena, at least in part. Certainly, *we* would expect arguments concerning musical change to be supported by musical evidence. It is never enough for historians merely to declare that, for instance, technological evolution and audience behaviour have certain consequences, which is an all too common strategy in pop music literature.

We realise, of course, that such approaches to musical history are seldom devoid of ideological undercurrents. For how a favoured music is described, particularly in terms of its connections with other musics and extra-musical events and conditions, can affect the status of that music in the mind of the reader. Thus a relevant question concerning the folklorists' perspective might enquire as to the reasons for their preference for rural, 'low-tech' song production methods. Does, for instance, this suggest a nostalgia for pastoral life and a rejection of the culture of modern working-class folk? This is not to argue that the ideological bias of any author, including ourselves, is the central issue in an assessment of musical history: such bias is never entirely absent from analysis. But it is important that a history of any subject concentrates upon the material issues involved.

Chapter 7

After the flood

In June 1967, the Beatles released *Sgt Pepper's Lonely Hearts Club Band*. Reaction was universally favourable, frequently euphoric, and the album became one of the best-selling of all time. Many critics still feel that it represents the Beatles at the peak of their artistic powers: some would regard it as the finest achievement in all pop music. That they are able to do so is largely due to the fact that it avoided a specific story-line and thus did not constitute an allegory which might be conceived as, at the very least, ephemeral, and which could ultimately be subject to acceptance or rejection by critic and record-buyer alike.

Yet for all this the album retains a unity invariably absent from the band's subsequent work together. Superficially, this is evident in the presentation of *Sgt Pepper* as a show, with opening and closing signature tune and the group decked out in band uniform. Admittedly, the songs have all the characteristics of being tailored by, or for, single group members – hardly surprising in view of the Beatles' emerging status as individual celebrities. The contrasting concerns expressed by these individuals did not, however, handicap the global vision of the complete product: on the contrary, one felt that McCartney's portrayal of a runaway teenager ('She's Leaving Home'), Harrison's contempt for cocktail-party phonies ('Within You Without You'), and Lennon's exploration of day-to-day existence ('Good Morning Good Morning') were all aspects *of the same personality*. If an underlying theme was present at all, it may be seen as the Beatles' perception of British life, a view reinforced by the specifically indigenous nature of the songs' content, references, and imagery. Such a theme was also commensurate with the Beatles' position as pioneers of wholly original and independent British pop music.

The aesthetic and commercial success of *Sgt Pepper* offered new possibilities to rock. There was now the opportunity of producing works on a larger scale with little or no reference to the American blues and R. & B. traditions. There was also the chance that such creations would elevate the status of their composers and performers – and by implication, pop music in general – to a level comparable with that of the European classical music of the past, and thus lead to acceptance within the circles of the musical establishment. This desire to 'legitimise' pop had been apparent at earlier periods in its history and proved to be equally counterproductive in the late 1960s/early 1970s. It is now possible to see how an album commonly held to be the epitome of a new maturity in rock music contributed directly to its decline. This process was further accelerated by new ambitions amongst instrumentalists, fed by an almost insatiable demand from audiences for displays of technical virtuosity. In this way a distance between performer and recipient was established, a separation which was both musical and physical. This situtation was enjoyed by both parties for some time: each was given full rein to indulge their fantasies. Even when songwriters began to concentrate on their personal trials and tribulations, they were welcomed by an audience keen to obtain a vicarious insight into the traumas of being a successful rock star. There came a point, however, when a feeling began to spread that things had gone too far.

Initially, 'concept albums' tended to follow the model introduced by the Beatles, that is, collections of original compositions loosely connected by a generalised theme or, in some cases, merely by an album-title of appropriate weight and significance. British bands led the way, partly as a direct result of the Beatles' influence, but also because the predominance of British acts in the United States guaranteed attention and probable success in that country. The Moody Blues' *In Search Of The Lost Chord* (1968) typified the new fashion. Its theme was rather more lofty than that of *Sgt Pepper* –it concentrated on the journey to spiritual fulfilment via mysticism and Eastern religion: as if to validate the serious intentions of the enterprise, poetry was incorporated as a prelude to the final track, 'Om'. Most of the songs, however, existed quite independently of each other as relatively self-contained items, though it is interesting to note that the single extracted from the ablum, 'Ride My See-Saw', was a commercial failure. It had been standard practice to issue a single from a potentially popular LP, both to advertise the album and thus attract buyers and to avoid all the effort, time, and costs required to produce an original and separate release. Bands who were sufficiently in control of their output began to discourage the continuation of this tradition (the Beatles had issued no singles from *Sgt Pepper*), no doubt believing that such extrapolations could not be appreciated out of context and would inevitably spoil the intended thematic unity of their album.

That the Moody Blues regarded themselves as custodians of Western civilisation is suggested by their next two LP releases, *On The Threshold Of A Dream* and *To Our Children's Children's Children* (both 1969). On the former, the protagonist quotes Descartes and is cautioned by an imagined mechanical deity who tells him that compared to his computer he is 'magnetic ink' (an image which might most kindly be described as unusual if rather obscure). Fears that technology will engulf humanity are largely allayed by the latter album which we can at least be sure will survive as a legacy for as long as mankind exists, just as we have survived so far from the time when prehistoric man made the kind of cave drawings depicted on the LP's cover.

Such developments reveal a complete contrast in attitude on the part of audience and performer with that shown during the 1950s. In spite of the efforts of various film-makers to make rock & roll palatable to parents, much of the enjoyment experienced by contemporary teenagers lay in the fact that the music represented anathema to what had become known as the 'older generation'. Many rock & roll songs celebrated the music and looked forward to its continued existence. Examples include Chuck Berry's 'School Days' (1957), Chuck Willis's 'Hang Up My Rock And Roll Shoes' (1958), and Ivory Joe Hunter's 'You Can't Stop This Rocking And Rolling' (1956). Yet the music was portrayed as something independent and distinct from established forms and styles: while Hunter saw rock & roll as having a place of its own within American music traditions, Berry was concerned with emphasising its separation ('Rock And Roll Music', 1957); in 'Roll Over Beethoven (1956) he admonished the serious music composers of the past to take notice of rock & roll, his light mockery serving to deflate their status.

In the work of the British rock bands of the late 1960s/early 1970s we may see the reverse process in action. There is the evident desire to *inflate* the status of their own music, thus soliciting favourable comparison with the acknowledged masters of the classical tradition. This they did with the complete acquiescence of their audience who, while wishing to retain the music as their own property, were anxious that its merits be accepted by their elders, by the critics, and by the establishment in general.

Variously described as an oratorio and as an opera, performed at London's Covent Garden, recorded by the London Symphony Orchestra, and adapted for the cinema by Ken Russell, the Who's *Tommy* fulfilled all such hopes and expectations. Released in 1969, the album sought to convey its message through a cast of characters and a continuous story-line. This format was new to rock (though there have been claims that the Pretty Things' 1968 LP *S.F. Sorrow* was the first in the field and the Who themselves had recorded a nine-minute narrative piece, 'A Quick One While He's Away', in 1966 for their album *A Quick One*). It was this fact, together with the Who's convincing renditions of the piece in live performance, that created initial attention. Despite retrospective denials by its composer, Pete Townshend, that *Tommy* was ever conceived as a serious operatic work, it was certainly regarded as such by large numbers of record-buyers and rock critics alike, undoubtedly encouraged by the plaudits already conferred upon *Sgt Pepper*. What was remarkable was that there was a tacit acceptance of *Tommy* as a great work; any close analysis of its thematic development, allegorical method, or overall meaning would have been against the tide of euphoria that its release inspired. The point was that *Tommy* was held to represent a new maturity in rock music.

It can now be argued that such a view was largely the result of the immaturity of rock criticism in 1969. Not only had the history of the music been relatively brief, but writers employed to cover the rise of the Beatles were now called upon to keep pace with new and widespread initiatives, while still keeping faith with the teenage record-buyer. The British publication *New Musical Express* had chosen, for example, to concentrate on the activities of the Monkees, no doubt in the belief that they might supplant the Beatles. It is hardly surprising, therefore, that in such a climate *Tommy* was accepted without opposition.

The critics of the late 1970s/early 1980s have been less accommodating. Dave Marsh (1980) states that *Tommy* 'veered between crackpot genius and plain farce, spiritual message and ludicrous conceit . . . its story line was skimpy, muddled, silly, a lot

of the songs were forced and forgettable' (p. 290) while Mick
Houghton (1980) calls it 'a vastly imperfect work . . . a millstone
rather than a milestone' (p. 166). Interpretation of the album's
meaning is indeed difficult, and is somewhat hindered by the
inconsistences of the allegory; even if we regard its subject as a
straightforward attempt at describing the problems of finding self-
awareness and spiritual fulfilment, we might question the wisdom of
tackling the issue in seventy-six minutes, given the additional
pressure of commercial viability. Such considerations did not inhibit
the Who either with regard to *Tommy* or in the creation of its successor
Quadrophenia (1973); neither did they deter the efforts of a host of
other bands in a similar direction; the concept album was now an
established medium.

The use of classical music terminology to describe rock
compositions did not originate with *Tommy*. The Nice's 'Ars Longa
Vita Brevis' (from the 1968 album of the same name) comprised a
prelude, four movements, and a Coda. While four of these sections
amounted to conventional rock music (the Prelude is a drum solo),
both the coda and the Third Movement use orchestral backing, the
latter being an adaption of Bach's 'Brandenburg' Concerto No. 6 and
constituting a framework for Keith Emerson's organ improvisations.
This extract followed the pattern initiated by 'Rondo' on the Nice's
first LP release (*The Thoughts Of Emerlist Davjack*: 1967) and
continued with versions of the Intermezzo from the 'Karelia' Suite by
Sibelius (also on *Ars Longa Vita Brevis*) and the Third Movement
('Pathetique') of Tchaikowsky's Sixth Symphony (on their third
album, *Nice*: 1969). Such items became crucial to the success of the
band's stage act, and though seldom accompanied in live performance
by a full orchestra, the Nice ensured that excitement was maintained
by investing such pieces with a driving beat, steady bass-line, and
virtuoso keyboard work by Emerson, complemented by a theatrical
and spectacular presentation. It is interesting to note that the Nice
never selected slow, reflective works for adaptation, indicating their
desire to use classical pieces only as a vehicle for audience arousal.

The next logical step was for the Nice to create a serious music work
of their own: this was realised in 1970 with *Five Bridges Suite*. While
the subject for the suite was fairly mundane – the bridges crossing the
River Tyne – its instrumentation was novel and ambitious,
comprising the Nice, a complete orchestra, and a horn section
manned by leading British jazz players. Unfortunately, it was hard to

avoid the impression that such embellishments were added merely for effect, the potential innovations suggested by such a line-up never reaching fruition; the jazz musicians in particular were grossly underemployed. There was the inevitable feeling that this was just rock music with too much backing and very little integration of its component parts. *Concerto For Group And Orchestra*, recorded at the Albert Hall in the same year by Deep Purple with the Royal Philharmonic Orchestra, befell much the same fate – if anything, this piece was even more cumbersome.

In spite of this burgeoning desire for credibility as serious music composers and performers, warning bells were beginning to ring among rock bands thus inclined. Albums such as *Five Bridges Suite* and *Concerto For Group And Orchestra*, though extremely popular amongst record-buyers, had not been greeted with the unreserved welcome from classical music critics hoped for by their creators. Might it not be better to dispense with terms such as 'opera', 'suite', and 'concerto'? To do so would, after all, confound the critics who wanted to analyse how closely their works corresponded in structure and content with those of the acknowledged masters. It might also help eradicate the epithet 'pretentious' which was being murmured amongst disgruntled blues fans and others. The answer would be simply to compose extended pieces – in effect tone-poems, but not to be described as such – based on sufficiently respectable subjects to retain the image of artistic competence already created. In this way, the medium of the concept album – which had proved to be such a banker for the Moody Blues, the Who, and the rest – could also be adhered to.

Emerson's composition 'The Three Fates' (from the album *Emerson, Lake and Palmer*, 1970) typified this pattern. Emerson is featured on the organ of the Royal Festival Hall ('Clotho'), on solo piano ('Lachesis'), and on piano with accompaniment by bass and drums ('Atropos'), and there any sense of formal presentation ends. Similarly, ELP's 'Tarkus' (from the 1971 album of the same name), while retaining a unifying theme – the by now familiar story of humanity versus the omnipotent mechanical adversary – avoids any conventional classical music structure. Keyboard-player Rick Wakeman went slightly further, basing his works on historical sources (*The Six Wives Of Henry VIII*, 1973), folklore (*Myths And Legends Of King Arthur*, 1975), and literature (*Journey To The Centre Of The Earth*, 1974). Choosing such specific material proved to be, however, just as restricting as adhering to a recognised classical format. Not only did it reduce the capacity for social comment, but it also inhibited individual improvisation, committed as the composer was to supplying a musical texture sufficiently varied to meet the sequential demands of his subject. *Journey To The Centre Of The Earth* exemplifies this dilemma. Verne's novel proved to be rather too mundane to provide for a statement of appropriate profundity (the spoken narrative by David Hemmings is particularly bathetic). Wakeman solved the problem by recruiting a full orchestra to play the piece: despite the fact that he could have simulated their part himself on moog synthesiser, the impression of artistic credibility might have suffered.

The safest course of action was to compose pieces of music of symphonic length (which could thus be fitted neatly on to an album and also constitute a complete set in live performance) which could accommodate individual group members' instrumental skills, principally on guitar and drums, but increasingly on keyboards; if a message about the state of the world could be incorporated, so much the better. This methodology was adopted by many British bands during the early 1970s, and led to enormous commercial success for groups such as Jethro Tull, Genesis, and Yes, especially in the United States where Anglophilia was still prevalent.

Though often placed in the same context, Pink Floyd did not completely follow the same precepts. For one thing, they avoided lengthy displays of instrumental proficiency. Their guitarist, Dave Gilmour, was the only member of the band to be featured regularly in solo, and even then his work was as economic and restrained as that of his accompanying colleagues. Floyd preferred instead to experiment with sound, their use of electronics corresponding to that of twentieth-century composers such as Stockhausen and Boulez – a distinct contrast to their contemporaries, whose grandiose projects had more in common with the Romantic works of the late nineteeth century. Pink Floyd were one of the few early 1970s bands whose popularity survived into the following decade.

The debate as to whether classical music might mix with rock was beginning to subside. Very few overt attempts at such a blend had met with a favourable reaction from serious music critics, and this, after all, was the kind of credibility such efforts aspired to, large-scale popular acceptance among rock enthusiasts being accepted as a matter of course. In any case, the issue was becoming increasingly redundant, for rock had now created its own aesthetic criteria, based not on the standards set by the great composers of earlier centuries but on the paradigms established by the Beatles, the Who, and the Moody Blues. In effect, the concept-album was now regarded as a medium in its own right.

While the star instrumentalist played an important role in this field, technical proficiency was still being pursued as an end in itself. Cream had laid the foundations, with the inauguration of the extended solo in rock and the adaptation of the blues guitar technique introduced by Eric Clapton. Yet they did not capitalise upon these developments: the band split up in 1968, and Clapton withdrew from a front-line position. No doubt influenced by the music of The Band, he was attracted to the 'down-home' approach of the American outfit Delaney and Bonnie, whom he accompanied as a sideman. Ironically, the success of his new colleagues in concert and on record (via the live album, *On Tour*: 1970) depended almost exclusively on his presence. British provincial audiences in particular, deprived for some time of the opportunity of seeing Cream in live performance, enjoyed Delaney and Bonnie only in proportion to the extent to which Clapton was featured. This state of affairs proved unsatisfactory to both parties. Without Clapton, Delaney and Bonnie's tenure as rock stars was brief; record-buyers had been slow to accept a return of simpler principles, even in the United States where The Band's *Music From Big Pink* reached only number 30 on the album chart. Similarly, Clapton's status as a guitar-hero was diminished, although he continued to persist with a more restrained approach to his playing, beginning with *Layla And Other Assorted Love Songs* (1971) and reaching fulfilment with *461 Ocean Boulevard* (1974).

The way in which Led Zeppelin were able to fill the void created by the demise of Cream has already been described (see Chapter 4). The British bands Ten Years After, Taste, and Free – featuring the guitarists Alvin Lee, Rory Gallagher, and Paul Kossoff respectively – were also able to cater for the demand for lengthy improvisations on a simple theme or riff. Such groups enjoyed particular success at rock festivals, outdoor events which had grown considerably in scope and duration since the Monterey show of 1967. Their magnitude had now increased to the extent that there were reportedly 500,000 rock fans in the vicinity of the Isle Of Wight Festival of 1970. For a time it seemed as if the marketing methods of record companies were undergoing a

change: attendances at festivals were so large that vast quantities of
albums could be sold on the strength of a band's appearances at these
events alone in front of what amounted to a captive audience, thus
avoiding the usual time restrictions of radio play and the whims of
station producers and disc jockeys. The resultant proliferation of live
albums served only to perpetuate the demand for marathon displays
of virtuosity.

Gradually modern jazz musicians were able to find themselves a
place in this scenario. John Mayall had introduced saxophonist Dick
Heckstall-Smith, bass-player Tony Reeves, and drummer Jon
Hiseman to rock enthusiasts on his album *Bare Wires* (1968), and
shortly afterwards these three musicians formed their own outfit,
Colosseum; similarly, trumpeter Henry Lowther and saxophonist
Chris Mercer left the same Mayall group to join the Keef Hartley
Band and Juicy Lucy respectively. There were parallel developments
in the United States where musicians of the calibre of Lew Soloff
(trumpeter with Blood, Sweat And Tears) and Jim Pankow
(trombonist with Chicago) were making new careers for themselves in
rock. It was not long before the term 'jazz-rock' was coined to describe
the work of these and similar bands. Yet in the context of rock music,
there were few opportunities for the jazz players to demonstrate their
talents in the manner to which they had previously been accustomed.
Their role was predominantly that of section-men, employed largely
to give emphasis to the pervasive riff of a piece, and on the occasions
when they were called upon to solo any possibility of rhythmic
variation and distinctive improvisational ideas was stifled by the
prevalent 4/4 time signatures employed by such bands and the
compulsion towards speed and volume to maintain the excitement.
While the importation of jazz into rock can be viewed as less than
aesthetically satisfactory, however, certain jazz artists were successful
in reversing the process. On his album *In A Silent Way* (1969), Miles
Davis retained the repetitive pulse and simple structure of rock, and
employed its characteristic instrumentation: electric guitar, bass
guitar, and electric piano. Yet such methods served to create musical
tensions and moods far removed from those of rock: guitar and piano
were used to punctuate rather than to dominate the proceedings, bass
and drums to support the soloists rather than battle with them.
Davis's intention of extracting the essential aspects of rock without
importing its excesses was much copied but widely misunderstood,
resulting in the creation of 'fusion' and 'jazz-funk', in which soloists

are as frequently shackled by disco rhythms as their predecessors were by the rock beat.

Such considerations did not, however, seem to concern the rock musicians inclined towards technical credibility. Indeed, the rock press did its best to encourage their ambitions. Elections were organised to determine the top individual musicians, a device borrowed from the jazz publications. Official recognition could now be conferred upon rock players: they could assume the status traditionally held to be the preserve of the jazz musician, whose technical mastery had long been taken for granted. In fact, the jazz artist was almost irrelevant to the new hierarchy. The results of the poll conducted by *Beat Instrumental,* announced in its edition of March 1970, demonstrate this clearly. Even allowing for the fact that *B.I.* was a British magazine and granting that its readership may have had little knowledge of modern jazz, the outcome of the voting was remarkable. There were five sections devoted to the leading instrumentalists (guitar, bass, drums, keyboard, and brass/ woodwind) and one section for vocalists: the top ten names appeared in each case. Of these sixty artists, only two were black (Jimi Hendrix and Roland Kirk), only six American (Hendrix, Kirk, Frank Zappa, Al Kooper, Jim Pankow, and Buddy Rich), and only two at that time playing jazz (Kirk and Rich). The implication of these results is evident. Just as rock musicians had aligned themselves with classical music by producing operas, suites, and concertos and, eventually, created their own criteria by means of originally conceived concept-albums, so had the star instrumentalists followed the example of jazz and thus elevated themselves to a position where comparisons were redundant and rock musicianship could set its own standards.

On the face of it, the increasing popularity of the singer/songwriters during the early 1970s might have provided an antidote to the developments described above: the danger that rock might overreach itself should certainly have been removed. Yearnings for acceptance in the classical or jazz fraternities would not enter into it – even the wishes of the folk enthusiasts need not be taken into account, as it was now permissible to specialise in contemporary as well as traditional folk music.

We might characterise the singer/songwriters as artists who combined the function of composer with that of musician, frequently performing alone, but occasionally accompanied by a small unit kept very much in the background. Invariably, the singer/songwriter would play acoustic guitar and/or piano and while concentrating on original compositions would occasionally record songs by artists of a similar type. Though this category could clearly include a large number of artists, we shall include those who were especially popular during the period under consideration: the Americans James Taylor and Carole King, the Canadians Leonard Cohen and Joni Mitchell, and the Britons Cat Stevens and Elton John.

The singer/songwriters appeared to write from their own experience or, at least, based their material on imaginary characters and events which seemed to be a product of their own environment and observations. This is a distinction which, in effect, is impossible for the listener to recognise. For once it was made known that certain songs by the singer/songwriters were based on actual events or real people, it was not feasible to separate them from those which were not. Normally, this issue would be of minor importance, it merely being a reflection of the creative process that forms a part of all songwriting. Yet it is fundamental to the impression that the singer/ songwriters wished to create and accounts to a great extent for their commercial success. An examination of the process and of the methods used should confirm the argument. We know that James Taylor's 'Fire And Rain' (*Sweet Baby James*: 1970) referred to his experiences in a mental hospital; what we cannot know is whether his version of Carole King's 'You've Got A Friend' (*Mud Slide Slim And The Blue Horizon*, 1971) was a message from King to Taylor, Taylor to King, or a consoling anthem for the lonely. Similarly, Joni Mitchell's 'Willy' (*Ladies Of The Canyon*, 1970) is commonly held to be about Graham Nash, but to whom is 'Carey' (*Blue*, 1971) addressed?

What matters is that all four songs – and this is true of the work of the singer/songwriters in general – are delivered with such a high degree of intimacy that the listener feels that he is being drawn into the performer's confidence, that personal secrets are being revealed as they might be by one friend to another. This impression is enhanced by the nature of the accompaniment – where backing musicians are present at all, their work is discreet and unobtrusive. The singer/ songwriters ensured that their image matched the day-to-day world in which their songs operated: T-shirts and jeans were preferred to ostentatious wardrobes (even Elton John did not assume his more flamboyant outfits until he had become an established album artist) – this added greatly to the intended authenticity of their compositions and helped the listener to identify more readily with them. Finally, the songs are almost invariably set in a restricted time-period: that of the present or, more commonly, in the immediate past, again underlining their credibility as statements of fact.

None of these considerations seemed to worry the large number of record-buyers who were drawn to the work of the singer/songwriters, in fact these were the very features that attracted them. Not only did they feel privileged to be invited into the lives of successful rock stars, but they were not at all confounded by the literal accuracy or otherwise of the songs: it *all* seemed true. They were indeed quite willing to enter into speculation as to who might be the subjects of given pieces; Carly Simon's 'You're So Vain' (1972) became a top three hit single in both Britain and the United States largely on the strength of such deliberations.

The paradox is that while the singer/songwriters seemed to be involving their audience to an unprecedented extent, they were in fact producing the reverse effect: the distance between performer and listener was as great as it always had been. In retrospect it is a complete illusion to think that it could ever have been otherwise. To begin with, the transmission of revelations was one way only, not a conversation between friends but a monologue. Thus when we enter the abode of Leonard Cohen in *Songs From A Room* (1969) our only course of action is passively to await whatever disclosures he will decide to make. Provided that these strike us as being authentic, we cannot dispute his implicitly superior role as producer since we must remain consumers. Furthermore, while we can make well-informed guesses about the mystery personalities in the songs of Mitchell, Taylor, and Simon, the sad fact is that we can never truly play an active part in their intrigues nor commiserate with them in their misfortunes – our involvement must be at best vicarious.

As we continue to dismantle the notion that we enjoyed some sort of personal relationship with singer/songwriters, we begin to notice how their material, once concerns about literal truth are stripped away, seems frequently to display many of the characteristics of a parable. An overt moral content becomes apparent in such individual items as Cat Stevens's 'Wild World' (*Tea For The Tillerman*, 1971), Leonard Cohen's 'Sisters Of Mercy' (*The Songs Of Leonard Cohen*, 1969), and Elton John's 'Daniel' (1973). It also seems to inform entire albums, in particular Carole King's *Tapestry* (1971) which, though it appears to be a collection of unconnected love-songs, leaves the impression that

King intended to deliver a more coherent and wide-ranging statement about her emotional entanglements to date. If the album's title is insufficient to make this clear, its content certainly should: for we find songs written at all stages of King's career, unified not just by the theme of her relationships with men, but also by her continual use of imagery alluding to nature: rain, earthquake, the seasons, and so on. Similar methods are apparent in the earlier *Writer* (1970) and the subsequent Carole King *Music* (1971) and *Rhymes And Reasons* (1972).

Tapestry sold over ten million copies, confirming that the techniques of the singer/songwriters had the effect of maintaining their separation as superstars from their compliant but remote supporters. Although their tactics were arguably more subtle (some might say insidious) than those who were aligning rock with classical music or jazz, the result was the same: the elevation of the rock musician to a status approaching deification.

Recognition of this turn of events pervaded the entire rock industry up to the mid-1970s: there was the irresistible feeling that rock had now established itself to such a degree that there were no further battles to be fought. Record companies were quite content: sales of albums, in particular, had reached new heights, and rosters consisted of bands whose followings were so devoted as to guarantee apparently permanent success. A new, less volatile audience was beginning to form, consisting primarily of those who during their teenage years had followed the emergence of the Beatles and the Rolling Stones and subsequently grown up in parallel to the development of rock. They were now gratified to see the music attain a maturity commensurate with their own advancing years. Now in their mid-twenties and almost certainly in work (something approaching full employment had been reached both in Britain and America in 1973), such enthusiasts possessed the resources to devote to what had become an essential leisure-time activity. As such, they were preyed upon not only by record companies eager to exploit a stable and affluent market, but also by similarly-inclined publishers and radio stations.

Rock histories and biographies appeared in great abundance. Such publication were characterised by two main assumptions. One was that rock had attained new and higher standards of quality. This was either expressed implicitly, or stated as a matter of fact, as in Bob Sarlin's *Turn It Up (I Can't Hear the Words)*, 1973, in which the author defines the work of certain singer/songwriters as 'songpoetry': he

claims that these artists 'combine elements of the best of rock-and-roll
with lyrical sophistication that has never been heard before in popular
songs', that they 'examine the kinds of emotional experience that have
previously been untouched in this area' (p. 15). The other was that
rock had now reached a plateau, a state which denoted both the peak
and the end of its development. Had the music been in a state of
growth or change, the publication of *The NME Book Of Rock* (1975)
or *The Encyclopedia Of Rock* (1976) would scarcely have seemed
appropriate. An unfortunate side-effect of some contemporary
surveys was that the sources of rock music seemed to be registered,
not as independent forms with a character of their own, but as more or
less primitive anachronisms, the contribution of which to the history
of rock appeared almost accidental. Thus in Tony Palmer's *All You
Need Is Love* (1976) rock & roll is allotted insufficient attention, while
the blues of the Delta and of Chicago are scarcely mentioned at all.

Radio stations were keen to cater for the new audience, especially in
the United States where, broadcast on FM, programmes combined
jazz and serious music with the work of rock performers and took care
to ensure that advertising jingles did not intervene at crucial
moments. British radio was rather slower to catch on, although Alan
Freeman's BBC Radio One show was suitably deferential to the rock
star's newly-acquired eminence – extracts from nineteenth-century
classical music were interspersed with the recordings of contemporary
rock bands of a similar persuasion.

Finally, the musicians themselves adopted strategies to appeal to
their legions of admirers. Stage shows became increasingly theatrical
and grandiose; albums were more lavishly designed and packaged.
Deep Purple were especially concerned with transforming the image
of the rock star. Not only were they spectacular live performers, but
they had been one of the first bands to produce a pseudo-classical
work – the *Concerto For Group And Orchestra* of 1970. That same year,
the cover of their album *Deep Purple In Rock* substituted the heads of
the band for those of the American Presidents carved into the peaks of
Mount Rushmore. Even if regarded as self-parody, it was an
indication of how rock musicians were beginning to view themselves,
and neatly anticipated the way in which things were to progress
during the succeeding five years.

It is commonly believed that punk rock represented a challenge to the
standards of composition and musicianship established during the

early 1970s, and it is certainly tempting to see its appearance as a spontaneous reaction to what had become, in effect, a musical hegemony. Without a doubt, there is a great deal of superficial evidence to support this conviction. The emergence of punk was, for example, extremely swift: within the first six months of 1977 its existence had been acknowledged in all corners of the rock music business. Records by the Sex Pistols, the Jam, and the Clash had reached the charts; the trade papers, particularly in Britain, were giving punk their almost exclusive attention; record companies were vying with each other to sign up its leading bands; and fashion-designers had recognised the commercial potential of its new sartorial styles. There is also no denying the radical differences in philosophy, presentation, form, and content between punk and the rock music which immediately preceded it. Pacifism had apparently given way to anarchy, musings on the fate of mankind and the vicissitudes of love, hatched in the Surrey countryside or in Southern California, were replaced by evocations of life on the streets of London and New York with specific images of violence, alienation, and unemployment. Instrumental proficiency was no longer desirable (in fact it was positively discouraged) and extended compositions were supplemented by the three-minute single.

Yet these ostensibly new attitudes had been forming some time before 1977 – the arrival of punk rock was by no means unheralded. Though much was made of the fundamental changes wrought by its practitioners, it is now possible to conclude that such developments were largely indicative of the thread of continuity traceable through all pop music. What, in this case, has tended to cloud the issue is the fact that the origins of punk rock are to be found in some unlikely sources.

As soon as the *aficionados* of punk got round to conceding that their music had any origins at all, they began to examine the work of the Velvet Underground and in particular that of Lou Reed. It seems the most logical place to have started, for the Velvets had represented an alternative to the prevailing methods and intentions of rock music as early as their formation in New York in 1966. Their first album, *The Velvet Underground And Nico* (1967), not only deals with issues seldom broached on the West Coast or in Britain, but also avoids any aspiration to compositional or instrumental virtuosity.

While it had been tacitly assumed that many rock musicians were drug users, references to drugs in rock songs were normally veiled, a

tactic which had the double benefit of signalling to the initiatied yet
retaining the support of record companies, advertisers, and television
radio stations. Furthermore, the drugs in question were of the
potentially less harmful variety: LSD, marijuana, hashish, and so on.
The Velvet Underground, in contrast, began to make overt mention
of drugs, particularly heroin, as in 'Waiting For The Man'. They were
equally explicit about other subjects previously regarded either as
taboo (for example, sexual fantasy: 'Venus In Furs') or commercially
inadvisable, especially mental disorder and disorientation, as in
'Sunday Morning'. This lack of lyrical inhibition was matched by an
uncompromising instrumental sound which dispensed with
pretensions to perfectionism in favour of a heavy and repetitive drum
beat, raucous guitar chords, and out-of-tune singing.

Such features betray clear links with punk rock, but it is important
to examine the essential difference between the music of the Velvet
Underground and that of the British performers who came to
prominence in the late 1970s. Unlike the Sex Pistols, the Clash, and
their contemporaries, the Velvets did not operate from a specific
political standpoint: one felt that their music was a reflection of society
as they saw it, rather than an apparent attack upon it. In addition,
their reduction of the music to the simple essentials employed so
successfully in rock & roll seemed to be a contrived and conscious
process, an effort to produce perfect pop rather than perfect work.
This impression is enhanced by the parallel experiments being carried
out in art by the band's early mentor, Andy Warhol. Whereas the
punks traded on their musical inabilities and, by implication, openly
invited their audience to emulate them (Siouxsie and the Banshees
were allegedly formed in response to just such a challenge), the Velvet
Underground appeared to be making an artistic decision to disregard
technical competence – bass-player John Cale was, after all, a
classically-trained musician.

Advocates of the connection between the Velvet Underground and
punk rock have also to consider that the American band achieved
negligible commercial success, even in their own country where all
their albums failed to reach the Top 100. It was not until Lou Reed
came to Britain to record his first solo album (*Lou Reed*: 1972) and the
subsequent *Transformer* (1972) that any members of the band received
popular acclaim. By that stage, however, the producer of *Transformer*,
David Bowie, had already established his own following, consisting
principally of teenagers who could have had no prior knowledge of the

Velvets or of Reed. Furthermore, they were responding to an artist whose music seemed to owe little to the intentions and techniques of the mainstream rock of the period and who had concentrated on the singles market to launch his career. This suited Bowie's audience very well: not only could they express the normal dissaffection with the tastes of older brothers and sisters, but collect the recordings he was making without overreaching their limited purchasing power – Bowie's studio work was always originally issued in single or single-album form.

What further enhanced Bowie's accessibility was the fact that he based many of his songs, and in certain cases whole projects, on pop music itself, thereby guranteeing a bond with his listeners; his particular skill lay in extending the potential for emotional transportation induced by pop into previously uncharted areas, to demonstrate by personal example that music could constitute a catalyst for the release of any moral or social inhibition. Thus the characters portrayed in 'John, I'm Only Dancing' (1972), 'Jean Genie' (1972), and 'Rebel Rebel' (1973) are celebrated for their self-indulgence, fecklessness, and complete immersion in the world of music and fashion. Similarly, *Pin-Ups* (1973) made it entirely acceptable to practise hero-worship; Bowie's use of cosmetics and glamorous clothes and his overtly erotic stage-act attracted heterosexual, homosexual, and bisexual admiration alike, allowing his audience total freedom to surrender themselves to his own music and momentarily forget repression and restraint.

Yet there was a darker side to Bowie's work, too: this had been evident from his first hit single, 'Space Oddity' (1966), which described the disorientation and loneliness of the astronaut. With *The Rise And Fall Of Ziggy Stardust And the Spiders From Mars* (1972), the protagonist became the pop star, the space-traveller trappings retained to underline the isolation imposed by the fulfilment of that role. The album demonstrates that the star's popularity becomes a vicious circle – the greater the acclaim, the wider the separation, both physical and intellectual, between performer and listener, resulting in the ultimate destruction of the star by his followers and the collapse of the myth.

While it is possible to view Bowie as a link between Lou Reed and punk rock, his achievement in integrating euphoria with pessimism constituted an independent foundation for the developments of the late 1970s; while his involvement with Reed awakened an interest in the Velvets' old recordings, Bowie attracted contemporary respect and admiration which continued through the emergence of punk and beyond it.

Bowie's re-introduction of the three-minute song, overtly commercial and easily absorbed, his preoccupation with pop and audience involvement, and his emphasis upon glamour and sartorial flamboyance, all wrought an influence upon the British singles artists of the early 1970s. T. Rex, for example, had a series of hits between 1971 and 1973 (including "Hot Love", 'Get It On', and 'Jeepster') which relied on a 'hook' simple enough to invite audience participation; Gary Glitter employed similar techniques for his hits 'Rock And Roll Part Two' (1972), 'Do You Wanna Touch Me?' (1973), 'Hello Hello I'm Back Again' (1973), while fashioning his appearance on that of Bowie; and Sweet capitalised on all three elements for their 1973 successes 'Blockbuster', 'Hell Raiser', and 'Ballroom Blitz'.

The fact that such efforts were regarded as ephemera by the vast majority of mainstream rock fans and critics was scarcely relevant to these performers. Indeed, they were intentionally celebrating pop music for its transitory qualities, aiming to release inhibitions and give pleasure in the present without concern for its future durability. To this end, rock & roll was invoked as an example to follow: music which had a limited life, but was fun while it lasted. The term became synonymous with any form of up-tempo, good-time pop music and was used to advantage by those artists who, it was supposed, would have had some contact with the original product, beginning with Rod Stewart ('Maggie May', 1971), and subsequently including Elton John ('Crocodile Rock', 1972), and the Rolling Stones ('It's Only Rock 'n' Roll', 1974). Even the new rock superstars got in on the act, bands such as Deep Purple and Emerson, Lake and Palmer performing rock & roll material during their obligatory encores; and for a time the original music itself underwent a revival.

The implications for the emergence of punk rock are clear: it was becoming acceptable – in some quarters, desirable – to play fast, aggressive pop music irrespective of technical complexity or hidden significance, music which could function without reference or comparison to more respectable forms or styles. Yet an audience accustomed to a diet of Top Forty acts only would have been insufficiently prepared for a music which had its origins in London's pubs, small clubs, and obscure theatres. The establishment of a thriving 'underground' movement was far more likely to provide the conditions under which a new musical fashion might flourish, just as it had done at the Cavern and the Marquee ten years previously.

In fact, the bands which now dominated 'pub rock' had clear stylistic links with their counterparts of the early 1960s. The standard fare was a rough approximation of American rhythm & blues, very much in the manner of the early efforts of the Rolling Stones, Yardbirds, and so on. The preoccupation of late 1960s rock musicians with instrumental skills had had its effect, however, resulting in the enhanced level of competence displayed by such pub rock participants as Nick Lowe, Brinsley Schwarz, and Dave Edmunds.

On the other hand, audiences were far more familiar with the type of material being played than they had been ten years previously. Those record-buyers who had investigated the sources of British R. & B. were, in particular, sufficiently knowledgeable to be able to assess the native efforts within the context of the black American originals. Access to the source material had also improved, owing to the many reissue programmes initiated by record companies during the early 1970s, a process which was to culminate in the formation of independent labels with the express purpose of leasing rock & roll and R. & B. recordings from the American majors, who by this stage had almost completely absorbed the small companies from which such items had invariably originated. Whilst it was gratifying, therefore, to witness the pub rock bands perform so vigorously the work of artists who were deceased, indisposed, or infrequent visitors to Britain, the commercial potential of such recreations was somewhat limited. Without the high level of record sales throughout the country such bands were reluctant to leave their circuit of venues in the capital, thus reducing their chances of widespread success still further.

The career of one of the leading pub rock bands, Dr Feelgood, illustrates this dilemma. On the strength of their live performances, they secured a recording contract with United Artists, who issued two studio albums by the band during 1975. The second of these, *Malpractice*, was a particularly faithful reflection of their stage work, including the popular original compositions 'Going Back Home' and 'Back In The Night', three songs from the rock & roll/R. & B. tradition (Bo Diddley's 'I Can't Tell', Huey Smith's 'Don't You Just Know It', and the Coasters' 'Riot In Cell Block No. 9'), and a blues – 'Rolling And Tumbling' – attributed to Muddy Waters, but in fact a constituent of the 'Minglewood Blues' song-family (see Chapter 1).

The band's own writing (mainly the work of their guitarist, Wilko Johnson) faithfully reflected the idiom in which they operated – no mean feat, but scarcely conducive to widening their commercial horizons. In fact, neither album sold especially well, but faced with the prospect of departing from a repertoire based so exclusively upon black American styles, the band chose instead to intensify their touring schedule, taking in not only British provincial cities but the United States, which they visited in 1976. This decision was vindicated when, during the year, they had a number one hit in Brtain with *Stupidity* which was, inevitably, a live album. Having settled on this course of action, however, the Feelgoods – despite retaining their popularity as a club and concert attraction – have since failed to repeat such commercial success.

A small number of artists did nevertheless, contrive to transcend pub rock and attain a more durable star status. One might cite, for example, Graham Parker and Elvis Costello (whose work will be discussed later in this chapter). Both were able to reflect the inherent aggression of rock & roll and rhythm & blues in their own compositions while still creating work which was original and distinctive in character. This led to their music being classified initially as punk, though once it became clear that both artists possessed the potential to encompass a wider range of styles they were dignified with the description 'New Wave'.

In general, however, the dependence of the pub rock bands upon American rock & roll and R. & B. material limited their prospects; while we may regard them as constituting the second generation of British performers to be influenced by the pop tradition of the United States, their appeal was too localised to catch the imagination of record-buyers on a national scale. Yet at the very least they revitalised a pub and club circuit that could no longer afford to present the leading mainstream rock acts of the day, many of whom had, in any case, already emigrated to the United States. They also established a close contact with their audience: while this was partly due to the physical proximity created by the small venues, it also resulted from the lack of self-indulgence on the musicians' behalf, the emphasis being placed instead upon short, aggressively delivered pieces. It is not difficult to see how punk rock was able to flourish in such an environment.

In the meantime, the rock bands that had followed the precedents set by Cream and Led Zeppelin, and who had become known as the 'heavy rock' groups, had begun to depart from the themes of peace, brotherhood, and tolerance so prevalent in late 1960s rock. Musically, these outfits were quite conservative and at pains not to deviate from the formula introduced by their predecessors – the simple bass riff underlying long and intense guitar solos and uninhibited, occasionally histrionic, vocals. Lyrically, they concentrated on dark and depressing subject matter to an extent hitherto unprecedented in any form of pop music.

Arguably the first of these heavy rock bands, Black Sabbath, covered a whole range of unpleasant issues. Their album *Paranoid* (1970), for example, included songs dealing with personal trauma – 'Paranoid' and 'Fairies Wear Boots' (which described the unsavoury side-effects of drug-taking) – as well as those confronting wider issues, such as the self-explanatory 'War Pigs' and 'Hand Of Doom'. Similar topics were a feature of the work of Sabbath's many imitators, in particular Uriah Heep, Budgie, and Babe Ruth, as well as the late 1960s bands whose careers were revived by their adoption of heavy rock principles: this category includes the Groundhogs, who enjoyed success with the anti-war concept album *Thank Christ For The Bomb* (1970), and Hawkwind, whose early 1970s albums were characterised by a preoccupation with social comment, as demonstrated by the songs 'High Rise', 'Kerb Crawler', 'Urban Guerilla', 'The Wind Of Change', and many others.

In the United States, Alice Cooper tackled a similar catalogue of subjects, but while the British bands, for all their musical excesses, operated from a rigidly moral standpoint, Cooper's use of self-parody and intentional bad taste served to obscure any such message he may have wished to deliver. Thus the portrait painted of the uncaring family in 'Dead Babies' (*Killer*: 1971) loses credibility when set against the gratuitous violence of 'Under My Wheels' from the same album. The moral ambiguity in Cooper's work – together with his introduction of bizarre and offensive subject matter – did not, however, detract from his popularity: on the contrary, it was the single most important factor in his success.

Heavy rock attracted a committed and loyal following, the majority of whom were completely impervious to the critical derision the music engendered. In fact, audience involvement was so great as to sustain its transition to an increasingly independent style during the mid-1970s. Conscious defiance of fashion and total physical and mental immersion in the music became prerequisites for the heavy rock enthusiast, as did the utter disregard for external opinion. While the heavy rock bands inherited the morality of the late 1960s, they switched the mood to one of foreboding, oppression, and gloom; while they developed the instrumental techniques established during the blues-rock era, they went no further, avoiding any experimentation with jazz or classical music principles; they made concessions to no-one but their own audience.

The emergence of punk rock in 1976 was a phenomenon much written about at the time, but scarcely considered since. We have seen how much of the substance of the music, and the attitudes adopted by its perpetrators, were already present in some form or other immediately prior to this date. David Bowie's work had combined the uninhibited celebration of the present with concerns about the future, and while the former philosophy had been taken up by the popular singles artists who purveyed good-time 'rock & roll', the latter preoccupation was paralleled in the thematic content of heavy rock; pub rock had re-established the demand for uncomplicated, R. & B.-influenced music in the small venues of London. All of these artists had consciously deferred to their respective audiences and averted the potential separation brought about by the search for credibility in jazz and serious music circles undertaken by many rock performers or by the deification of the singer/songwriters. To summarise, the challenge to what was threatening to become a rock music 'establishment' was *already* in progress by the time of punk's arrival.

To maintain that the early punk rock bands set out to amalgamate these elements to create a new form of pop music would be to attribute to them too great a degree of premeditation; musical change seldom results from such a conscious contrivance on the part of the artist. Yet it is clear that the features itemised above all contributed to the climate in which punk was able to develop; it is equally evident that they formed the basis for the success of its leading exponents. The Sex Pistols, for example, integrated euphoria and nihilism, often within the course of one song, as in the celebratory renditions of 'Anarchy In the U.K.' (1976) and 'God Save The Queen' (1977) in which the 'no future for you . . . no future for me' refrain is bestowed with an anthem-like character. In other cases, bands concentrated upon one or other of the polar opposites: while the Damned placed the emphasis upon trivia, the Clash opted for themes of violence and insurrection. All punk rock bands played pieces of short duration, normally with the minimum rock instrumentation of guitar, bass guitar, and drums; most made their public debuts on the circuit worked by the pub rock bands, with whom they often shared the billing, notably at such venues as London's 100 Club or the Hope and Anchor. Finally, every punk rock outfit tried hard to create a rapport between themselves and their audience. This was frequently achieved by unorthodox methods: bands such as the Pistols and the Buzzcocks indulged in the abuse of their followers, both **verb**ally and in their ragged and apparently unprofessional execution of their stage-act; yet such was the attractiveness of the punks' overt defiance of anything that might be regarded as musical convention that audiences were not only quite happy to comply with this arrangement but were often moved to reciprocate – mutual contempt denoted mutual respect.

It was this kind of paradox that provided punk with a sense of style which distinguished it from any type of rock music that had preceded it. The celebration of social decline and degeneration, moral decay, and personal disorientation had inevitable consequences for the content and presentation of the music: there was no way that traditional standards of composition and performance could possibly be adhered to. In fact much early punk resembles the more amateurish attempts at R. & B. perpetrated by the British 'beat' groups of the early 1960s, characterised by impossibly fast tempos, primitive drum figures, crashing guitar chords, and wailing, out-of-tune vocals. Yet it was philsophically appropriate to employ such techniques: not only could notions of musical quality be reversed, but also an invitation issued to all would-be musicians to ignore any worries about instrumental competence and join in.

The British rock music press, in particular the leading weeklies *Melody Maker* and *New Musical Express*, fostered and encouraged the development of punk; there was even a feeling in the provinces that such publications were responsible for its emergence in the first place. In the BBC Radio One series *From Punk To Present* (broadcast between 19 January and 6 April 1985), Bob Geldof related how a gig he attended at the 100 Club, at which the pub rock band Roogalator shared the bill with the Damned, was said in a subsequent rock press review to be 'packed' when in fact the audience had consisted of some thirty-five to forty spectators. Greil Marcus (1980) has stated that 'Punk was a carefully orchestrated media hype, the latest version of a tried-and-true scenario of pop outrageousness that elicited a hurricane of Establishment hysteria – a hysteria that was in many ways as cynical and self-serving as the provocation' (p. 454). As Marcus points out, it was in the rock journalists' own interests to promote punk – but not merely for the reason that it represented the latest pop music trend. Prior to the appearance of punk, the rock weeklies felt obliged to reflect the wide variety of forms and styles that made up the music. Thus *aficionados* of jazz-rock, concept album bands, Top 40 artists, heavy rock, and the singer/songwriters all had to be catered for; *Melody Maker,* in addition, carried columns serving the minority tastes of folk and jazz. As such, rock music publications attracted a fragmented readership, very few of whom could be satisfied by their complete content. By devoting widespread – in some cases, almost exclusive – coverage to punk, there was a likelihood that the music would gain the universal popularity needed to ensure high circulation figures and a homogeneous market. Such an approach would also help to ward off the competition of the independently produced 'fanzines', designed to reflect the activities of punk artists and publicise their music.

A further feature which distinguished punk from the rock music of the early 1970s was the initial concentration of its principal practitioners upon ideological concerns. While the heavy rock bands had composed songs with a pronounced moral content, they lacked a specific political base. The punks, on the other hand, seemed to find a solution to society's problems in revolution and anarchy. The extent to which these beliefs were sincere or to be taken at face value has been a matter for subsequent debate. Marcus (*ibid,* p. 451) explains the position as follows:

> It may be that in the mind of their self-celebrated Svengali, London boutique owner Malcolm McLaren, the Sex Pistols were never meant to be more than a nine-month wonder, a cheap vehicle for some fast money, a few laughs, a touch of the old *épater la bourgeoisie.* It may also be that in the mind of their chief theorist and propagandist, anarchist veteran of the Paris insurrection of 1968 and Situational artist McLaren, the Sex Pistols were meant to be a force that would set the world on its ear . . . and finally unite music and politics. The Sex Pistols were all of these things . . .

In *From Punk To Present,* Joe Strummer of the Clash claimed that by referring to 'sten guns in Knightsbridge' ('1977': 1977) he was observing terrorism rather than advocating it, that such material amounted to prophecy (of, for example the London and Liverpool riots of the summer of 1981) rather than incitement. Whatever the case, it was not long before principles – whether genuine or not –

began to be compromised; self-interest supplanted ideology. We may trace this process not only in the particular case of the Pistols, whose singer, Johnny Rotten, eventually opposed McLaren in court, but also in the speed with which many leading punk outfits moved from the small independent record labels to the major companies; such concessions, as we shall see shortly, also had implications for the nature of the music.

While punk retained and exploited certain key elements present in the rock music of the early 1970s, it also benefited from what we might characterise as extra-musical factors: its capacity to outrage, its unique audience-performer relationship, its apparent commitment to nihilism and anarchy and evident celebration of both, and its unrestrained endorsement by the rock music press. Its reduction of rock music to its basic instrumental and compositional structures – whether seen as the continuation of a process already in motion or as a conscious attempt to reverse standards – did, however, accelerate change. In spite of its relatively brief existence as a recognisably distinct musical form (spanning, at most, the years 1976–8), punk had the effect of rendering unfashionable the excesses present in the work of so many rock musicians pre-eminent at the end of the 1960s and still considered important five years later. In this respect, punk was to have a long-term influence quite out of proportion to the *actual* musical objectives it had set itself. Few of the original punk rock performers maintained their popularity once their classification became outmoded, though some, by following policies of compromise and/or diversification, were able to survive as members of the New Wave.

Deviation from the standard punk formula became an option early on, and resulted from a number of considerations. Firstly, the music itself imposed too many restraints – there was clearly no opportunity for instrumental creativity nor imaginative songwriting: while displays of technical competence were frowned upon, punk also offered a narrow range of subject matter: essentially insurrection, violence, adolescent trauma and the like. Secondly, the innate conservatism of the major record companies meant that the bands who had joined them with such alacrity now felt under pressure to produce music which was rather less extreme in content and execution. Thirdly, it was becoming apparent that the emergence of punk had not brought with it the commercial bonanza that many had anticipated; chart success was limited in Britain and almost non-existent in the USA, where there was widespread bewilderment at the fact that the music had achieved any recognition in the first place.

Various attempts were made to resolve such dilemmas. The Jam, whose first album *In The City* (1977) recalled the early work of the Who in style and presentation, continued to derive inspiration from 1960s pop with their subsequent releases *This Is The Modern World* and *All Mod Cons* (1977 and 1978 respectively), using the Beatles and Byrds as models in each case. They even produced a concept album, *Setting Sons* (1979), for which numerous embellishments (including strings) were employed to add drama to the storyline of a future civil war.

Regarded as one of the first punk bands, the Clash were in an especially vulnerable position: their followers naturally expected the continuation of the style that had made them popular. The band responded by introducing changes in their music gradually, so that by the time of their third album, the double *London Calling* (1979), they had achieved a seamless blend of punk and selected aspects of rock & roll, R. & B. and soul, as well as the reggae which they had used from the start. Thus Bo Diddley's shuffle rhythm is present in 'Hateful', the horn theme of Frankie Ford's 'Sea Cruise' is featured in 'Wrong 'Em Boyo' and the accompanying riff in 'The Right Profile' resembles that of 'Everybody Needs Somebody To Love' by Solomon Burke. In addition, the band make use of their instrumental abilities: there are fluent, if brief, guitar solos on 'Brand New Cadillac' and 'Lover's Rock', and Topper Headon's drumming, though crisp and propulsive throughout, is heard to particular advantage on 'The Guns Of Brixton'. Finally, the band continued to develop their use of humour, with instances ranging from the evocation of mediocrity of 'Lost In The Supermarket' to the self-deprecatory implications of 'Revolution Rock'.

It would have been understandable to categorise as punk the early work of the Police, as the title and label of their first single 'Fall Out' (Illegal, 1977) might suggest. All three band-members were, however, experienced musicians, and soon integrated more conventional rock elements into what had seemed initially to comprise a routine imitation of the medium in which the Clash were operating. Examples of this process are 'So Lonely', 'Roxanne', and 'Can't Stand Losing You' (all from *Outlandos D'Amour*, 1978). In all three songs, two distinct moods are present: while the verses are taken at a slow pace, are sung plaintively, and possess a ballad-like character, the choruses are fast, repetitive, and aggressively delivered, both vocally and instrumentally.

New Wave artists were essentially those who adapted the musical and lyrical principles of punk while still adhering to the standards of rock musicianship and composition established in the late 1960s and early 1970s, frequently making reference – as in the cases of the Jam and the Clash – to specific artists and/or styles of the past. Thus the uncomplicated song structures and band instrumentation of the late 1950s and early 1960s were revived but the presentation and execution were both now more competent. Furthermore, largely through the efforts of the Clash, the reggae rhythm had become absorbed into punk, and its standard 4/4 time signature, corresponding to that of much early rock music, now suited the purposes of many New Wave acts who also undoubtedly benefited from the simultaneous increase in the popuarity of reggae itself. Finally, the uninhibited approach to songwriting adopted by the punk performers meant that subjects and imagery previously considered to be taboo were now acceptable; while there had been some inclination towards moderation, largely as a result of commercial pressures, New Wave composers were still able to write candidly and provocatively.

There were certain New Wave artists who, though associated with punk rock at the time, could scarcely be considered to have been punks at all – they espoused the principles described above from the outset of their careers. Some, such as Graham Parker and Ian Dury, had been investigating similar methods even before the emergence of punk; others, like Elvis Costello, absorbed its influence almost imperceptibly.

Costello contrived to retain his own identity as a performer in spite of the numerous musical and lyrical strains he derived from external sources. This was accomplished by harnessing diverse elements to correspond to his own intentions. Many of Costello's songs operate within narrow terms of reference, specifically his reaction to the vicissitudes of emotional relationships: while his responses taken on various forms, there is a marked absence of resignation and conciliation. More common are expressions of anger, resentment, aggression, and unrepentant self-interest. Steve Taylor (1980) has stated that Costello's lyrics 'attack the sexual mores of the last two decades from the embittered viewpoint of a jilted, nerve-jangled

victim, (p. 319), but we might add that the attack varies in character
depending on the guise of the protagonist.

Thus there is jubilation at the prospect of revenge in 'Pay It Back'
(*My Aim Is True* 1977), an added admission of self-disgust in 'Lipstick
Vogue' (*This Years's Model*, 1978), and a vacillation between feelings
of tenderness and violence in 'Alison' (*My Aim Is True*). The latter
song is remarkable for its economy of expression. The dismissal of
both marriage and sentimentality are clearly related to the singer's
frustration and jealousy: within a single line his impulse towards
aggression is counteracted, and complemented, by his continuing
infatuation – Costello's articulation of the words 'Sometimes I wish I
could *stop* you from talking when I hear the silly things you say'
translates, at the word 'stop', from harshness to dejection. This
relationship between apparent polar opposites is further emphasised
in the play on words of the refrain 'my aim is true' which implies both
the threat of vengeance and the sincerity of the protagonist's feelings.

Given the confines of Costello's approach to his subject matter, it
was entirely appropriate that he should have chosen to rely on an
undiluted rock instrumentation of guitar, keyboard, bass guitar, and
drums, and that he should have made musical reference to such
latently aggressive styles as punk and rock & roll. While his
integration of the former is on a relatively superficial level (as in 'No
Action' and 'Pump It Up', both from *This Year's Model*), his
invocation of the latter often operates on a more sophisticated level.
'Mystery Dance' (*My Aim Is True*) is in structure, sound, and
execution a re-creation of a rock & roll song, but that fact alone is
insufficient for Costello's purposes: the frustration of a protagonist
unable to relive his own nostalgia ties in perfectly with the idiom
employed. Elsewhere, his use of rock & roll tends to reinforce the
potential for a song's interpretation, as in the examples of
'Luxembourg' (from *Trust*, 1981) or 'Everyday I Write The Book'
(*Punch The Clock*, 1983) with its allusion to the Monotones' 'Book Of
Love' (1958). In other words, there is nothing gratuitous about
Costello's application of rock & roll: it is treated as an entirely viable
entity within his work.

Costello's relationship with country music seems to be rather more
ambiguous. Whilst he adapts it from time to time in the manner
described above (as, for example, in 'Different Finger' from the
album *Trust*), it is more difficult to devine the intention of a whole
album devoted almost completely to standard country material,

Almost Blue (1981). Although a degree of belligerence is present – for instance in the near-rockabilly rendition of Hank William's 'Why Don't You Love Me' or the reworking of Johnny Burnette's version of the Joe Turner composition 'Honey Hush' – the prevailing mood is one of melancholy. We might conclude that the project amounted to a labour of love; Costello's aptitude for premeditation may suggest it was the acknowledgement and/or fulfilment of the preoccupation with self-pity in his own work. A third possibility is that the album represented the recognition of the continuity inherent in pop music, rather as 'The Beat' had done on *This Year's Model*.

In the United States, there were few counterparts to Costello or any of the other British New Wave artists. For one think punk, although temporarily fashionable in New York and one or two other big cities, had failed to capture the imagination of the nation's rock enthusiasts. There was thus no context in which any equivalent progression to New Wave might develop. For another, the attention of record-buyers, concert-goers, and the attendant media had, by the late 1970s, become focused on the one native superstar to emerge during the period, Bruce Springsteen.

At the beginning of his career, numerous comparisons were made between Springsteen's work and that of Bob Dylan, but unless taken at the most superficial level such analogies appear to be ill-founded. By the time of Springsteen's first album, *Greetings From Asbury Park, N.J.* (1973), Dylan had been an established artist for over ten years and had undergone various changes of style, image, and subject. Thus while such items as 'Lost In The Flood' (*Asbury Park*) bear some resemblance to contemporary Dylan, it does not seem sensible to relate one or two albums of one artist to many years' worth of output by another. It is even difficult to extrapolate features characteristic of individual phases of Dylan's work and connect them directly to Springsteen's early recordings in the way that one might, for example, compare Elvis Costello's critical view of personal relationships with the Dylan of 'Like A Rolling Stone' or 'Positively 4th Street' (both 1965). There also appears to be little evidence to link Dylan and Springsteen in terms of vocal technique, the timbre of Springsteen's voice and his frequent use of vibrato more closely resembling that of – if anyone – Elvis Presley.

It is possible, however, to detect some correspondence between Springsteen's work as a whole and the themes of dissatisfaction and disillusion common in the rock music of the mid-1970s and beyond.

In this respect he was rightly associated with the British New Wave artists, who were also taking a similar approach to the presentation and execution of their material. There is nevertheless a clear contrast between Springsteen's songwriting method and that employed by, for example, Elvis Costello. While Costello writes from an entirely individual point of view, creating his own tableaux with little sense of time and place, Springsteen's compositions are less abstract. The listener's potential for complete identification with a Costello song is controlled by coincidence – in Springsteen's work it is almost unavoidable.

Springsteen normally writes in the first person, although we are unable to gain much insight into the personalities he assumes for his songs. He concentrates instead upon providing a narrative, frequently locating the action in a particular state, city, or – occasionally – a specific state or district. Examples are numerous, and include '4th Of July, Asbury Park', 'Incident On 57th Street', and 'New York City Serenade' (all from *The Wild, The Innocent And The E Street Shuffle*, 1974), 'Tenth Avenue Freeze-Out' and 'Jungleland' (*Born To Run*, 1975), 'Jackson Cage' and 'Hungry Heart' (*The River*, 1980), 'Darlington County' (*Born In The U.S.A.*, 1984), and, by implication, the complete contents of *Greetings From Asbury Park, N.J.* and *Nebraska* (1982).

Having set the scene, Springsteen extends the listener's identification of location to recognition of circumstances. In his earlier work, he focuses on adolescence, sometimes portraying innocent nostalgia as in 'Spirit In The Night' (*Asbury Park*) but more commonly alluding to the attractions of delinquency, as in 'It's Hard To Be A Saint In The City' (*Asbury Park*) and 'Jungleland', which takes the preoccupation with gang warfare to its inevitable violent conclusion, and, as such, typifies the new realism of the whole *Born To Run* album. We find, for example, songs confronting such subjects as drug-dealing (Meeting Across The River') and harsh working conditions ('Night'). Yet equally predominant is the yearning for escape from the constraints of poverty, dreariness, and inertia. While the central character of 'Night' obtains his freedom by remaining within the city, the protagonists of 'Born To Run' and 'Thunder Road' look forward to a new life elsewhere: in the first case the timing and destination are still uncertain, but in the second the prospect is more immediate.

Springsteen does not attempt to analyse the causes of oppression;

indeed there is a degree of passivity in his matter-of-fact acceptance of the social evils he describes. His interest lies in the consequences for the individual and the opportunities for eventual release. In this way his compositions recall those of the country blues singers, in whose work the 'protest' motive is virtually absent. This parallel becomes even stronger when one considers the manner in which Springsteen uses the images of day-to-day life to reinforce the authenticity of his songs. References to car travel, for example, permeate *The River*, supplying the framework for 'Cadillac Ranch', 'Stolen Car', 'Drive All Night', and 'Wreck On The Highway' among others, while 'Downbound Train' (*Born In The U.S.A.*) links the relentless momentum of the locomotive with the inevitable decline of the protagonist's fortunes. Similarly, 'The River' (from the eponymous album) represents a sanctuary where suffering can be temporarily washed away.

The result of such methods is that Springsteen's songs are characterised by an almost universal application: environment, theme, and imagery are uniformly related to the familiar and the ordinary. Throughout, individuals are portrayed sympathetically in their losing battle to overcome forces over which they have no control. As such, his work reaffirms the relevance of the picaresque tradition in American culture.

It is therefore hardly surprising that Springsteen has avoided any attempts at musical innovation. It is essential to his purpose that his songs be set in an appropriately recognisable idiom, that no pretensions to progress or instrumental complexity hinder the potential for mass communication. Though generically a rock singer, Springsteen has drawn increasingly upon rock & roll as the medium to suit his needs. *Born To Run* shows a close correspondence with the work of Phil Spector, the 'wall-of-sound' production reflecting the urban concerns of the lyrics. *The River*, on the other hand, relates to earlier strains of rock & roll: the impression given is of a collection of songs recorded in one take with, excepting the occasional use of echo, the minimum of studio technology. Heavy back-beat is employed at various times, most notably in 'Hungry Heart', 'I Wanna Marry You', 'Cadillac Ranch', and 'Ramrod' which is particularly evocative of the 1950s with its simple organ riff and lyrical idea of the emancipation to be derived from car ownership. The band sound on many tracks, with its tenor saxophone-and-rhythm emphasis, recalls that employed by Gary 'U.S.' Bonds for his 1961 hit on Legrand, 'Quarter To Three'.

After the acoustic departure of *Nebraska*, Springsteen returned to rock & roll for *Born In The U.S.A.* Again, extensive use is made of the off-beat rhythmic stress: it assists the anthem-like nature of the title track while complementing the message of 'Glory Days', itself a warning against the dangers of over-indulgence in nostalgia. With this album, however, Springsteen alludes to the influence of country music upon rock & roll, most notably in the rockabilly character of 'Working On The Highway' and in the ballad 'I'm On Fire' where the prevailing mood is one of sentimentality.

It is difficult to determine the extent to which such artists as Bruce Springsteen and Elvis Costello were governed by the return to fundamental pop music principles during the mid-1970s. What *is* clear is that they have both demonstrated the durability of rock & roll, not through indiscriminate imitation, but by a process of careful assimilation, allowing for a greater freedom to express their individual, if contrasting, concerns.

Pop music is, by nature, susceptible to change – certainly to a much greater degree than, say, jazz or classical music. The pressures applied by successive generations of teenagers, and the businessmen who depended on them for their livelihood, have, since the mid-1950s, accelerated a progression that had originally been dictated by such factors as the transmission of regional variations via population movement in the United States. No music could produce the amount of genuine innovations required to cater for such demands. It is therefore not surprising that we are able to identify particular stylistic features that have been periodically recycled and reworked. Commonly, this involves the almost unconscious absorption by an artist of a performance (invariably a recording) or series of performances during his formative years. In this manner a complex of influences is built up which defines his work as distinctive and, occasionally, as innovative.

Throughout the evolution of the music it is possible to detect an underlying continuity composed of certain key aspects of theme (especially the use of the picaresque, from the Delta blues singers, via Dylan, to Bowie, Costello and Springsteen) and technique, where we might point to the essential pop music elements of voice and guitar. We have already noted, for example, how Bob Dylan employed the 'talking' style of Mississippi blues artist Bukka White and others (see Chapter 4). It became evident during the 1960s that a vocal technique using wide variations of range and pitch was potentially unsuitable for pop and was more conducive to success in the opera or popular music field, hence the revival in the 1970s of Dylan's 'flat' vocal delivery by Bryan Ferry, Elvis Costello, and the like. We might contrast this process with the way in which the methods of playing electric guitar have fluctuated since the 1950s. The close relationship between guitar solo and rhythm in rock & roll has once again become apparent in the 1980s, and has superseded the predilection of rock guitarists, who derived their technique from that of the urban blues players, for creating their own rhythmic variations while soloing. Similarly, the staccato style of guitar-playing has been reintroduced at the expense of the concentration on sustain, especially in the top register, so prevalent in the late 1960s and early 1970s.

Technology, which once played a crucial role in the formation of pop music by assisting the dissemination of American regional styles throughout the country as a whole, now has a more direct bearing on the nature of the music produced. It is now possible, using a synthesiser, to simulate the sound of any musical instrument, and this facility has been widely indulged in during the 1980s, appearing to some observers to threaten the continued existence of pop itself. Some musicians, however, notably Bruce Springsteen, have refused to make use of the new technology merely because it is available, and it may be that the synthesiser will meet the same fate as the electronic organ, hailed in the late 1950s as a panacea but destined for a sharp decline in popularity. We may find that the presence of a drum-machine will, in future years, date a recording as having a '1980s sound', just as we can now locate by aural evidence the time period in which the recordings of previous eras were made. Above all, we are consoled by the fact that people still enjoy learning to play musical instruments: anxieties about the impending death of pop music might yet prove premature.

Appendix A

Musical analysis

This appendix has the purpose of providing a *written* explication of the evolution of pop as a musical tradition. As such it will concentrate upon the musical parameters of that tradition, in terms of those structures and elements which characterise it. This will involve the careful description of the blues-boogie-gospel family, the first and founding generation of pop, for it was in that family of musics that the parameters of pop were given form. And, like any sociomusical tradition, pop music owes its coherence *as* a tradition to the musical elements and structures which provide its musical parameters, thus distinguishing it from other traditions.

Essentially, pop is distinguishable from other traditions, such as popular music and jazz, because it characteristically employs certain melodic, harmonic, rhythmic and lyrical patterns (i.e. structures) in the construction of songs. That is, the various types and sub-types of pop involve characteristic chord and melodic sequences, plus lyrical forms and rhythms, which together serve as their identifying characteristics. Thus Delta blues is characterised by its employment of the 'blues pentatonic' mode, its unique use of the I to VIIdim. (or IIIdim.) melodic harmonic sequence and its common twelve-bar AAB stanza form. And rock & roll is characterised, in part, by its use of boogie melodic and harmonic sequences and its gospel-derived 'off-beat' rhythmic stress.

Sociomusicologists typically combine the orientations of musical theory and musicology, as traditionally practised, with the cultural orientations of ethnomusicology. That is, 'musical theory' – a term used in art music to denote the structure of musical pieces, or types – is combined with 'musicology' – traditionally seen as the study of musical history. And together they are used as tools for the provision of rigorous descriptions of music as a cultural product.

In order to describe the characteristic structures (therefore the parameters) of pop music's evolution, we shall use a number of methods of measuring the *melodic, harmonic* and *rhythmic* (as well as the *lyrical*) aspects of that music.

In our description of the melodic structures we shall employ the criteria of 'mode' (i.e. the *actual* scale, or number of tones, used), 'tonal prevalence' (i.e. measurement of those tones most and least employed) and, most importantly, 'tonal sequencing' ('melodic contours'), which details the construction of melodies in terms of their characteristics of tonal patterning.

Modes, tonal prevalence scales and melodic contours

A mode is the selection of two or more notes from the seven making up the diatonic scale (see Figure 1),

Figure 1: The diatonic scale (in the key of C major).

or from the twelve available in the chromatic scale – which includes the half-steps of C#, D#, F#, G# and A# that are omitted from the diatonic C major key.

Some musical types typically use a particular scale of less than seven tones. Among these is the Delta blues, in which many songs are either in the 'Delta blues pentatonic' or in modifications of that mode (see Figure 2).

Figure 2: The Delta blues pentatonic (in E major)

Thus country blues numbers (and many of the modern blues songs derived from them) can be readily identified by means of their modal construction. This has led to the employment of the term 'blue-notes' in the characterisation of this musical type: a method of description which is oriented towards the way in which *some* blues songs use a scale which differs from those conceived within a diatonic framework.

Those songs and musical pieces which belong to the 'boogie' (or 'boogie-woogie') sub-type cannot, however, be recognised in terms of their modal characteristics. This is because boogies typically use all the notes in the diatonic scale. The boogie can, in fact, be regarded as a particular and novel employment of the diatonic major triads, in that it consists of what may be called a melodic adaptation of basic diatonic harmonic 'theory'. By this is meant that in boogie numbers, including vocal and instrumental pieces, the basic diatonic triads provide a template for melodic sequencing. Thus the basic chords (triads) of, for instance, G major (see Figure 3)

Figure 3

are played sequentially, instead of simultaneously, thus providing the chords seen in Figure 4.

Figure 4

As boogie melodies do not have characteristic modes (i.e. actual scales) they are best evaluated according to their tonal prevalence and tonal sequencing structures. 'Tonal prevalence' is ascertained by what has become known as 'stem counting'. This involves, as it implies, simply a count of the number of stems of each note, thus producing a measurement of the prevalence of each tone. Taking as an example the music shown in Figure 4 we get a count of

G = 2, A = 1, B = 1, C = 1, D = 2, E = 1, F# = 1

This count yields an 'order of prevalence' which, as commonly expressed, equals

$$G + D > A + B + C + E + F\#$$

(where '>' means 'occurs more often than')

for the notes in Figure 4.

From such a short piece of music we obviously derive a rather inconsequential result. But, as we shall demonstrate, this measurement can be very revealing when stanzas from two or more song examples are used as the materials for investigation.

To illustrate boogie structure in terms of tonal prevalence and sequencing we can use a typical stanza (verse), derived from the template shown in Figure 4, which is often used in rock & roll and rhythm & blues records as an accompaniment to the vocal – examples are Fats Domino's 'Ain't That A Shame' (1955) and 'Blueberry Hill' (1956) (see Figure 5).

Figure 5

The count for the twelvebars in Figure 5 is

$$G = 19, A = 1, B = 8, C = 6, D = 10, E = 3 \text{ and } F\# = 1$$

From this we get the order of prevalence

$$G > D > B > C > E > A + F\#$$

'Melodic contours', which are a simple but effective method of highlighting characteristics of tonal sequencing, are nothing more than the reduction of a transcription (or part of the same) to a line which shows changes of pitch over the course of the musical item, or items, to be analysed. The first line (four bars) of Figure 5, shown as a melodic contour, looks as follows:

(Nb '————' denotes the keynote line)

Melodic contour maps are very useful in comparisons of musical 'shape'; that is, the types of ascending and descending curves which characterise the products of musical traditions.

Harmony and rhythm

As much of the 'folk' music from which pop is derived was modal – that is, designed to be song-unaccompanied and, where more than one voice was used, in unison, it is no wonder that melody is a stronger orientation for pop musicians than is harmony. Much of the modal approach to music has, for instance, been preserved via the country blues. An aspect of this in the Delta blues is the use of the guitar as a 'second voice' echoing the tones carried by the vocal or providing inversions of them.

However, a common method (particularly among jazz and popular music writers) of describing the harmonic structure of 'twelve-bar blues' *does* serve as an harmonic rendering of many boogie pieces – including that of Figure 5. This 'harmonic shorthand' usually looks like Figure 6.

Figure 6

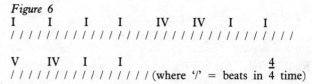

Among members of pop bands such harmonic shorthands are regularly used as 'quasi-arrangements'; that is, as a rough guide to the instrumental accompaniment required for particular musical pieces.

Previous to the research published here, boogie, as a sub-type, has ubiquitously been distinguished in rhythmic terms. Sometimes it has been referred to as a 'fast blues' – though at least in much of Jimmy Yancey's work this is a misnomer – and as typically being 'eight (beats) to the bar'. Boogie, or at least piano-based boogie-woogie, *is* usually played at a faster tempo than the average country blues. But more important is probably the use of eighth notes in combination with quarter notes, which from the early thirties onwards developed the syncopation and stress which later came to be associated with rock & roll. The off-beat 'feel' so essential to rock & roll is often understated in piano boogie. In the early days it was more prominent in country gospel and many varieties of hillbilly than in boogie-woogie. And by the late thirties it was to be found even in the Delta blues, through the work of Robert Johnson. All these developments combined boogie melodic patterns (or boogie patterns modified by Delta patterns) with syncopations organised around off-beat stress. This characteristic combination of quarter notes ( ) with eighth notes ( ), producing a 12/8 feel to the music, is illustrated in Figure 7.

Figure 7

The pattern in Figure 7 has provided a template for many pop numbers, particularly in the rock & roll sphere. It forms the basis, for instance, for the piano introduction to Joe Turner's 'Shake, Rattle & Roll' (1954) and the main theme of Bill Doggett's 'Honky Tonk' (1956). But an early utilisation of the pattern can be found in Robert Johnson's 'From Four Untill Late' (1937) (Figure 8).

Figure 8: 'From Four Untill Late' – Robert Johnson

'From Four Untill Late' was Johnson's version of a song family which is probably best known through Leroy Carr's version of it – his 'Midnight Hour Blues' (1932). Charley Patten also recorded adaptions of it; 'Tom Rushen Blues' (1929) and 'High Sheriff Blues' (1934). And Frank 'Springback' James cut a piano-accompanied version called 'Will My Bad Luck Ever Change?' in 1936. Musically, the song family seems to be distantly related to the old 'joint-stock' family of 'Betty And Dupree'. But what is most likely is that both melodic patterns stem from the period when the then new diatonic musical practices were encroaching upon the traditional modal folk musics.

Both 'Betty And Dupree' and the 'Midnight Hour'/'From Four Untill Late' family are closely related, in terms of melodic structure, to that melodic pattern known as the "boogie walking-bass' figure. This pattern was gradually adapted, first by blues musicians and latterly by rock & roll performers and composers, as both a vocal and a lead instrumental pattern. Though there are many variations on the walking-bass pattern, the 'logic' of its melodic development provides for ascending phrases followed by descending ones (thus the concept of 'walking' up and down the scale). These patterns involve movements from the first (tonic) of the scale, through the third (mediant) to the fifth (dominant) to the sixth (submediant), then descending via the same steps. The pattern is then repeated, but with the fourth (subdominant) acting as the base (instead of the tonic), and finally with the fifth (dominant), or one of the tones in the dominant triad, becoming the base. Figure 9 is an example of the walking-bass pattern.

Figure 9

The sequential arrangement of the walking-bass boogie was a standard structure by the time pop music was born. The many modifications, include those which merely *imply* part of the structure (such as the first two steps of the initial ascent – the first two notes in Figure 9). Many of the modifications of the boogie structures involved their combination with tones, figures, phrases and structures we now associate with Delta blues.

The two musics have many areas of structural compatibility, whilst having as many points where they represent very different approaches to musical construction. They both, for instance, have a strong tendency to use pitch changes involving steps in thirds (e.g. first to third, to fifths, etc.), yet boogie is, at least loosely, based upon the diatonic scale whilst Delta blues has strong orientations toward a 'pre-diatonic' pentatonic mode. The boogie conception has thus contributed a great deal, if not most, of the harmonic practices common to pop music, whilst country blues has contributed an approach to melody unlike any other in *modern* Western music.

In the evolution of pop these two sub-types, boogie and country blues, have been so closely related that they are best thought of as two parts of a musical complex from the point of view of the pop historian and musicologist. In fact the many ways in which they have appeared as distinct *and* in combination brings as close to the central mechanism of pop development as it is possible, at present, to reach.

The boogie-blues complex

There are many early recordings which are not only called 'blues' but which also exhibit all of the typicalities associated with country (even Delta) blues except their mode. One of these is Richard 'Rabbit' Brown's 'James Alley Blues' (1927). Brown's number is in the major key throughout, and uses truncated boogie walking-bass patterns as its melody. The first verse of the song employs an abbreviated *ascending* walking-base figure for its initial four bars, whilst in other verses (including Verse 8) it uses part of the *de*scending figure for those bars. These are given in Figure 10.

Figure 10: 'James Alley Blues' (fragments of Verses 1 and 8)

Verse 1:

Oh times ain't now   nothin' like they used_ to be   etc

Verse 8:

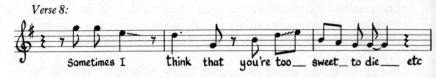

Other songs combined the melodic properties of boogie and blues. A particularly important method of boogie-blues melody construction, throughout pop history, is that which uses the modulation of the major scale at the third and/or the seventh. That is the walking-bass figure (as in Figure 9) is used but the third (mediant) and the seventh (the 'leading note') are 'flatted'. Often this figure begins its ascent at the fifth (dominant) note of the scale, rather than the first (tonic): then moving through the sixth to the 'flatted' (i.e. minor) seventh (see Figure 11). This particular modification is especially interesting in that commencing a melody with the fifth note of the (diatonic) scale is a very common feature of Delta blues.

Figure 11: Boogie-blues melodic progression

Often the tonic (in this case E) is inserted at points marked ' △ ' as a base 'drone'. Such an addition to Figure 11 would, for instance, produce something very close to a transcription of Bill Doggett's 'Honky Tonk' (1956).

This progression permeates pop music from the twenties to the eighties. It is the basic figure in, for instance, John Hurt's 'Got The Blues, Can't Be Satisfied' (1928) (Figure 12).

Figure 12: 'Got The Blues, Can't Be Satisfied' (first line)

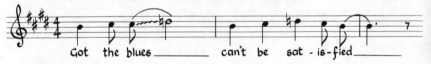

Elmore James used the same progression for his 'Shake Your Moneymaker' (1961). It was an important progression in the work of Presley, Chuck Berry, and many others, in the rock & roll era.

Interestingly, it was used to great effect by Dion for his 'Ruby Baby' (1963) to provide one of the last examples of classic rock & roll; and, more recently, by Bruce Springsteen as the basic pattern for his 'The River' (1980), in which he commences with the tonic and moves to the flatted third (via the major second), and for his 'Downbound Train' (1984).

The progression seems, however, to predate the pop era. It is a prominent feature in the joint-ballad 'John Henry', for instance: an early recording (1927) of which, by a band called the Williamson Brothers and Curry, who called it 'Gonna Die With My Hammer In My Hand', is transcribed for Figure 13.

Figure 13: 'Gonna Die With My Hammer In My Hand' (first 5 bars)

The progression also found favour with Jimmie Rodgers. It is featured, for instance, in his 'Train Whistle Blues' (1929?) (Figure 14).

Figure 14: 'Train Whistle Blues' (first 3 bars)

The analysis of songs having the aim of determining the relative weight of boogie to blues components usually requires both the tonal prevalence and tonal sequencing methods. In a comparison of boogie and Delta blues structures, for instance, the tonal prevalence counts should be very different. Thus the boogie walking-bass given in Figure 9 has a tonal prevalence scale of

$$G+D+E>B>>A+C>F\#$$
(Where '>>' is an intensifier of '>'.)

This is as expected for any boogie structure wherein the first, fourth and fifth tones of the diatonic scale are of great importance. But fairly prevalent also is the second (A), and even more prominent is the sixth (E), neither of which are of *great* importance in Delta blues structures.

An analysis of a randomly selected sample of forty-five Delta and Delta-derived Chicago blues tracks yielded a tonal prevalence scale of

$$G>B^b>F>C+D>>E>>F\#$$

Blues structures

Beginning, as we have, by limiting our subject matter to songs which can reasonably be thought of as 'country blues', that is, those with the least musical connections with vaudeville and jazz blues, renders the resulting range of materials a great deal more manageable, and also more homogenous. The distinction between boogie and Delta blues melodic structures also contributes to this homogeneity. Yet unless we limit our analysis to a straightforward comparison between boogie and Delta blues (as in the above tonal prevalence scales) we are still faced with a complex set of structures.

A number of writers have argued for the existence of a *general* 'blues scale' (or 'mode'). Baker (1973), for instance, gives this as that in Figure 15.

Figure 15: 'Blues scale' (Baker (1973), p. 13)

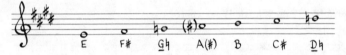

Yet in terms of the 'blues' available on record this mode itself appears to hold an optional status. In our sample of just over 200 blues transcriptions the major thirds and major sevenths (G# and D#) occur almost as often as their minor forms, and more often than does the leading note, or second (i.e. F#). Our research in this area is in agreement with that of Titon who states that, of all the tones in the major and minor scales, 'Least important, but significant none the less, are the 2nd note and its octave' (1977, p. 156).

Blues fans and writers often propose a 'blues pentatonic' mode, particularly in connection with the Delta blues. This is usually similar to that given in Figure 2.

Though a fair number of Delta blues use a scale only slightly divergent from the pentatonic, Robert Johnson's 'Travelin' Riverside Blues' (1937) and other members of the 'Minglewood Blues' family being prominent among these, the pentatonic mode is not, as it stands, a very useful guide to blues scales as used on record. It is probably more rewarding, from an analytical point of view, to treat the combination of the major, minor, blues and blues-pentatonic modes as allowing a series of options for modulation and, therefore, experimentation. Thus a blues musician can modify the major scale via minor modulation, extend the pentatonic by moving to the major, and so on.

Much of the confusion surrounding 'blues modes' stems from the ubiquitous discussion, in blues and jazz circles, on the topic of 'blue-notes'. These phenomena are the 'flatted', or minor, thirds and sevenths of the scale (as given, for instance, in Baker's 'blues scale', Figure 15). A great deal of the discussion concerning 'blue-notes' centres on their exact manifestation in blues. They have been described in terms of 'microtones', 'slurs' and 'complexes', as well as 'flatted' and 'minor' tones, over the years. However, all of these terms describe some examples of the phenomenon, with a reasonable degree of accuracy. Titon's notion of 'complexes' (1977, p. 155 *et passim*) has the merit of being both explicit and reasonable. It describes, via transcriptions, the relevant notes as a series of microtonal availabilities (see Figure 16).

Figure 16: 'Blue-notes' as tone-complexes: the G-complex

In this method of transcription the arrows ➤ ➤ indicate that the actual pitch is somewhat less than a semitone above or below the position shown. The ~ device indicates a slurred tone, either between two notes, or a microtonal vibrato around a single note.

The actual mode used for blues is, of course, affected crucially by the choice of alternatives within the third and seventh note complexes. And many factors are involved in such compositional, cum improvisational, choices. The structure of the lyric, particularly the number of syllables contained, is an important factor, as is the basic rhythm of the piece. There are, of course, innumerable other factors involved, most of which act in combination.

A basic compositional element in blues is that of the melodic phrase. As in boogie, blues phrases act rather like prescribed routes from one part of the territory to another. Within a musical tradition such as the blues, routes of different statuses and purposes can be discerned, much like train and road, including main *and* secondary routes in transportation.

Four of the most common phrases to be found in Delta blues are transcribed in Figure 17.

Figure 17: Delta blues melodic phrases

The recorded work of Robert Johnson, as well as that of Charley Patton, Blind Lemon Jefferson, and many other blues 'giants', provides a great deal of evidence to suggest that country blues, as a musical tradition, should be described as a continuum stretching from the pentatonic (or quasi-pentatonic) Delta blues to the songs with a 'blues' form married to a boogie structure, as instanced by 'James Alley Blues' (see Figure 10).

In between these two poles reside the various mixtures of blues and boogie structures, and, giving another dimension to the model, those blues which are combined with country ragtime structures.

In terms of being a source of 'recipes-for-song-production' the boogie-blues continuum has thus always combined elasticity with clarity as a song-producing model. In other words, the structural alternatives within the continuum are more than adequate in number without this resulting in an indistinct tradition wherein 'anything goes' in terms of compositional structures. In fact most of the alternative choices for blues composition are linked to each other. Thus certain rhythmic patterns 'fit in' with particular melodic structures, and *vice versa*. This also applies to the relationships between lyrical and melodic structures, and so on. Also the tonal prevalences and melodic contours of songs composed within a boogie structure limit the ways blues musicians may provide them with pentatonic modulations. A very good example of this is provided by the various recorded versions of the song 'Sitting On Top Of The World'. The original, as recorded by the Mississippi Sheiks (1930), was in a straightforward major key, with the melody beginning on the keynote (tonic). Such a melodic contour rules out modifications initiated by the fifth or flatted seventh notes of the scale (which have always been popular as the initial notes among Delta musicians). Thus Delta bluesmen like Robert Johnson and Howling Wolf would modify the melody by flattening the thirds and sevenths. Figure 18 gives the melody as a major key melody, whilst indicating the points where Delta-style modifications could be made.

Figure 18: 'Sitting On Top Of The World' in E major – with optional melodic variations

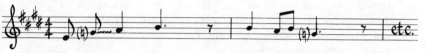

(Where (♮) indicates tones which are likely to be played as 'naturals' by some blues musicians.)

The structural elasticity of the blues-boogie complex, and the many diverse approaches this allowed, has probably been the key factor in its persistence as an important musical tradition. As our title *From Blues To Rock* indicates, the history of pop music can be adequately summed up by detailing the various mergers of types of blues and boogies. Thus we get country blues, hillbilly blues (*à la* Jimmie Rodgers), boogie-blues and rhythm and blues, rock & roll and soul, and finally the rock musics from the sixties onwards, as an evolutionary map of pop from its inception to the present.

On the whole the blues-boogie-gospel family has, with the exception of the rock & roll revolution, changed very little in sixty-odd years. And this is almost certainly due to the extremely important emphasis upon subtlety in that tradition. Very *small* additions to, and modifications of, the 'state of the art' have seemed revolutionary at the time, and *usually* (rather than occasionally) have taken years to be properly worked out in practice. In some cases (instances are the contributions of Charley Patton, Blind Lemon Jefferson, Robert Johnson and Muddy Waters), these small but important modifications to the tradition's musical potential have still to be adequately worked out. Certainly, nobody has really attempted to carry further the compositional and instrumental ideas begun by Robert Johnson. It is therefore *not* so surprising that blues numbers originating in the twenties and thirties were recorded virtually in the manner of 'belated cover-versions' by rock bands in the sixties and seventies, without seeming archaic to their new audience.

The subtlety of the blues-boogie-gospel structures is well illustrated by the way song-family development exploited the variety of melodic, rhythmic, harmonic and lyrical elements and structures compatible with the song to be developed. Country blues (and its musical kin) can be said to have, as its compositional elements, components we may call 'thematic phrases'. These elements are melodic, lyrical, rhythmic and harmonic. They are also instrumental and 'executional' (where we mean to indicate not only instrumental choice but also methods of playing the instruments chosen). 'Executional' choice and the interdependence of phrase choice are well illustrated by the song-family which is usually known as 'Poor Boy Long Ways From Home' (or the 'Poor Boy' family). Though this family produced a great variety of versions (members) it is remarkable how many involved 'bottleneck' guitar accompaniment. Also the various members could be linked via either lyrical phrases, or melodic (accompanying) phrases, which provided thematic links. Lyrically the 'poor boy' theme became linked with train/general picaresque (i.e. 'long ways from home') themes. And an accompanying phrase structure seems to have become a universally recognised 'Poor Boy' instrumental theme by the mid to late twenties (though 'universal' in this context includes only those within the country blues community). (See Figure 19.)   *Figure 19*: The 'Poor Boy' instrumental theme

Both Furry Lewis and Frank Hutchison used the theme as an introduction and 'fill-in' on their versions of the 'Cannonball Blues' (see Figures 24 and 25), as did Willie McTell on his 'Love Changing Blues' (1929). And Bukka White used an inversion of the theme for the melody of the chorus on his part-instrumental 'Panama Limited' (1930) (see Figure 20).

Figure 20: Chorus of 'Panama Limited' – Bukka White

Some of the earliest recorded versions of the 'Poor Boy' theme show both its versatility and its typical exploitation of the boogie-blues musical range. Gus Cannon's 'Poor Boy Long Ways From Home' (1927) presents the song in a straight major form (see Figure 21).

Figure 21: 'Poor Boy Long Ways From Home' – Gus Cannon

'Poor Boy Blues' by Willard 'Ramblin' Thomas (1928), on the other hand, is one of the few versions recorded in the pentatonic mode (see Figure 22).

Figure 22: 'Poor Boy Blues' – Ramblin' Thomas

Willie McTell's 'Mama 'T'ain't Long Fo' Day' (1927) uses a truncated 'Poor Boy' figure as the melody line (see Figure 23).

Figure 23: 'Mama 'T'ain't Long Fo' Day' – Willie McTell

Whereas many of the 'train-song' developments, particularly the 'Cannonball Blues' variety, tended to use the 'Poor Boy' riff as either a vocal chorus or guitar embellishment (sometimes thought of as a 'second-voice'). The latter method is exemplified by both Frank Hutchison's and Walter 'Furry' Lewis' versions. Both use the 'Poor Boy' riff (as Figure 20) as a guitar theme whilst employing inversions of the riff as the vocal line (see Figures 24 and 25).

Figure 24: 'Cannon Ball Blues' – Frank Hutchison

Figure 25: Cannonball Blues – Furry Lewis

The various members of the 'Poor Boy' family thus exhibit a range of modes; one fitting our proposed boogie–blues continuum, as they range from the blues pentatonic (e.g. 'Poor Boy Blues' by Ramblin' Thomas) to the boogie-structured major mode (e.g. 'Mama 'Tain't Long Fo' Day' by Willie McTell).

The members of the 'Minglewood Blues'/'Rollin' & Tumbling' family exhibit a similar range, though with some bias towards the pentatonic and minor modes. This bias is typified by three of the earliest recorded versions of the song family, by Gus Cannon's Jug Stompers, 'Hambone' Willie Newbern and Charley Patton (see Figures 26, 27 and 28).

Figure 26: 'Minglewood Blues' – Gus Cannon's Jug Stompers

Figure 27: 'Roll and Tumble Blues' – Willie Newbern

Figure 28: 'It Won't Be Long' – Charley Patton

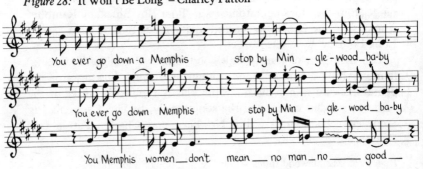

Later versions differed from those detailed here mainly in terms of rhythm and instrumentation. Robert Johnson's 'Traveling Riverside Blues' (1937), for instance, is in 12/8 time, though his melody is very close to those of Cannon and Patton, whilst his guitar accompaniment, for this and for most of his recordings, owes as much to the style of Willie Newbern (as illustrated on 'Roll & Tumble') as to any of his predecessors. After Johnson the off-beat syncopation he developed became the normal rhythmic approach to this as to many other blues and boogie songs. Whether Johnson received his concept of syncopation (which was unusual for Delta bluesmen) directly from gospel, or even from hillbilly or 'western swing' recordings (or live performances) may never be known. Certainly there were contemporaries of his in Mississippi, though not in the Delta area as far as we know, who, by the thirties, were mixing blues and boogie structures with gospel syncopation. In the south of Mississippi, for instance, the Graves Brothers (Roosevelt and Uaroy) made a number of records which show their profound ignorance of (or disinterest in) Delta blues, but which also showed that they were brilliant musicians, with a penchant for doing imitations (perhaps even caricatures) of run-of-the-mill vaudeville blues singers (complete with imitation female vocal tones) and, more interestingly for our present subject matter, also for doing both gospel numbers which seem to have been in the most up-to-date style, in terms of their syncopation, and for producing numbers which merged these rhythms with boogie melodic and lyrical elements – thus producing what must be thought of as proto-rock & roll.

The interactions between blues, boogie and gospel intensified during the forties and fifties. In the case of many rhythm & blues records of the early and middle fifties the blues-boogie-gospel mix seems to use each 'ingredient' in an almost ideal way. In this period, it is important to remember, records by Sam Cooke and the Soul Stirrers, by the Staple Singers, and a number of other groups, could hardly be distinguished from secular records by people such as Ray Charles, Bobby Bland and, very shortly, Sam Cooke himself. Whether, as one soul fan we interviewed told us, 'rock & roll was just a bi-product of black people developing soul music' (an idea which would not, we feel, find too much support from either Chuck Berry or Bo Diddley), certainly the difference between sacred and profane musics seemed, during the fifties and sixties, to be slight.

Ray Charles gradually developed, during his years at Atlantic, a very interesting, and eventually financially successful blend of blues, gospel, rock & roll and rockabilly elements. Also, of course, he was closely associated with the 'soul' movement in modern jazz. In 1959, just before he left Atlantic records, Charles produced what many critics think of as his masterpiece – the double-sided single 'What'd I Say'. The vocal style of the track is taken from gospel vocalising, the melodic progressions are derived from Delta blues, as, it would seem, is the rhythm, which is syncopated yet on the 'on-beat' – a very unusual phenomenon for Atlantic Records in the fifties. This syncopation is particularly noticeable in the solo guitar introduction with which the track begins (see Figure 29).

Figure 29: 'What'd I Say' – introduction (fragment)

The introduction of the piano, with an off-beat syncopation, provides a neat polyrhythmic effect.

It was particularly the rhythmic experimentation and improvisation of the gospel-rhythm & blues complex that characterised the important soul records of the sixties and seventies. Thus Aretha Franklin's magnificent 'I Never Loved A Man' (1967), as a prime example, was a blues in terms of its melodic progressions, yet was sung with the rhythmic emphasis and the vocal inflections derived from gospel musicianship (see Figure 30).

Figure 30: 'I Never Loved A Man' – Aretha Franklin

Yet another great blues *singer*, whose career began prior to both that of Ray Charles and that of Aretha Franklin, yet was to receive most of his public acclaim after theirs had 'peaked', provided, during the fifties, sixties and seventies, a different model of blues perfomance, and one which had a profound effect upon the *rock* music of the sixties and seventies. This was Muddy Waters. As a musician his reputation suffered, like that of Blind Lemon Jefferson and Sam Hopkins before him, from his constant availability. Yet his mastery of the blues vocal, a greatly underrated art, could be matched by few of those still recording in his last three decades. Perhaps he could not reproduce the brilliance of Robert Johnson's guitar work, and he never quite achieved the song-writing brilliance of Son House, but his vocal ability, like Aretha Franklin's, was at times very close to perfection. The techniques of blues singing in the Delta-Chicago 'downhome', style is illustrated well by Muddy's 1951 recording of 'Long Distance Call'. The song, with its melodic echoes of the Delta and the singer's role of bridging the gap between the early days of pop musicians like Charley Patton and Robert Johnson and the explosion of Delta-influenced 'blues-rock' in the sixties, through the work of the Rolling Stones, Eric Clapton and Cream, the Grateful Dead, Canned Heat, and others, makes it a fitting item with which to conclude our explication of pop music – from blues to rock.

Figure 31: 'Long Distance Call' (final verse)

Appendix B

Discography

Records are listed according to their importance to the arguments contained in the book. We have listed only issues believed to be currently available and likely to remain in catalogue for a reasonable amount of time. For those readers who do not have easy access to record stores which stock a wide range, the following mail-order firms are suggested:

Red Lick Records, P.O. Box 3, Porthmadog, Gwynedd, Wales

Blackmail Records, 170 Hainton Avenue, Grimsby, South Humberside DN32 9LJ

Rapid Records Ltd, P.O. Box 325, London E1 8DS

Down Home Music, 10341 San Pablo Avenue, El Cerrito, California 94530, USA

Where individual tracks given prominence in the text do not feature on albums, these are available as reissued singles, or in some cases in their original form. All albums listed are single-LP issues except where a figure is given in parentheses, indicating the number of records in the set.

The Mississippi Blues (1927–1940) Origin OJL 5

Includes the only two widely-available commercial recordings by Willie Brown ('Future Blues' and 'M. & O. Blues'), together with Bukka White's 'Panama Limited', Skip James's 'Hard Time Killing Floor Blues', and Son House's 'Preaching The Blues' Parts One and Two.

Ragtime Blues Guitar 1928–30 Matchbox MSE 204

Contains 'Old Country Rock' by William Moore, 'Brownie Blues' by Tarter and Gay, Bayless Rose's 'Jamestown Exposition', 'Black Dog Blues', 'Original Blues', and 'Frisco Blues', and 'Dupree Blues' by Willie Walker.

Mr Charlie's Blues Yazoo L 1024
Includes Larry Henseley's 'Match Box Blues' and Dick Justice's 'Black Dog Blues' and 'Cocaine'.
20 Of The Best Jimmie Rodgers RCA International WL 89370
A Collection Of Mountain Blues County 511
Contains 'Cannon Ball Blues' by Frank Hutchison, 'Johnson City Blues' by Clarence Greene, 'Brownskin Blues' by Dick Justice, and 'Careless Love' by Jimmy Tarleton.
The King Of The Delta Blues Singers Volumes One and Two (2) Robert Johnson CBS Blue Diamond 22190

Country Blues: The First Generation Matchbox MSE 201
Includes 'Don't You Leave Me Here' by Papa Harvey Hull and Long Cleve Reed and 'James Alley Blues' by Richard ('Rabbit') Brown.
In The Spirit Volume One Origin OJL 12
Contains 'I Am Bound For The Promised Land' by Alfred G. Karnes.
Roots Of Rock Yazoo L 1063
See Chapter 6.
King Of The Country Blues (2) Blind Lemon Jefferson Yazoo L 1069
Founder Of The Delta Blues (2) Charley Patton Yazoo L 1020
Furry Lewis In His Prime 1927–29 Yazoo L 1050
Tommy Johnson (1928–30) Complete Recordings Wolf WSE 104
20 Of The Best Carter Family RCA International WL 89369
The Piano Blues Volume One (Paramount) Magpie PY 4401
Includes Little Brother Montgomery's 'Vickburg Blues', Louise Johnson's 'All Night Long', and James Wiggins's 'Forty Four Blues'. Other albums in this series are also of interest.
Muddy Waters (2) Chess CXMD 4000
The Sun Collection Elvis Presley RCA NL 42757
Elvis Is Back Elvis Presley RCA SF 5060
Original Golden Hits Carl Perkins Sun 111
Motorvatin' Chuck Berry Chess CXMP 2011
New Orleans Rock 'n' Roll (3) Fats Domino Pathe Marconi 155 183
The Ray Charles Story Volume One Atlantic 40264
The Ray Charles Story Volume Two Atlantic 40265
This Is Sam Cooke RCA DPS 2007
A Shot Of Rhythm And Soul Arthur Alexander Ace CH 66
The Very Best Of Eddie Cochran Liberty FA 3019
Rock 'n' Roll Music Volume One Beatles Music For Pleasure MFP 5056

Please Please Me Beatles Parlophone PCS 3042
Bob Dylan CBS 32001
The Freewheelin' Bob Dylan CBS 62193
Fresh Cream Cream Reaction 594 001
Music From Big Pink The Band Capitol GO 2001
The Band Capitol 038 EVC 80 181
My Aim Is True Elvis Costello Stiff SEEZ 3

An Anthology Of American Folk Music (6) Folkways FA 2951–53
Contains early hillbilly, blues and the like: many tracks not easily
available elsewhere.
Cannon's Jug Stompers (2) Herwin 208
Praise God I'm Satisfied Blind Willie Johnson Yazoo L 1058
The Early Years 1927–1933 Blind Willie McTell Yazoo L 1005
The World's Greatest Blues Singer (2) Bessie Smith CBS 66258
Blind Roosevelt Graves (1929–36) Wolf WSE 110
Crawlin' King Snake Big Joe Williams RCA International 1087
Aberdeen Mississippi Blues 1937–1940 Bukka White Travellin' Man
TM 806
The Best Of Elmore James Ace CH 31
Mardi Gras In New Orleans Professor Longhair Nighthawk 108
The Best Of The Delmore Brothers Starday SLP 962
40 Greatest Hits (2) Hank Williams MGM 2683 071
The Sun Box (3) Sun Box 100
The history of Sun Records *sans* Presley.
Honky Tonk Polydor 2310
Includes Bill Doggett's 'Honky Tonk' Parts One und Two.
41 Hits From The Soundtracks Of American Graffiti (2) MCA MCSP
253
Includes Buddy Holly's 'That'll Be The Day', Chuck Berry's 'Almost
Grown', the Flamingoes' 'I Only Have Eyes For You', Bill Haley's
'Rock Around The Clock', and Booker T and the MGs' 'Green
Onions'.
Bo Diddley (2) Chess CXMD 4003
Little Richard – His Biggest Hits Specialty SNTF 5028
Keep A Drivin' Chuck Willis Charly CRB 1074
Cry To Me Solomon Burke Charly CRB 1075
The Best Of Aretha Franklin (2) Atlantic ATL 50751
With The Beatles Parlophone PCS 3045
Sgt. Pepper's Lonely Hearts Club Band Beatles Parlophone PCS 7027

Animal Tracks Animals Columbia FA 41 31101
The Rolling Stones Decca LK 4605
The Rolling Stones No. 2 Decca LK 4661
Bringing It All Back Home Bob Dylan CBS 32344
Blues Breakers John Mayall with Eric Clapton Decca LK 4804
Layla (2) Derek and the Dominos Polydor 2625 005
The Rise And Fall Of Ziggy Stardust And The Spiders From Mars David
Bowie RCA Victor SF 8287
Malpractice Dr Feelgood United Artists UAS 29880
Tres Hombres Z Z Top Warner Brothers WB 56003
The River (2) Bruce Springsteen CBS 88510

Appendix C

Bibliography

Allsop, Kenneth (1972), *Hard Travelling: The Story Of The Migrant Worker*, Hodder & Stoughton, London, 1967 (Penguin, Harmandsworth.)

Bane, Michael (1982), *White Boy Singing The Blues*, Penguin, Harmondsworth.

Bastin, Bruce (1971), *Crying For The Carolines*, Studio Vista, London.

Belz, Steve (1972), *The Story Of Rock*, Oxford University Press, New York.

Berendt, Joachim (1976), *The Jazz Book*, Paladin, London.

Broughton, Viv (1985), *Black Gospel*, Blandford Press, Poole, Dorset.

Charters, Sam (1963), *The Poetry Of The Blues*, Oak Publications, New York.

—— (1959), *The Country Blues*, Rhinehart, New York. (Also Michael Joseph, London, 1960.)

Collier, James L. (1981), *The Making Of Jazz*, Papermac (Macmillan), London and New York.

Collis, John (ed.) (1980), *The Rock Primer*, Penguin, Harmondsworth.

Cook, Bruce (1975), *Listen To The Blues*, Robson Books, London.

Dixon, R. M. W. and J. Godrich (1970), *Recording The Blues*, Studio Vista, London.

—— (1982), *Blues And Gospel Records: 1902–1943*, Storyville, Essex.

Escott, Colin and Martin Hawkins (1975), *Catalyst: The Sun Records Story*, Aquarius Books, London.

Fahey, John (1970), *Charley Patton*, Studio Vista, London.

Gillett, Charlie (1983), *The Sound Of The City*, Souvenir Press,

London.

Groom, Bob (1971), *The Blues Revival*, Studio Vista, London.

Guralnick, Peter (1971), *Feel Like Going Home*, Omnibus, London and New York.

—— (1979), *Lost Highway*, David R. Godine, Boston, Massachusetts.

Hamm, Charles (1979), *Yesterdays: Popular Song In America*, Norton, New York.

Hardy, Phil and Dave Laing (eds.) (1975), *The Encyclopedia Of Rock Volume 1*, Panther, London.

—— (1976), *The Encyclopedia Of Rock Volume 2*, Panther, London.

Hoare, Ian, Clive Anderson, Tony Cummings and Simon Frith (1975), *The Soul Book*, Methuen, London.

Kennedy, Stetson (1959), *Jim Crow Guide To The U.S.A.*, Greenwood Press, Westport, Connecticut.

Kerman, Joseph (1985), *Musicology*, Fontana, London.

Lang, Iain (*c.* 1942), *Background Of The Blues*, Workers Music Association, London.

Leadbitter, Mike and Neil Slaven (1968), *Blues Records: 1943–1966*, Oak Publications, London.

Logan, Nick and Rob Finnis (eds.) (1975), *The N.M.E. Book Of Rock*, Star Books, London.

Logan, Nick and Bob Woffinden (eds.) (1977), *The N.M.E. Book of Rock 2*, Star Books, London.

Malone, Bill C. (1968), *Country Music U.S.A.*, University of Texas Press, Austin.

Marcus, Greil (1977), *Mystery Train*, Omnibus, London and New York.

Mellers, Wilfred (1984), *A Darker Shade of Pale*, Faber and Faber, London.

Miller, J. (ed.) (1981), *The Rolling Stone Illustrated History of Rock & Roll*, Picador, London.

Norman, Philip (1981), *Shout!*, Hamish Hamilton, London.

Oliver, Paul (1960), *Blues Fell This Morning*, Macmillan, London. (Published in the US as *The Meaning of the Blues*, Collier, NY, 1963.)

Palmer, Robert (1981), *Deep Blues*, Papermac (Macmillan), London and New York.

Palmer, Tony (1976), *All You Need is Love*, Weidenfield and Nicholson, London.

Pidgeon, John (1976), *Eric Clapton*, Panther, London.

Russell, Tony (1970), *Blacks, Whites and Blues*, Studio Vista, London.

Sarlin, Bob (1973), *Turn it Up (I Can't Hear the Words)*, Coronet, London.

Schuller, Gunther (1968), *Early Jazz: Its Roots & Musical Development*, Oxford University Press, New York.

Southern, Eileen (1971) (1983), *The Music of Black Americans*, Norton, New York. (1983 edition enlarged and amended.)

Titon, Jeff Todd (1977), *Early Downhome Blues: A Musical and Cultural Analysis*, University of Illinois Press, Urbana.

Watson, D. R., and D. J. Hatch (1974), 'Hearing the blues: an essay in the sociology of music', *Acta Sociological*, 17(2).

Whitburn, Joel (1983), *The Billboard Book of U.S. Top Forty Hits*, Guinness Superlatives, London.

Woods, Fred (1980), *The Observer's Book of Folk Song in Britain*, Frederick Warne, London.

Index